Magic at the Helm . . .

The metal-hulled ships set forth on the final stage of their journey. They cut through the sea like friction-less knives, leaving the mainland coast unseen beyond the southern horizon.

Then they heard it, the wild growling of the fortress as it turned on its stone foundations.

"Here we have arrived!" Nemed called across the sea. "War Crows, are you ready to fly?"

"Yea!" Bava answered. "Our wings are strong and our beaks hard!"

"All you sorcerers, are you prepared and strong with magic?"

"We are! Our weapons are hungry!"

"And my men!" Nemed thundered. "Are you ready to fight the Freths?"

They shouted like wild men and threw up their weapons, then crashed the butts of them on the oak planking, then twice again.

"Victory, then!" he said. "Shake their fortress down!"

Ace Books by Keith Taylor

The Bard Series

BARD
BARD II
BARD III: THE WILD SEA
BARD IV: RAVENS' GATHERING

The Danans Series

BOOK ONE: THE SORCERERS' SACRED ISLE
BOOK TWO: THE CAULDRON OF PLENTY *(coming in October)*

THE
SORCERERS'
SACRED ISLE

KEITH TAYLOR

ACE BOOKS, NEW YORK

This book is an Ace original edition,
and has never been previously published.

THE SORCERERS' SACRED ISLE

An Ace Book/published by arrangement with
the author

PRINTING HISTORY
Ace edition/June 1989

ISBN: 0-441-77565-9

Ace Books are published by The Berkley Publishing Group,
200 Madison Avenue, New York, New York 10016.
The name ''ACE'' and the ''A'' logo
are trademarks belonging to Charter Communications, Inc.

PRINTED IN THE UNITED STATES OF AMERICA

10 9 8 7 6 5 4 3 2 1

In memory of my father,
Jack Taylor,
with love and pride
and in the knowledge that,
like all his family and friends,
I was lucky

Chapter One

"Ahe! We might as well be droving snails!"

The youth hurled his free hand outward in an extravagant gesture. Eyes blue as the morning glittered with impatience even as he laughed. Slender and lively, he gripped his roan horse's sides with bare knees as it pranced on the spring grass, sensing his mood. Tarb, the herdsman walking beside him, swallowed barley beer from a flask and wondered what the youth would do next to alleviate his boredom.

"Sen Mag has room for everyone, lord," he said placidly. "We will get there."

Garanowy, son of Siala, nephew of Loredan the Honeymouthed, and brother to folk no less remarkable—as well as being fairly important in his own estimation—did not feel content with that. He surveyed the back ends of the ambling red cattle, slapped at a fly, and yearned for a clear road to stretch his horse's legs. Besides many other droving parties, every family and craft in the island seemed bound for Sen Mag, most of them obstructively afoot. He couldn't just ride through them, of course, much less over them; not the girl with her waddling flock of geese, or that tumbling child, or the train of laden air-wagons floating above the ground as if they weighed nothing—but, womb of the fertile Earth, they were slow!

His restless glance passed over a band of Freths, and darted back. A grin of delight suddenly glowed on his face. *They* didn't belong at the spring gathering! He could make them jump out of his path with a light heart.

"Do without me for a while, Tarb!" he laughed. "I'm for some fun with those lobs yonder!"

"Lord!" Tarb yelled, noticing what Garanowy had not—the standard in the center of the Freth band. "Wait, you blind cub!"

But Garanowy was away. Whooping, he raced towards the heavy, buckskin-clad figures walking beside their shaggy cattle. His horse scarcely left hoofprints in the rich plain. The Freths turned their weathered faces towards him as he shrilled "Danu forever!" and rushed upon them, the wind of his racing approach flapping his cloak with its pattern of interlocking spirals, yellow, orange, and blue.

One of the party had somehow come from the center to confront him. Garanowy had not seen him move, and certainly he did not seem to be moving fast, yet he was there, standing calmly before the onrushing horse. Garanowy glimpsed a broad face, a shaggy mop of hair and grey-speckled beard, before he reined his horse back to its very haunches to avoid riding the Freth down. That had never been his intention; he had merely looked to see them scatter, and have to round up their cattle in the travelling crowd.

The momentum of his rush wasn't so easily halted. He felt his mount's chest slam into the standing Freth, and thought in dismay, *Oh, fool, too proud to jump!* In the next instant, he felt amazement, for he might have ridden into a boulder. The Freth grunted explosively, and his heels scraped foot-long grooves in the grassy soil of Sen Mag, but he absorbed the impact which should have flattened him as if he had been butted by a small, impetuous child. Garanowy shot forward along the roan's neck, and had to fling his arm around it to maintain any kind of contact with the horse at all. He had very nearly gone over its head and over the Freth's terrific shoulders together.

Gasping, he slid back to a more dignified position in the saddle. His gilded bridle-ornaments chimed as the roan struggled fully upright. The Freth still held it with its four feet on the ground, his grip forbidding it to rear or stamp—and incredibly, it did not resist such treatment. The horse had always been as impatient of restraint as Garanowy himself. This was a new thing under the sky.

Flushing carnation, Garanowy blinked at the Freth. He saw great ugliness by his own standards, yet it did not matter. Never would this man fumble abashed because of his looks, in any company. Brown eyes looked into the youth's from a net of radiating wrinkles, with a steady, penetrating gaze. His forehead was folded like an ancient lava flow—what forehead he had—and his wide, nearly bridgeless nose squatted thick below massive brow ridges, between wide strong cheekbones. His full moustache and beard covered the lower part of his face, which expressed enormous strength and patience. He didn't look angry—yet—but Garanowy felt suddenly that the Freth was making up his mind at his own unhurried rate, and with all his fiery courage he found himself hoping the other would decide to be tolerant. He was holding the tall Danan horse dead still yet, and he betrayed no effort. Garanowy felt light as thistledown fluff before him.

The brown stare enveloped him. It saw youth, rashness, and impatience at once, but searched deeper—for malice, perhaps. Whatever it found remained the Freth's own concern.

"Young fool," he said, in a deep, slow voice. "We don't scatter aside so easily. If you didn't care for us, what about your horse? You Danans love them well, it's said. Now I put a bond on you. Dismount, and walk from here, leading your beast. You will get exercise and it will rest."

"What?" Garanowy reddened more deeply. "You can't lay bonds on me! I'm royal, stranger—one of Siala's sons."

More than hot-headed pride spoke then. Royal Danans were always trained in magic. While Garanowy was far from the most gifted of his family, he did have sound reason to believe that nobody could impose a sorcerers' bond on him as simply as that.

The Freth was not even interested. "Dismount."

He seemed ready to stand like a huge rock, gripping the horse, until the island was swallowed by the sea. Unless—

Garanowy wore a sword.

"What of the law?" the Freth asked.

The law protected all who came to the spring gathering. No exceptions were recognized. Even a prince could be outlawed for violence. With a shrug, Garanowy dropped to the ground, as lightly as if it had been his own idea.

"Now let go my horse," he said. "I want to be sure he's all right."

"Ought he to thank you for it, if he is?"

The roan seemed sound. Garanowy decided to lead it for a while, just to be sure. The Freth's command had nothing to do with that; so he assured himself. Why, he couldn't be of much importance even among his own folk. He wore a peasant's hooded leather tunic and horsehide wrappings around his calves, though his feet were bare, and he smelled strongly. There wasn't an ornament on him.

"Who's your lord?" Garanowy demanded.

"Only the bear, and the Mother."

Garanowy looked at the stranger's band, then, and finally noticed the short wooden pillar they carried in their midst. Above incomprehensible designs, it was carved in the shape of a bear's head.

"The Bear Tribe? Huh." Garanowy looked at the group, now banded in a circle with its men facing outward, flint spears and axes ready. Four or five actual growling bears were among them. "No lord? Who are you?"

"I'm called Sixarms."

Garanowy boggled like an idiot. The greatest of all the Freth chiefs released his compelling stare and returned to his tribesmen. The youth, bemused, led his roan gelding back to his own party and never thought of mounting it again.

"You chose your man to offend, didn't you?" Tarb said furiously. "If he'd struck you, we'd have had to fight, you know, peace or not. The outlaw life's no fun in the winter. I'm too old for it."

But he'd have fought for his lord. Even if he wasn't calling Garanowy lord at this moment. The youth whacked him on the shoulder, moved.

"Tarb. You know who that was? Sixarms himself. If he didn't lie."

"Your sister's own guest." The herdsman whistled. "That must be why he didn't change you into a rock. Well. Can we get on?"

They did, Garanowy walking through the warm haze after having shed his cloak and fastened it behind his saddle. He walked unusually deep in thought.

At the center of Sen Mag, the First Created Plain, they penned their cattle in an enclosure of hurdles. By then Garanowy's spirits were high again. He led his horse to the stables of his clan, where he saw the grey and sorrel stallions of his brothers and the white mare of his sister, the Rhi. Whistling, he went to find them.

They were together, near the open-sided wooden temple of the Mother, with its many pillars and thatched roof. Garanowy gave them a cheerful hello. In the back of his mind was the knowledge that Cena would not be pleased to learn that he had nearly trampled her most important guest. He worked hard at being blithe.

Since he seldom had to work at that, the others soon noticed. They were not fools. Cena, gowned in blue, looked at him searchingly and said, "What girl has refused you, little brother? You are pretending that nothing has jolted your pride again. Now I suppose you will be showing all the day how little you care, and by morning you will be over it indeed."

"It's cattle I have been chasing, not girls, all the way from Glen Obar," Garanowy laughed. "Can you not tell?"

"Now that you mention it, yes." Cena had been used to farmyard smells all her life. "Did you see any of the Bear Freths travelling in the same direction? Sixarms is with them, so they would carry their tribal standard."

The subject had been raised. Knowing himself in the wrong, Garanowy said ruefully, "I saw them indeed. It was Sixarms I nearly rode down, by accident, trying to scatter their beasts all over Tirtangir."

Silence. Oghmal and Carbri looked at each other, the one sardonically, the other showing amused sympathy. Cena caught fire with anger.

"You nearly rode him . . . ! You fool, Garanowy! Half my chieftains are thinking it is allowable to play such tricks as it is. Must my brothers show them the way? Did he know who you are?"

"He knew. I wasn't for hiding it. Would you have had me do that, sister?"

"I would like to hide you! In the shape of a squirrel, for a

year! It should make no difference to your brain. Did you ask his
pardon when you learned who he was? Not that any other Freth
would have liked it better, but—did you? No.''

"Ask pardon of a Freth?'' Garanowy protested.

He asked pardon of a tree when he felled it, a deer when he
killed it, but the Freths were rivals for the island. While
Garanowy did not hate them, he wouldn't have minded a war
with them, to extend the Danan lands in Tirtangir.

"Of this Freth, yes. I want you to do it when you see him.
War with them would be a harder business than you seem to
think, Garanowy. They are older in the land than we are. They
know more in some ways. Oh, we could win, but the cost might
be as high as though we lost.''

Oghmal said, ''We will have to fight them again one day,
Cena. It's certain that we must, as long as our numbers grow.
They will swallow us, or we them.''

Oghmal was the dark one of the twins; dark-natured, not in
hue. In fairness of skin, blueness of eye, in height and strength,
they resembled each other closely. But whatever Oghmal had in
him that had made him the Danans' battle champion set him
always a little apart. Speaking seldom and always to the
purpose, he was the one who uttered the unpleasant truths some
would rather not see.

His sister had never been among the cheerful avoiders. She
said, ''Maybe. But we are too few. If it comes to war, it had
better be in another generation, and I look to you to help me.
The Freths are my guests! If I let them be mistreated, it hurts my
honor—so you will ask Sixarms's pardon, little brother. I lay
the bond on you.''

She looked at him with her sorceress's eyes as she spoke.

"Two bonds in one day,'' Garanowy said angrily. ''You
should not have done that, Cena. I would have done it because
you asked me. Now I'll do it because I must, and I have already
walked in the muck because of that Freth who hasn't even a right
name!''

"If that's all he made you do, he cannot be too much
offended. But, goddess! I will be, by more of this. Little
brother, it's I you are hurting. Maybe you cannot see that. I, and
the tribe. There are too many who think we cannot live with
them, too many who won't even try. Then there are those like
you, who think it fun to stir the brew. I cannot always be softly
persuading you. This thing you will do!''

Garanowy nodded, looking as though he had eaten too many green apples. Carbri watched him go.

"I'll wager he was a trial to Tarb. Were we ever as young as that?"

"No," Oghmal said definitely.

The Freths found Cena on her apple-wood throne, atop a turf dais, before the feasting tent which could expand to cover a host. She wore a gold belt, and chiming gold bracelets, and her own wealth of tumbling red-gold hair. Although not as beautiful as some, she had strong bold features, warmth and laughter, combined with the strength of a ruler. Most men desired her, many loved her, and only a few plotted against her.

"Welcome, Sixarms," she said, standing and walking to meet him, ignoring the grunts of outrage from some of her nobles. Loredan, her mother's brother, gave her support by walking with her. "Glad am I to see you. Did you journey safely?"

"The width of the land," he answered. There was no mention of Garanowy's act, and she did not think there would be. She knew Sixarms from many a council, many a feast, and some armed clashes. He'd never been petty. He smelled like one of his bears, though. He always had.

Standing now in his massive height and width, he had not changed from his coarse travelling garments to greet her. Huge, big-bellied, with muscles like slabs of seasoned wood, Sixarms smoldered with maleness. The grass itself seemed to grow greener where he trod.

Cena, tall and striking, was fully as much a woman as he was a man. The rulers of tribes made their lands fertile and caused their folk to prosper. It was disastrous to have a weakling or a miser on a throne. Those who reached one seldom stayed there long.

"That isn't what I heard," Cena said, "about the safety you enjoyed. I'm told you were nearly trampled less than a mile from my door! Isn't it so, little brother?"

"It's so indeed," Garanowy said. "I was thinking to teach you a lesson for daring to come here, lord. As it befell, I was taught one myself. I ask your forgiveness—" He choked a little. "—for my bad manners."

"Bad manners? You nigh trampled him!"

"Nothing so deadly," Sixarms said. "It was a little thing."

"I'm glad." Cena raised her voice. "Yet I want no more of these *little things*, by chance or plan. Let none pretend that he hasn't heard. The lord Sixarms and his folk have the benefit of the spring fair's peace, as much as any Danan—and they are my guests." She took the great Freth's hand in hers. "I make you free of my houses, my goods, and these lands. While you stay within these borders, harm done you is harm done me, and may the powers destroy me if I fail to avenge it. May they obliterate me and all my blood."

It was no rote gabble, but a living pledge, and all who listened knew that her words had the force to come true if she allowed them to be defied. Sixarms was as safe as he could be in his own country.

Cena feasted him that night, and exchanged friendship-gifts with him. Many a Danan stared in disgust at the way the Freths ate, and objected to sharing their great tent with bears, which growled at the Danan hounds. The Rhi sat beside Sixarms and cautioned him with a quiet word now and then, while other attendants helped his companions. Yet this "help" was given with sneers, and many a Danan commented freely. They had cause; the Freths were crass. Besides, they had weak heads for the fiery Danan distillations, the making of which was high art and sorcery in equal parts. Cena had held more successful feasts.

Sixarms's appetite was not disturbed, though. He ate calmly, massively, and if someone like Gui of Lost Star Lake ventured to mock, he had only to turn upon him the steady, encompassing look which had quelled greater men than Gui.

Cena leaned towards him and said, "What complaints have you for me this season?"

"The same ones, only more of them. Raids, incursions, a killing or two—and retaliation from us, which is no better. They increase while you increase, Cena."

"We can't consent to decrease." Clear yellow light from glass orbs made gold of Cena's sun-browned skin. Behind her, the figures on a tapestry moved slowly, acting out one of the legends of her race, their battle with the Poison Warriors among the stars.

"If it were only you, we would not have to fear. But you must have grazing for your horses, ground for your wheat. Always more. The forests suffer."

"Still an old tale, Sixarms. Maybe my forebears"—a beast of Sixarms's retinue licked her arm as she spoke, making a joke of it—"were wrong to come here, but come they did. I was born here, like my mother, and her mother. These lands are my home. I know blood feuds are starting. The question is, can they be stopped, and how? You are wiser than I if you know."

"I have a way." Sixarms looked at her. "If our peoples were joined, if we showed them how, there might not have to be war—for that is where we are moving. You can take any man you like. Will you mate with me?"

"What?" Cena's eyes widened, then narrowed. "You mean, for all my life? With meaning in law?"

"Yes. And work with me to make Danans and Freths one folk. It will be a long lifetime's work, that, and we'll leave it unfinished. But I think it must be tried."

"And you ask me here? By the goddess, you choose a strange time! I can't answer you like that. Sixarms, it is more than joining two peoples. Our joining would have to be good. I do not know that I could live with you, or you with me. What if we quarrel, favor this man or that in a lawsuit? What if I knife you? My temper is not mild."

"What if I strike you?" Sixarms countered. "I've long desired you. We have lain together as host and guest . . . True, that is not the same thing. You have no single man you prefer—or has that changed?"

"No. It's the same yet. There was Macha's father, before he was lost at sea." Cena glanced at the little girl tugging at a bear's shaggy flank and vowing to climb its side. Carbri picked her up and set her on his own shoulders, before she provoked the beast. "Would you strike me? I think I would kill you if you did—or my sibs would. That is what I mean. If we deal together ill instead of well, we would cause war, not avert it. Sixarms, I like you well, and there is no question of desire or of manhood! But you are so strange to me.

"I'll name one thing, just one. With this in your mind, you come to my feast new from a cattle drive, and you do not think to bathe."

"I washed in the river."

"Not enough. Garanowy was ripe, and he spent all afternoon in the bath-house, then changed his clothes. See him yonder, with a girl on each arm? We Danans are picky. That is one thing you will have to do for me, maybe the least of them. So you have long desired me. Nothing else?''

"Rhi of the Danans, I like you well. That you are fierce, I know. We both have strength, and love. But I cannot make songs like your brother Carbri's. They sound to me like a bird beating its wings against walls. The folk in his songs come to bad ends. I can offer my love to content you, my strength to ward you, the earth's bounty to feed you—and a long task for which you will receive no thanks, from my people or yours.''

"To announce it alone would bring a war." Cena was growing angry. "We'd make strange-looking children together. Did you not think of that? Would Danan or Freth want any part of them?''

"I would, very greatly," Sixarms said. "Would you?''

Cena looked at her daughter again, crowing on Carbri's shoulders. She thought of bearing low-headed sibs for her, with great long upper lips and faces which jutted forward. Sixarms was different; he was only himself, with a power and kindness which made his looks no great matter. But who could say what their half-breed children might be like?

"This asks for thought," she said. "Goddess! I'm not even sure you will find the idea good when you are sober. But—you are the greatest male Rhi in Tirtangir, and between us we might do the thing. Will you dare ask it of me in the daylight tomorrow, in front of all my clan, in front of the people, not knowing what I will say?''

"I would dare. Yes. But is this some Danan joke like your brother's, Cena?''

"You may think so. You will have to trust me. Sixarms, I am not a harebrain like him. The tribe must learn to respect you as I do. Then we'll see. Strength, prowess, courage, and the skills of a craftsman; those they respect. Wisdom they revere less.''

"You plan to test me?''

"Not for myself. Will you do as I say?''

A long pause followed. Cena wished she could follow the thoughts being turned and trimmed in that deliberate, strangely shaped head. Sixarms, for his part, wished that he knew Cena better. Asking for her as his mate openly might get him torn to pieces, yet—she would never contrive that. And a risk to his dignity was less important than the growing certainty of a war.

"Yes," he said.

Cena smiled like the first dawn of summer through winter mists. "Indeed that is well." She kissed him with the warmth of old friendship. "Now I make you free of my own quarters tonight, but you should do nothing there but sleep, since you may need all your strength tomorrow. Eat nothing more, either."

That came as disappointing advice, for Sixarms ate mighty servings and called for more, as a rule. He wondered what Cena was up to, and chuckled to think that it would astonish her own people as much as it did him.

Before sharing her bed with him, she took Sixarms to the bath-house and saw him cleansed thoroughly, doused, sweated, scrubbed, trimmed, and even smoothed with pumice. His protests rose to animal roars by the end, and the rinsing water ran black.

"Ah, don't fuss so, giant," Cena laughed, helping her women do the work with a merry will. "You have suffered this before and it was worth it."

This was true. Cena had insisted on the strange ritual the other times as well; perhaps there was sorcery in it. The old women of his tribe would doubtless say so, but he trusted Cena. Sixarms fell asleep on her coverlet feeling refreshed and strangely fine.

He awoke at dawn, willing to wrestle a bull if that was required of him. It wasn't, but the brightly colored Danan garments Cena had magically altered to fit his body almost gored out his eyes by themselves. Orange breeches, black and sky-blue jacket, an indigo cloak embroidered with golden triskeles—and the many-tinted weave of the shirt!—would have made them choose a new chief in the Revolving Fortress. After Sixarms had put them on, he hardly recognized himself.

Walking out, he was at once aware of the belly-knotting giggles the servants had to suppress, and the roar of laughter Gui could utter unrestrained. He laughed too hard. Sixarms had the pleasure of seeing him choke painfully over breakfast.

"That accursed Freth did it," he said angrily, when he could speak again. "He spoke a charm against me. I heard him. By the night powers, I won't forget it."

Carbri grinned when he saw Sixarms, too, but it was a friendly grin. With his copper hair and flowing moustache, the harper seemed an older image of Garanowy, for whose sake

Sixarms walked on bruised heels this morning. Yet one couldn't dislike Carbri.

"Cena would have tossed your garments on the midden," he said. "I rescued them; maybe they are your enchanter's clothes? Never blame Cena. She doesn't understand how a man can grow fond of something rank."

"Thanks. I built the Revolving Fortress in them."

Carbri believed it. "Eat with me. It's bannocks and bacon only, but Nesth cooks them well."

Sixarms could have eaten a hill of them. With a pang, recalling Cena's words, he said, "I must fast today."

"Fast, at the spring fair? The Earth-Mother comfort you! You'll find Cena in her temple, should you be seeking her. Hai, Garanowy! You look decently hungry, little brother. Join me."

Walking under the temple's thatched roof, between the many carved pillars, felt like walking in a forest—the more so since there were no man-made walls to enclose them, and sweet grass underfoot. Sixarms stopped near Luchtan's image of the Earth-Mother, hewn from one great tree. She sat cross-legged, with swelling, fecund belly and full breasts, holding forth her hands. One held nuts, fruits, and grain, the other, mold and bones. A living brown bull was stalled on each side of her.

Cena asked the goddess's favor for the days of the fair. Many of her people watched, and made offerings; not alone the tall, red-headed Danans, but a goat-legged urisc and a tree spirit or two. They were learning, these newcomers. They did not know the earth of Tirtangir, yet, as the Freths knew it. He doubted they ever would. But they were the Earth-Mother's children for all that, returned from a long exile.

Oghmal the Champion was there, Sixarms saw, in his bronze-bossed leather kilt, his weapons laid aside. This was a man the Freth might one day have to fight. Nemed, the lord from Alba seeking new land for himself and his warriors, was there also; they kept coming. He would not favor peace.

Sixarms walked limping through the cookfires and shelters of Sen Mag to the camp of his own party. Seeing the heavy, skin-clad bodies and wrinkled brows gave him joy. The Danans set a great value on beauty. If they could see none in a Freth, they were fools, for all their cleverness.

"There may be trouble," he warned them. "The Danans are

not going to like what I say when I present our case. The old women, if we succeed, are going to like it less. Stay together and fight only if you have to."

"If the Danans gave you those clothes, they are your enemies," Winter Elk said. "You look like a colored fungus on a log!"

"It's their notion of finery. Bring me the Grinder."

"They could have dressed you as a jester for all you know."

"I trust Cena. But now I have a lawsuit to bring, and I will do it as a chief."

The Grinder was a yard-long club few Danans could have swung in one hand, a stone-headed pestle counterweighted below the grip. No weapons were allowed to be borne at the gathering, save by men of the highest rank, who were deemed able to control themselves. Sixarms considered that he had already proved his self-control.

He needed more of it when Gui met him with several friends, all armed. It seemed they were out enforcing the laws of the spring peace.

"You must give that up, Freth," Gui said, smiling nastily. "What if you grow drunk? No weapons is the rule."

"Then give up yours."

"We are Danans, and noble. We hold our liquor like men, not like half-beasts who couple with beasts. Hand it over."

"Does the Rhi know of this?" Sixarms asked. "I don't think she does. Ask her. I am a chief, and this is my talisman, like the Wailing Spear for you."

"It looks more like a maul for stunning cattle. Give it up, Freth—or must we prod you until you do?"

Gui's smile was now an open smirk.

"If you begin prodding," Sixarms said, his voice like a first low rumble of thunder, "I will begin smiting, and none of you with your puny sticks will be whole when I have finished. Let us ask the Rhi."

"She isn't here. Nor would I trouble her about you if she were. You are far beneath her attention, Freth."

"She'd think it no trouble," Oghmal assured him. Unarmed himself, he casually plucked the spear from Gui's hand and leaned on it. "Maybe I know more of her mind than you do. You've insulted her guest. She won't like that. You had better go."

"But the law—" Gui began.

"Will you gainsay me?" Oghmal asked in his gentlest voice. He no longer leaned negligently on the spear.

"Well," Gui shrugged, "the champion is equal to six men. If you'll be responsible for the beast, lord—"

"He's a chief. Speak to him as one before you leave." Oghmal turned to Sixarms. "Unless you want to complain of them, sister's guest."

"Too little a matter."

"Then—farewell, chief of the Freths," Gui said.

"The word," Oghmal told him, "is lord."

"And farewell to you, lord champion. Nay, I made no error. I will die before I say *lord* to such a walking pustule—"

"ENOUGH!" Sixarms bellowed. He advanced upon Gui, let a great thick-fingered hand fall on his shoulder, and began squeezing. "Go! If I see you after the gathering I'll break your bones!"

Gui whitened in that terrible grip, though he made no outcry. Sixarms released him as he was about to sink to the ground from the pressure of the Freth's hand. Gui left as he had been told. His cronies were already moving.

"Gui," Oghmal called. "You forgot your spear."

He threw it, casually. The lord of Lost Star Lake caught it, and raised it in a malevolent salute before he departed.

"Now," Oghmal said, "I had better take you to the judgements before you make more friends."

"First," Sixarms said, "I change these clothes. Wearing them was a mistake. Carbri knows where my own are—but a cowhide will do."

"A cowhide, to appear before Cena?" Oghmal's face grew stony. Then he considered the big-bellied form of Sixarms, and shrugged. "Maybe it is more fitting, at that. Do as you like."

Thus Sixarms appeared before Cena, Rhi of all the Danans, wearing a hairy cowhide tunic of the simplest kind, his splendid cloak discarded, and with a forest bear snuffling at his heels. He rested his stone-headed club on one massive shoulder.

Cena's blue eyes kindled like sulfur burning. Her advice had been ignored, her gifts rejected. She listened to the charges Sixarms brought against her lords and chiefs, of invasion, slaying, tree-felling, and the like. It all amounted to one thing, taking more land. In awareness of her anger, and, yes, hurt, she strove even harder to give a wise judgement, but she knew as Sixarms did that such things would go on while the situation remained the same.

The Danan lords brought counter charges, of cattle-slaying and sorcery, against the Freths. Unlike Sixarms, they could not name individual culprits, and for them to accuse others of sorcery was like eagles accusing hawks. None of which made their charges any less true.

Sixarms owned it. "Now I would speak," he said. "Have I leave?"

"My guests speak as they wish," Cena said. "You are bringing your own lawsuit."

"Not my lawsuit!" Sixarms's voice crashed forth. "My people's! There is more on both sides that this cow stolen, that forest defiled. We were here before the Danans, and the Danans are taking what is ours. Yet you cannot leave Tirtangir and find another place to live, even if you would. We must live together, or make war.

"I favor living together. Not because I believe my folk would be defeated. Some things you can teach us; some we do not want to learn. And there is a deal we can teach you.

"Our cases in law are better than the horse lords', but we will withdraw them if the Danans will do the same. Laws are needed that both sides think are good, both will abide by, and livers which know both peoples to make them. There must be those who belong to both races to give judgement in the future, so that all sides can accept their rulings without ill-will or suspicion.

"I am Sixarms, of all Freth chiefs the mightiest. Cena is Rhi of all the Danans, your judge, war-leader, and high sorceress. Lady, of all Tirtangir's women you are the best, and the only partner to fashion such a joining.

"Sixarms asks you, then, if you will wive him. I will bring honor to cherish you, fortresses to defend you, and the deep powers of earth to uphold you. I bring my club Grinder to the bones of the one who offers you harm or slander. There is no more that I have."

Cena sat on her throne, listening to the declaration she had expected, though never so eloquently. Sixarms spoke her language better than any other Freth. Yes, she believed the thing would work—or if it would not, nothing would. Yet a sound began among the gathered Danans, and grew. It was laughter, incredulous, scornful laughter.

Cena stood, raising her arms in a demand for silence. Then she came down from the turf dais to face Sixarms on a level.

"You say that of all Tirtangir's women I am best? Then truly, I can't be for any but the mightiest of chiefs. If you are that, show me! I'll unite with no man who cannot eat, drink, love, and fight as greatly as he talks. For a beginning, lord, show me how you can eat!" She pointed to some nearby cooking trenches and vats set out in the open. "There is a full vat of porridge which has bubbled all night. I know its quality. Empty it to the bottom by sundown, you alone, and Cena will . . . take thought to your offer. If you fail I will never accept it!"

Sixarms stood there. Cena's voice sounded only mocking, while the wicked Danan pride sparkled in her eyes. Then, in the background, laughter began again, laughter of the lords, ladies, and people, laughter which approved Cena's answer, laughter of expectation. They thought Sixarms would walk away in defeat.

"Come, then," he said.

With the bear shambling behind him, he walked to the steaming vat. Cena followed, her handsome, jewelled court at her heels. Sixarms glowered at the bubbling porridge, his great arms folded. At least it was good porridge; so its smell declared.

The vat was a hollow, seasoned log a fathom long, in which hot stones were dropped at intervals to cook the contents. Sixarms hoped they had all been fished out. Behind him, the Danans laughed over the joke and offered him the advice of their choosing. Their anger at his audacity had been diverted; they were happy. Their laughter increased while Sixarms thoughtfully tasted the stuff. Yes, it was excellent, cooked slowly the night through, with generous chunks of bacon and pork therein.

"Dive in and splash about!" a kitchen girl dared cry from a safe distance back.

"You hesitate to begin," mocked Gui, stroking his little forked beard. "Do you fear poison?"

Sixarms glanced at him once, a glance to be sure of remembering the man; then he swung his club, the Grinder. Seasoned warriors scattered out of the path of its terrible stone head, though his stroke was hardly more than a playful swat.

"So you little people offer me this and call it a meal," he

rumbled. "You think it will fill me? Stand back, all of you! Stand away and give me space. I'll show you how a man eats!" The rumbling became a bellow. "I want a stool, and a ladle, *large!* Bring me cream in buckets and milk in barrels! Do you think Sixarms will eat porridge without cream? Do you think I'll meekly die of thirst in the meantime? JUMP!"

Cena, choking with stifled laughter, said, "Do as he . . . requests."

Sixarms placed his buttocks on the swiftly produced stool, and scratched his attendant bear behind the ears. His people squatted on the grass, watching the Danans, who watched Sixarms with something akin to awe. He scowled disparagingly at the big wooden ladle a cook gave him.

"My own at home can dip up entire carcasses at a time," he declared, "but this will do."

The ladle vanished into the steaming porridge. Sixarms tasted, savored, then tilted it into his mouth and swallowed. He emptied the ladle again, and a third time, slowly at first, building to a steady, unhurried pace which nonetheless disposed of porridge as though it were beer in the hands of a drunkard.

The cream arrived, thick and yellow in the demanded bucket. Sixarms poured it over the surface of his vast meal, tossed the emptied vessel aside, and went on eating, if anything more contentedly than before. Some of the Danans had already begun to boggle.

"I take my sworn oath, he's reduced it a hand's width," Carbri said. "It may be he can actually do it."

"No man can," Luchtan the wood-worker said with certainty. Then he added, "But Freths are not men."

"I think he'll succeed," Carbri decided. "Will you wager, cousin? The next colt of my mare Skyborn against your gold belt with the fish-buckle."

"I'll take you, cousin. I think you want that blotch to win! Have you considered what it will mean if he does? Your sister in his bed? *Him* to rule us?"

"She only said she would not have him otherwise, or even hear his suit. As for ruling us—by our laws he can't. You know that as well as I. Cena's our Rhi, no other. That won't change, whatever man she takes."

"He spoke of changing the laws, didn't he? Making new ones to govern both Danan and Freth? As if such laws could ever be!"

"He set us a large thing to swallow there, aye—but trust Cena to set him a larger in her turn! Sky, earth, and sea! Will you observe him?"

Sixarms had paused to sluice his gullet clear with part of a pail of foaming new milk. Then he proceeded to demolish the porridge. He ate a third of the way along the vat before he ceased to eat for the pure pleasure of it, and another third before showing signs of distress. By then it was afternoon, and his progress had grown painfully slow. He overlapped his stool all around.

His ladle had uncovered one of the hot stones used to cook the porridge. Now it encountered another. Frowning intently, he made sure no others had been left in the vat, then reached for his awful club. He brought it down a dozen times. Porridge, rock dust, and oak splinters flew about, and then nothing remained of the offending stones but grit. Luchtan gasped.

"He's eating the stones as well!"

"Yes, I have eyes, cousin. None can say he cheats. A little effete, though, he must be, to pulverize them first."

Again the colossal Freth paused, to wash down his victuals with milk. Then he went on towards the end of the vat, doggedly plying the ladle, scooping, tilting back his besmeared head, sucking the rich porridge in. An ugly sight, and Carbri's conscience stirred.

"I say it is enough, my people!" he called out. "Sixarms has kept his promise to show us how a man eats; shall we demand that he burst? I'm ready to agree that he has passed the test. Now, what say you?"

"Cousin!" Luchtan protested. "We've a bet!"

"And I'll forfeit it," Carbri said. "The next colt is yours. Now let's be hearing your voice, master of chips and shavings! It's enough?"

"It's enough," Luchtan agreed, shamed or bribed, running nicked and callused carpenter's fingers through his brown hair. "Sixarms has won. Declare it ended."

"Declare it ended." Other tongues began to wag to that slogan, which became a chant in moments. Before it could spread throughout the crowd, though, voices as loud challenged it. Gui's was first among them.

"To the hungry void with that! He has the vat to finish, and he will last it out or stand shamed! Let him eat it all."

Many echoed his last words. Carbri nodded slowly, his mouth wryly puckered as if he tasted something bitter. Then he strolled forward, thumb in his ornate belt, buckles, brooch, and sword-hilt glittering in the sun, each step an insult, his stance an affront. He halted before the lord of Lost Star Lake and surveyed him disgustedly from crown to foot.

"Gui," he said pleasantly, "you are not a dog. I've known some worthy dogs. You must have been born a Danan by mistake." Half turning, he yelled with all the power of his bard's voice, "Declare it ended!"

Sixarms had more volume yet. He shouted like a thunderclap, "NO!" and heads turned his way. He brandished his ladle like a weapon.

"I will finish what I began. None of your scornful generosity so late in the day, Danans! It's too late."

Before them all, he scraped the sides and bottom of the vat until it contained no more than smears of his repast. Cleaning the ladle for the last time, he broke its bowl in his great misshapen hands and hurled the fragments across the plain. Forcing himself to his feet, he swayed drunkenly, half a yard behind his own distended belly, the plain with its mortal and faerie crowd blurred to his vision. He began telling them all what he thought of them.

When he had finished, he shouldered the Grinder and turned his back. He walked step by step to his people's cattle-camp, sick and nigh to bursting, his stomach a-joggle with each labored pace. Thick-limbed, thick-bodied Freths went before and behind him, while the forest beasts paced on either side. No Danan could go near him.

He fell with a grunt on a pallet of herbs and grass, to sleep until cock-crow.

When he awoke he felt heavy and dull, but interested in living. His half-animal senses had told him even while he slept that someone sat beside him, perfumed and warm-breathing. A woman; Cena.

"Wasn't the sport good enough?" he growled.

"Come, old friend, do not be sullen. You said you trusted me."

"I was mad."

"Not you. The test was uncomfortable, I know. Still, I knew you would pass it, as no other could. My people were angry when you asked me to marry; they liked it when I seemed to make a public butt of you. Now their anger has vanished, and they admire you.''

''Hunhh.'' A deal of scepticism can be conveyed in a grunt. Sixarms's effort approached the possible limits.

She patted the humped, scarred muscle of his back. ''They do, most of them. You did the impossible, without complaint. You would take no concessions or insulting mercy, and at the end, when you could barely stand, you called my proud Danans weaklings, children of spite, toadspawn, and challenged their worst. None came to shut your mouth. Why do you think that was?''

''They did not dare.''

''I know my own people better than that. Dare? There were *women* in that crowd who would fight with a blunt broomstick against a war-band fully armed, to make a tiresome day lively. There were men who would lift spears over the best portion of a meal, because it should go to the best warrior, and die rather than draw back a step. Do you think they were frightened of bears? No. They were ashamed.''

Again Sixarms grunted, as doubtfully as before.

''But they were! They had cause. You came among them as my guest, and they subjected you to insult.''

''Insult? I offered them peace, and asked for marriage. They laughed. If they do get war with the Freths, they will not find it the game they think.''

''We know that. They do not. But they like you for facing them down when you were helpless, and telling them what oafs they were.'' A throaty chuckle came out of the dimness. *''Weasels with the guts of stinking fish-market offal.* You could make a poet.''

''They did not attack me because they were too fair-minded, eh? I cannot believe that.''

''Some were not,'' Cena said. ''Gui for one would have made short work of you and never thought about it again, but he had my brother Oghmal's spear-tip jammed half up his nostril at the time. Carbri led the call to end the test; he should have done it sooner. Still, I was proud of him.''

''Your own closest kin. They won't be enough, and your people won't change because of this. They laughed at my cost and felt good afterward. Nothing more.''

"They admired your feat. The story of Sixarms's porridge-feast will be told for a thousand years! Surely they laughed, but you passed my test and they must accept that. Now we can talk of what's next to be done."

"You bought your people's consent by making me look a fool." Sixarms took her by the wrist with the hand that had throttled wolves, and worked stone by the ton in building his fortresses. "Will you say you didn't enjoy the joke at all?"

Cena was a warrior herself. "I delighted in it. You may avenge yourself for that if you like."

Sixarms's capacious belly rumbled. He felt bloated yet. But—one did not reject the offer of a Rhi, or of a friend, if Cena remained that. He changed the grip of his hands, opening and sliding them. Like one of his bears, he sniffed her hair, throat, and breasts. Then he kissed as she had taught him to do. That hadn't been a Freth custom, though mothers licked their children. Some Danan customs the Freths could copy, Sixarms thought.

The pallet rustled. Scents of bruised herbs, perfume, and aroused flesh rode the milk-warm air. The bears muttered in their sleep. Cattle called nearby. A wolf howled, somewhere away across the plain.

For the rest of the gathering, Sixarms was Cena's guest in every way, to both their rich satisfactions. All knew and none were offended, though Gui and a few like him pretended to be. Danan women conducted themselves as they wished, the more so if they happened to be rulers. Still it was discussed and gossiped about.

"Between themselves, it's their own concern," Oghmal growled, pouring birch wine into a cup of purple glass. "But marriage! Few do that unless they want to raise children or unite two septs, or both. Between two peoples, it's our concern. I foresee a storm, brothers."

"You have all the second sight of a mussel," Carbri said, "as you well know. Would you rather see your lands wasted?"

"*He* could never be our Rhi," Garanowy protested. "The laws say a Rhi must be fertile and have no blemishes. Why, he's a walking blemish, bent-kneed, big-stomached, ugly as a banshee!"

"Infant, surely he couldn't," Carbri agreed. "Cena's our Rhi, and will be no matter whom she marries. If she can endure

his looks, it's her affair, and if she cannot she has the privilege
of closing her eyes. Gui's handsome, but I'd sooner trust
someone I cared about to Sixarms than he. Peace. It's a fine
thought to me, who have lands and kine. Those who haven't
would find themselves waiting on endless judgements. What
would you think of that, Nemed?''

The man addressed, a lean, quick-moving fighter with a
hungry mouth and auburn hair thinning early, answered at once.
"If you make a lasting peace with the Freths, there is nothing
for me here. I came with my war-band to win land by the points
of our spears. Forbid that, and we may as well return to Alba.''

"You don't seem perturbed," Carbri commented.

"I am not." Nemed smiled. "A lasting peace is as likely as a
cloudless sky forever.''

Gavidu, the master flint-worker, had been listening in silence.
Now he spoke with his slow, half-Freth tongue. "And what do
you all think of calling Sixarms's get nephew and niece? If his
plan works, there will be children of Freth and Danan as surely
as there will be the clouds you mentioned, lord. There are even a
few now.''

Garanowy pulled a disgusted face. Nemed shrugged. While
Oghmal said nothing, he set down his wine and grew very
attentive. Carbri played an odd, questioning chord on his harp.

"Has that marked you?''

"No. You all saw that it should not. Besides, I'm the master
of a craft, which means respected. But those who are not? My
mother was a Freth bond-woman, as any can see, and the chief
sent her away from his rath lest it even be whispered that he had
fathered me. Worse than that could befall.''

"You oppose the thing?" Oghmal asked quietly.

"I don't oppose peace. But on my ten fingers, I doubt that
this is the way to reach it.''

"There is no way," Nemed said with assurance. "One
people will swallow the other in the end. The question is
which.''

His words left an echo in the minds of those who heard them.

Chapter
Two

Luchtan considered the long curving spine of seasoned oak, decided that one more stroke of his adze would be a stroke too many, and lowered the tool. In the cool of the spring morning he strolled to where Cena and Loredan, her mother's brother, had been watching.

"If you must give him a floatwain, lady, we can spare a dozen," the wood-worker said. "This one will never be finished before you leave."

"It needn't be," Cena answered, "but it must be new. I won't give Sixarms a gift of something we have discarded. He's not our beggar, or anyone's. However, I won't be taking this until I go to visit him by land. You have time to make it as it should be crafted, cousin."

"First find a road to Bronagh that airwains can follow."

"Sky and sea!" Cena yelled. She had heard too many such sullen, half-patronizing comments of late. "You might as well call me idiot to my face! I know what floatwains need as surely as you, and I can trace power courses better, any day of my life.

Make the thing! Leave transporting it to me, and be more careful of your words.''

Luchtan flung down his adze with violent force. ''If I'm to speak only with my hands, I'm a bondman! What use is a gift you can't take to the Freth? Or that may not float within his borders, because the goddess's power doesn't flow there?'' His freckled bony face set more stubbornly. ''All I asked was why you hadn't searched out these things before you set me to work.''

''You implied that I was such a fool as not to think of them. Did you not? Well, cousin, I have my reasons. But what they are I will not say.'' She leaned towards him, emanating mystery. ''Keep silent yourself. What you build may be more important than you know.''

''You play on me, as when we were children,'' Luchtan retorted. ''This is a floatwain like many another, or it will be. What's the importance of that?''

''It will be the first such in Sixarms's country, and when he sees how useful it is, he will want more. Now do you see?''

''Shh,'' Luchtan breathed. ''And Danans will have to trace the power-courses for him . . . you were always tricksy, cousin.''

''Will you build, then?''

''The best wain you have seen!''

They left Luchtan cheerfully selecting timber. Cena's uncle looked at her whimsically. Round-faced and well fed, in the long tunic of a poet, he stood high in her councils.

''Now he believes he's the sharer of a vast secret.''

''He also believes Sixarms is stupid enough to allow Danans to survey his land in that way. He never will until he trusts us better.''

''He may not accept your gift until then, either. Luchtan will be aggrieved.''

''Goddess! The temperament of craftsmen! And my warriors are as bad. Tell me, my mother's brother, how can I keep them from raiding the Freths until I visit Sixarms?''

''The truth?'' Loredan pinched his round chin. ''Cena, short of casting the lot into ensorcelled slumber, I do not believe you can.''

He was being proved right as he spoke, in Gui's home on Lost Star Lake. The supercilious lord gazed across the water, in

which stars were reflected even on cloudy nights. Behind him
rose his house, with its sun-balcony and pillars of red yew,
secure within three rings of fortification. It wasn't as splendid as
many. Gui's wealth lay in fine cattle and finer horses, of which
he never could get enough.

All around him, the men of his household were saddling to
ride. He waved to his mother Sanhu, and to the child she held up
to receive his farewell. The sorceress watched the riders stream
into the dark, cloaks flying and hoofs beating softly.

"There, boy," she said harshly. "Your father will come
home with more beasts we haven't grass or grain to feed, and
maybe a Freth head or two which isn't even fit for soup. I would
we had a Rhi who would capture some land and parcel it out,
instead of the dreaming trull we have! Cena, you are your
mother's shame."

The little boy listened big-eyed to her strictures for a while.
She pinched him when she caught him yawning, and began her
fierce recriminations again.

"No, Cena," she said at last, to the waters of the lake. "You
shall never have your union with that dirt, or your ugly lover to
dwell at Ridai with you. The Danans will rule Tirtangir."

Gui's men crossed a waste of forest and bog on their
wind-swift horses, their hoofs never breaking the treacherous
surface. Owls hooted a warning to the village of sunken-floored
huts which was their prey, but the raiders were not far behind the
sound, shadowed by Sanhu's magic.

Bronze spearheads flickered, to be stained a deeper red. The
heavy flint hatchets of the Freths answered, though at too short a
range to match the elusive Danans. One powerful man, seeing
his mate ridden down, sprang chest to straining chest with a
mare and heaved, raising horse and rider together. A constant
grinding roar came from his mouth as he lifted, lifted, lifted,
then pushed. Horse and rider collapsed backward, the man
convulsively trying to leap clear, but failing. His agonized
scream as his own mount's falling weight crushed his thigh
filled the clearing.

Gui heard, saw, and spat a curse. Riding forward, he struck
out with his sword, calling to the fallen man to mount behind
him. Hopping, the Danan rose on one foot with a cruel effort, to
be felled again by a Freth stone which broke several ribs.
Another whizzed by Gui's head.

The lord threw a javelin, and had the satisfaction of hearing a squeal before he rode away. From the shadows under the trees, Freth men and women, clutching their children, watched their shaggy little cows being driven away. They smelled the blood of their own kind on the night air, and the blood of at least one raider. He was conscious when they came out of the woods, gathering around him. He remained conscious for a long while after that, but wolves and crows fed on his remains at last.

Gui came home coldly angry. His raid had been intended as sport, and the Freths had spoiled it, the foul, man-killing animals. Cena meant to marry one? No, she should not!

"So it is Cena," his mother said contemptuously. "What of the man you left to those beasts? You have no care for him, I see."

"I was the one who pulled him clear and tried to get him on my own horse! He couldn't ride with a broken leg."

"So you abandoned him again, without even a death-blow of mercy. My brother would spit on you if he were alive." Erect, twig-thin, and dry, she looked at her son with black scorn. "He was a man. They had to cut him to pieces before he left the spot where a kinsman had died. Oh, but you brought the cattle back!"

"I was there, and you were not," Gui snarled. "My uncle probably died where he stood because he hadn't the wits to do anything else. Myself, I had twenty men and a band of cattle to bring out through nigh-trackless forest and bog, with the wilderness against us. Lead a cattle-raid yourself if you think it is so easy."

"May your tongue shrivel in your mouth when you speak so of Mahon again!" Sanhu hissed. "So! A little raid after cows is difficult? How will you face a war, brave hero? How will you clear the Freth chiefs from Tirtangir when you are routed by one pigsty village of theirs?"

"How? With armies, old hag, that is how, and men will die in those battles too. If you mean to shriek at me for every life that is lost along the way, we may as well stop now. The Freths won't yield their lands for the polite asking, and that rancid pile of horsehide called Sixarms will never have Cena. She's mine. If she doesn't understand that the Freths must be fought, she had better learn."

"Good. There is some sense in you, though how you can think to touch Cena after a Freth is more than I know. She visits him in his own stinking kennel at Midsummer, did you know? I want you to be part of her retinue, so keep your raids as secret as you can.''

''It can't be done. Men will boast of things like that.''

''Not with spells of silence upon their tongues.'' Sanhu's face, smooth flesh stretched over bones so sharp they appeared to be cutting her from the inside, grew tauter yet. ''And we have few guests here.''

''Since you poisoned Airvith, we do not. It was admitting defeat for you, wasn't it? You could never bend her abjectly to your will, and I think you will have less success with Cena.''

''If you care about her, you should hope that I have more. Your little mate was a fool, son of mine, soft, and she left you a soft child. I grant you that Cena would be a better choice. Now. On second thoughts it would be better if you did not go with Cena to Bronagh your own self. All know how you despise Freths. She wouldn't take you. We must suborn one of the men she does take, to do what is necessary. I will see to that. You raid the Freths and cause them all the grief you may.''

Gui needed no urging. The Freths had slain his mother's brother when he was a boy, and he had never forgotten it. Nor had she. Striking swiftly by the hidden trails through the bogs, he lifted cattle from other Freth villages and left the turf huts burning. Strong enough to resist, the older inhabitants of the land were generally too slow to prevent, and without horses they could not pursue. Nor was Gui the only one who harassed the Freths, simply the most purposeful.

They had their own ways of taking revenge. Bullhide drums boomed in the night, and Freth women gathered in caves which smelled of aconite and apples. Danan horses began to die after thick gnarled hands had added something to their grain. Wolves came boldly into the plain, banded in packs, unnaturally, during the summer, to cripple steeds and flee back to the forest. Men who followed met birch tree spirits, and fell dead at a touch of white hands over the heart, or came back mad after the same white hands had stroked their heads. Flax, grain, and fruit grew stunted and scrawny in the Danan fields. Children of the Earth-Goddess the Danans might be, but the Freths were senior ones who knew her body better.

Cena sought those of her own people who were responsible, and found some, though never the worst offenders. She sought to compensate, to make amends, after the wrongs had been done, and that was too late. Meanwhile Gui traded his surplus cattle to bronze-smiths for weapons.

When Sanhu came to court, the Rhi was surprised and not overly pleased to see her. A bitter woman, though cunning and adroit in sorcery, she had lived a secluded life at Lost Star Lake for years. She should perhaps not be blamed for having mothered Gui, though Cena suspected her of hiding her son's raids with all her powers, after inciting him to make them in the first place. Loredan concurred.

"I knew her before you were born," he said. "She was different then, but pride was her curse, always. When the Freths slew her brother, she swore to take Tirtangir from them and give it to the Danans, until no Freth had so much as a grave-mound to call his own. Those were her words. She tried to become the Rhi, but of course she couldn't. No man or woman of her line had ever been that. I wonder what she has been doing since."

"Fighting with her son's woman for control of the house and winning at last, perhaps. I'll talk with her."

Sanhu was willing to talk, indeed. She held her biting opinions in and made herself pleasant, with Gui's little son Mahon as her pretext for visiting the court.

"He was named for a hero," she said fondly, "my own brother. He should see what heroes are like."

"Oghmal is away," Cena answered, "but I can offer the lad Prince Nemed, from Alba, who has a great name for fighting the Firbolgs. Was there really a need to come from Lost Star Lake to show him heroes? I never heard your son called anything but a fighter, and he has many good men in his war-band."

"They soften for lack of practice," the grey sorceress said, her tone sharpening, "and weaken for lack of food. Must we suffer this Freth spellcraft, lady? The land suffers."

"Yes. I'm guesting with Sixarms at the Revolving Fortress soon, but I doubt that he can stop it—any more than I can stop my own folk raiding for cattle."

"Then it seems war will come," Sanhu said, "whether you and Sixarms desire it or not."

"If I find who is leading the worst of these forays, I'll stop it by calling him to fight, and punish him myself!"

Sanhu's cold eyes glimmered with amusement. "I'd wish you

luck in that event, my lady. You would need it. From all I've heard, the leader is a man of his hands.''

"I grew up with three brothers, one of them Oghmal, so it is not for me you'd be needing to fear." Cena's hot pride flamed. "If you should meet the one we're speaking of, take him that challenge from me."

"It isn't likely that I shall meet him, my lady."

Cena drew an exasperated breath. *I'll go to Lost Star Lake myself and watch as a she-wolf. Gui hasn't bred those cattle he barters. He will learn what it means to defy me.*

She had noticed the boy, Gui's son, as he stayed unobtrusively behind her crystal pillars, peeping at the court, shy as a violet. *No wonder*, she thought, *when he shares that lonely house with such a detestable hag.* She approached him quietly, not to startle him.

"Good day to you," she said. "I am the Rhi, and so you are my guest. You are Mahon the son of Airvith, not so?"

He nodded. She did not smile too sweetly, or overwhelm him with hospitality. She who had never been shy found his reticence irksome, even if she did feel sorry for him.

"You're welcome here. Have you been away from your father's house before?"

"No, lady."

"Well, you are about of an age to be fostered. Has he spoken of that to you?"

"N-no, lady. I don't want to leave the lake."

"It's a fair place, as I've heard. But not the only one." Cena went impulsively to one knee. "No doubt he has a friend in mind, though it's none of my affair. If you care to go riding, tell my stable master you can choose your own horse, within reason." She had noticed that he did not have one of his own with him, and that was odd, for a boy whose father was a masterly horseman.

"My thanks, lady, but—I'm a poor rider." He blushed.

Gui would not like that. Cena assured the boy he was free to choose any other amusements he wished, and found a playmate or two for him, then gave her attention to other things. She was to remember, later, that the first words she spoke to young Mahon had been of fosterage, and wonder at their appropriateness.

His grandmother watched, listened, and divined, looking behind the faces of those she met by her sorcery. Those at Cena's court with most to gain from a war with the Freths were Prince Nemed and his band of exiles. His captain, Valf, was to take the Rhi's party to Sixarms's Revolving Fortress in the sea, and Valf proved open to a bargain. Although it was not easy to drive one surreptitiously, with Loredan so watchful, and able to hear any spoken word in the royal rath that he desired to hear. Sanhu chose moments when he was sleeping. She well knew the master-poet did not trust her.

Her sojourn at court ended. She returned to her home with Mahon, who had come unwillingly, and now looked back at the feather-bright roof of Cena's house with regret to be leaving it. Sanhu did not look back at all.

"Look to your weapons, and be sure they are sharp," she told her son with grim joy. "When this embassy is over, you will have need of them, and nothing will keep them dry until winter."

"My mother, that is excellent hearing," Gui said, his face alight. "Do you think this Alban captain will fail you?"

"There is always the chance, surely. But I am certain he knows better than to do it."

She rested a hand grown too bony, too young, on her son's shoulder. Rarely did the sorceress make such gestures, though Gui was her only child.

"Cena may be killed in the strife," he said bleakly. "I suppose that does not trouble you."

"Less than the life of a fish in the lake. It has not troubled you enough to speak of it, until this hour. Come, son of mine! I know you crave Cena for your mate, but as well I know that you want this conflict more. If there is a new Rhi—why, he will have so much more to avenge on the Freths."

"Unless he is Loredan."

"Not even Loredan will be able to avert war, should he be chosen. But Cena's named heir is another. No, that will make no difference."

"It's well. You have wrought greatly, my mother." He kissed her. "Now we shall see."

Nemed's fleet of seven ships lay in the curve of a shining blue bay with basalt cliffs at one end, a dark bluff where more than one vessel had been wrecked. But Nemed's did not wreck easily. Their thin metal hulls floated lightly upon the sea, a strange, shimmering mirror-blue which remained cool to the touch on the hottest day. Even the Danans no longer knew the secrets of building such ships, and unless they rediscovered them, when the remaining ones were gone there would be no more. Within the hull lay oak flooring, a pine mast and bronze fittings, with sails from the sorcerous Danan looms, woven all in one multicolored piece. The enchanted race had lost old knowledge and discovered new since it had returned to the Earth.

With Cena, Garanowy, and twenty others aboard, the gifts for their host securely stowed, and a wind in their sails which Carbri had called on his harp, the ship raced north. Its hull clove the water without resistance, and even the wind had to hasten to catch it. The bard Uisfrel tuned his harp and sang, a fine carefree song of a voyage to wondrous places which encouraged the Danans to join in the refrains. White and brown throats together pulsed with merriment. Cena trod and sprang in a whirling dance with a kilted young sailor, for it would be long and long yet before the idea became common that such pleasures were beneath royal dignity.

They passed the purple capes of northern Alba, and the steersman turned them westward by the Giants' Cliffs.

None knew any longer, unless he was immortal, why they had their name. Ancient lava flows had solidified there in masses of six-sided stone pillars a hundred feet high, like blue-grey honeycomb. Other such masses lay farther west, with the sea booming against them. Sixarms had fetched much of the rock for his fortress from those formations.

Westwards and farther west they sailed, beyond the remotest Danan settlements and outposts. Their last encounter with folk of their own race happened on the isle called Furtherest. It was nothing of the kind, except from their tribal point of view. Ample coast and many an island lay ahead of them yet, but it was all Freth territory, holding Freth secrets, Freth powers.

The chief of Furtherest welcomed them, making them guest-free. A zestful pirate named Shaui, he had an endless supply of fiery liquor and not the least aversion to sharing it. Though most of his followers were Danans, he numbered a few crouching, splay-footed bog-men among them, and one shark-skinned blue giant with cold eyes. Shaui himself had a faint tinge of green in the bronze-red of his hair, suggesting Lyran blood.

"The Revolving Fortress?" he said. "Lady, if you follow the shore towards the sunset, you can scarcely miss it. Let me advise you; turn around. I don't say it cannot be taken, but it has powdered the bones of every sea-host that ever came against it, Danan, Freth, or Lyran in ships invisible. I've seen it twice, when I was blown out of my way, like a mighty growling quern set on the waves. I, Shaui, prosper because I have never deliberately gone near it. The master of it, Sixarms, is a Freth demon."

"Well," Cena said, "that Freth demon was my guest on the First Created Plain, and now he has invited me to be his. Maybe the way to return from the Revolving Fortress is to go there as a friend."

"If you believe that, lady, you do not know Freths," Shaui retorted, "and less do you know Sixarms."

Cena might have told the island chieftain precisely how well she knew Sixarms, but didn't. She asked, "What will you wager that you don't see us return?"

"My head's the most precious thing I own," Shaui said, and roared at the joke, "I'll set that against all the goods in your royal house."

He'd drunk freely, as had Cena. She said, "I'll take that."

"Done!" Shaui bawled, and clasped hands on it there.

Hours afterward, as she walked on the shore to cool her head with two spearmen warding her, she halted by a rock carved in the likeness of a three-faced god. To the older warrior, Ith, she said:

"Did it strike you that something was wrong in the terms of my bet with Shaui?"

"The stakes, lady," Ith said in a dry voice.

"Apart from those."

Ith shrugged. "If we don't return, he wins. However—if we don't return, how can he claim his winnings? Go to the Revolving Fortress and ask for it, when he's deathly afraid of the place? That's what comes of wagering drunk. I've done it too."

"He wasn't all that drunk. No. There's a way he could both win and collect, my braves . . . if we do not come *back* from the fortress because we never arrive there."

They digested that, and grew thoughtful.

"We have one ship, and there are forty of us. Shaui musters half as many again."

"Whom we would eat in equal fight!"

"Not all fights are equal," Cena reminded them. She sprang to the top of the stone head. "Do you remember what he said about invisible ships?"

"Lyrans?"

"I mean nothing else."

"The man has a green tinge to his own hair," Ith said. "I marked it. He's also followed by everything, except Lyrans. Maybe they're only absent, waiting."

"And none of us can see them."

"I came prepared," Cena said. "Go aboard the ship with me, and be sure none disturbs us. Perhaps I wrong Shaui."

"Perhaps, lady," Ith said ironically, "but I'd make no wagers on that."

Within the vessel's sides, Cena opened a chest divided into several drawers. The lid held carved wands of oak, rowan, beech, and yew. Each drawer contained a garment of some sort of skin; a cloak of eagle feathers, a tunic of swansdown, a wolfskin, a doe's hide, and lastly a dolphin's.

Cena chose two wands, lay down between them, and put on the dolphin's hide from the tail forward, all the while singing a song that ranged in pitch from deep to inaudibly high. The two spearmen did not flinch from such evidences of sorcery. They were also Danans.

The Rhi endured spasms, torments, ecstasies, and shiftings. Then a white dolphin arched upward from the tiny foredeck, flipped forward on its tail, and vanished into the water. Nothing was left where Cena had been but two ornate wands and her human clothing.

Sleek as Prince Nemed's ship, she drove through the sea, powered by muscles and flukes strong enough to dismay a shark. Currents and eddies spoke to her through her skin, which stung with living. She could not see far, or clearly, but every pop, gurgle, groan, and slap of water reached her ears with tenfold meaning.

Her own throat poured forth sounds which came back to her as echoed clicks and shrillings. They made pictures in her brain. A rock, a school of fish, the metal ship behind her . . . a wooden hull, lithe in the sea, a mile away. Another. She raced forward, high above the earth, circling the unknown ships at a wary distance.

Lyrans for certain they were, children of the sea as Danans were children of the land. To mortal eyes their ships were impossible to detect. Not, however, to the senses of a dolphin. Laughing and playful, Cena made a great leap, letting the air rush past her until the water received her again.

Mastering the dolphin's urges, she swam within the sight of her own ship and made two leaps. Her spearmen knew by that signal she had found two Lyran craft lurking, and indulged in some soft-voiced, heated discussion of Shaui's character. They were for rousing their whole party and confronting the pirate then.

"No," Cena declared, once ashore in her proper form. "That wouldn't be wise. Besides, I have a bet to win from him."

The Danans put to sea with the next daylight tide. A white dolphin frolicked ahead of their vessel, guiding them, and when the unseen ships of Shaui's Lyran friends began to close in, she led the way to safety. For Valf to outsail them was easy, once he knew where they were. Shaui's dreams of a rich ransom vanished like the bubbles they had been.

His erstwhile guests came to the island of the Revolving Fortress. Shaui had not given a false description. It could be seen for miles, a squat tower within an encircling wall which turned and turned on its foundations. Its gateway came level with an opening in the stationary outer wall three times each hour, and then one might enter—if the Freths allowed it. If they did not, the only way in was to climb the walls of precisely fitted stone, at the risk of falling to the base and being milled there like grain. Old rusty stains at the base of that wall showed where attackers in other days had failed.

"Blazing thunderbolts!" Garanowy cried. "Sixarms built that? No! It must have been here before he was born! Giants made it, or I'm a herring!"

"You will be cooked for breakfast like one if you say many more foolish things such as that," Cena told him. "Sixarms is the builder. He's older than you think, little brother, and a man of more power."

She fell silent then, marvelling at the forces which upheld and turned that immense mass of stone. Drawn from within the earth, in the same way that the Danans' wagons were made to float above the ground without wheels, they awed and appalled the mind in a way that common floatwains never would. This island must be a seething focus of earth power to make the little channels of force across the Danan country look puny. Cena thought of her people's common belief that the Freths were too ignorant to use it, typified by Garanowy's outcry.

This visit should make some of them learn, at least.

She felt the forlornness of that hope as Prince Nemed's ship glided to its moorings among the heavy dugouts and leather curraghs of Sixarms's people. So much swifter, more graceful, delicate, and light it was that any Danan's pride would lift at the comparison—even under the walls of the Revolving Fortress.

Sixarms lumbered down the crude quay to meet them, clad now in a tunic with long sleeves, and cowhide leggings. A necklace of hammered gold nuggets winked about his massive throat. Other Freths in sewn deerskins came behind him, unarmed to show good faith.

"Cena!" he rumbled, gripping her silken shoulders. "A long voyage and dangerous you had to come here. We'll requite you for that. It is good to see you!"

"And you, Sixarms!" She kissed him in greeting, with a laugh. "I'd never have thought you could grow uglier, but you have succeeded. Goddess! Do you live here all the time?"

"No more than part of the year." He laughed himself, showing big square teeth. "And you are as bold as ever. Shaui must remember your passing. Did you clash with him?"

"No! We were his guests. A good fellow, who saw to it that we were not bored."

The fortress's gateway opened again. They had ample time to walk through it, though Cena felt some concern for the sailors bearing the chests and bales of gifts.

"It's nothing," Sixarms assured her. "I can make the fortress turn slower or faster as I wish."

He showed that he could, and the burdens were safely carried within his walls. Freths bearing solid wooden shields ambled along the ramparts, while catapults with great stone counterweights and long arms stood below in the yard. The squat tower, its stones partly melted together with fire, provided a final haven if the walls were overrun.

The tower's double walls contained stairways and rooms.

Cena stumbled more than once, going up. From ledges on the inner wall, rough ladders led down, into a circular grassy enclosure with vats and cooking pits at the center. Throughout, the place was filled with a soft, constant rumbling.

They feasted that night on food which was clearly plentiful in the Freths' country. Despite its slovenly comfort, the fortress showed health and abundance in its every corner. The Danans ate better than they had lately done at home.

"Your people have cursed us," Cena said. "You must know that, Sixarms. It's a slow curse, of the kind that our magic can't counteract."

"The old women of all the villages are sending it," Sixarms admitted. "I cannot stop them if I would, Cena. You still do not know how it is with us. The paramount chief is always a man, but the old women rule. They know the body of the Mother in ways men never can. You Danans, you trace courses of power and you marvel at this fortress, but you know nothing at all."

"Are our horses and metals nothing? Our workmanship? Sixarms, I can't stop my young men raiding you, any more than you can stop your old women making magic! But lately there is a plan and a direction to the worst raids. The men responsible for that, I can find and stop. I need only time. With the hunger there will be in our lands this winter, though, my folk will come harrying in force just to eat. Did your old women stop to think of that?"

"They do not see that they have much to lose."

"They do! And so have we."

"What will you do for food?"

"Hunt," Cena answered. "Butcher the last of our cattle, those that haven't sickened. Already I have sent for grain from Alba. Whether we get it will depend on their harvests."

"I don't say this to gloat. A lean winter may teach your people a lesson. *We* are not here for them to hunt! You have your horses, but we can force you to eat your horses."

"I'll ride my own across your last river before I do that! Sixarms, are we so helpless, then? I am not. If I have to fight half of them and talk the rest to death, I'll put sense into them yet! I know the man who does these things. By winter I'll have caught him. Yet you must leave me to deal with him. He's one of my own. As for your powerful old women—I can't advise you there."

Sixarms hacked at a joint of venison. Flies buzzed around him. His broad nose and corrugated brow stood out in the firelight. With her red-gold hair and tall carriage, Cena showed beside him as a goddess beside a forest boar. Yet she knew the quality of the thoughts that turned over in that backward-bulging head.

"I'll do what I can," he said at last. "Listen, you Danans! Before the Day of Autumn, I will send a thousand cattle of my own herds into your land. Rough they are, but they can live on roots and bark if they must, and still give more milk, and richer, than your own beasts have ever done. This is a gift. But I will not have you think the Freths weak. The cattle your folk have stolen will cause trouble with hoof and horn until they are returned to us. If you butcher them for meat in your tribal lands, the place where you slaughter them will lie barren for years. The meat will cause such aches, colics, and vomiting that those who devour it will be sorry they were born."

"A thousand cattle!" Cena said. "Chieftain, that was the offer of a Rhi. I accept gratefully."

How many cattle do you have, that you can be so generous?

Outside, within the turning wall, the sea-captain Valf was also being generous. He had trundled casks of barley beer ashore, to drink and to share with the Freth warriors. He ladled it out freely.

"There isn't much food to go with it," he grinned, "but you and I needn't be bothered by that."

While the Freths brewed good beer of their own, they had seldom tasted the like of what Valf gave them. Soon they clamored, and passed their beechwood cups for more.

"It's fine!" they said unanimously. "It is the best."

"It ought to be, you browless fools," Valf said to himself. "There's a keg of Shaui's strongest spirit in it, that I won wrestling."

The bard Uisfrel had grown bored in the vitrified tower. He did not speak the Freth language, for one thing, and did not care for their food, for another, much less their way of eating it. He said so, loudly, and would have composed a satire on the subject had Cena not stopped him.

"Och, it's harmless sport, lady," he said plaintively. "These lobs do not even know what I'd be singing."

"That doesn't matter. It's insulting to your host. What's

more, Uisfrel, some of these . . . lobs . . . speak our tongue passing well, while you do not understand a word of theirs. Go out, by the Mothers, and walk yourself sober. Come back when you can think.''

Uisfrel went out with his hurt bardic dignity, and walked into uproar.

Reeling, laughing Freths filled the circular yard. Some swayed with their arms about one another's shoulders, chanting their own songs to a rhythm of beaten sticks. Two were down on their hands and knees, butting their heads together. Others were fighting with their flint axes and spears, roaring. Uisfrel took one swift look and raced back to the tower. He knew what happened when Freths went mad on water-of-life.

He crashed into Sixarms as he reached the tower's doorway. It was like colliding with a tree. He rebounded, into the arms of a warrior Freth who had chased him simply because he ran. The Freth cuffed him aside. From his own standpoint it was only a rough tap, but it knocked Uisfrel stunned to the paving-stones, bleeding from his nose and ears.

Striking a bard was a deadly crime among the Danans, and two of them, crowding behind Sixarms, saw it happen. They hadn't come to the feast armed, but they saw a rack of spears nearby and seized a couple.

"Danans forward!" one of them shouted. "There's treachery here!"

Together they lunged at the Freth who had struck down Uisfrel. Cena cried in her most commanding shout, *"No, you triple fools!"* and springing forward, seized their necks to bang their heads together. As they stumbled, she knelt beside Uisfrel. She lifted him without stopping to see whether he lived, and strove to carry him to safety. His slack limbs weighed as heavy as stone.

Sixarms thundered, "Stop, or have my curse!" The stones of the outer walls vibrated to his voice, and it might have quelled even the drunken brawl in the liss. A furious Danan, convinced they were the victims of deliberate treachery on Sixarms's part, hurled himself on the Freth's wide back. Holding his bronze eating-knife in both hands, he drove it downward into the thick muscle of the shoulder, so hard that the point snapped against bone. Sixarms reached upward and back with his good arm, closed a hand like a clamp on the Danan's neck, and dragged him from his position. He studied the choking man as a fisherman might study a piece of rubbish which has found its way into his net and damaged the meshes. Then, taking a grip on the fellow's thigh with his bleeding arm, the chief threw him at the tower wall. He rebounded and lay still.

Many Freths saw the act, and cheered it. Some saw the blood spilling from their chief's shoulder, and were thereby moved to greater rage. If they thought at all, they believed his cry to halt or be cursed had been meant for the Danans. A Freth warrior kicked Cena's legs from under her. She fell flat beneath the dead weight of Uisfrel.

The two warriors she had manhandled came to her aid, not asking what it was about. They saw their Rhi menaced by swinging weapons; that was enough. They reddened their spears in Freth bodies with the Danan war-shout on their lips, and others raised the same call in response, from within the crude tower.

Sixarms rushed back there, climbing the dark stairway between the double wall, ignoring the pain of his wound that was as nothing to the anguish in his huge heart.

What he saw confirmed his worst thoughts. Danans and Freths were at one another's throats with knives, both sides convinced the other had begun a treacherous slaughter outside. In the firelit tumult he recognized Garanowy, the raw lad who had nearly ridden him down at their first meeting. Tears shone on his beardless face. He was fighting like a red-haired demon despite them.

Grunting in pain, Sixarms clambered down the ladder and dropped the last few feet to the grassy circle at the bottom of the tower. Far, far above, smoke escaped to a patch of starry sky. Sixarms instinctively lifted his club, the Grinder, with contradictory passions tearing him. Then he began whirling it, not to kill, but driving the Danans back to the walls of the tower and the ladders propped against them.

"Go!" he advised them forcefully. "Go from here while you can!"

Poorly armed, trapped in a confined space with men and women who could dismember them bare-handed, the Danans went up the ladders like squirrels. When it came to fumbling their way down the crude stone stairs in the dark, they progressed more like moles, despite their night-vision; but they couldn't delay.

Emerging into the paved liss, they met the drunken Freths and a remnant of desperate Danans who tossed them what weapons they could. The turning walls, five times a man's height, made of upright stone columns as lesser stockades were made of tree-trunks, could not be scaled.

"Where's the gateway?" Garanowy asked.

"Here, little brother," Cena answered, over the brisk cracking noises her spearshaft made on a Freth shield. "Here! But it's moving so slowly, and it isn't aligned with the outer gap yet."

The youth did not care, so long as it was a place to make a stand and guard his sister's side. Cutting at a broad face with his recovered blade, he saw the Freth flinch. He made a powerful salmon-leap, landed with his feet on the Freth's hard shoulders, and launched himself over two more shaggy heads, dropping nimbly to the ground before the gateway. He disabled one warrior with a drawing cut to the thigh, and rejoined Cena after dodging the grip of a broad, clutching hand.

"Where are the rest?" he panted, sensing in that first instant how few his companions were.

"Lying back there," Cena answered as tersely, before an axe-blow to her shield split it across. She fell bruisingly to her knees, hissing with the pain of a broken arm. Garanowy screamed a war-cry and drove his sword into an open mouth.

"You catch flies that way," he said as his blade came free with a grate of bronze on bone.

The Freth onslaught eased for a moment. Cena struggled to her feet, aided by her brother. The firelight caught their hair, red-gold and copper-hued, reflecting from it to sheen on the deeper reds of bronze and blood. Cena's bold-featured face was milky.

"Now all they need do is stone us," she whispered.

There was a rush of cool air at their backs. At the same time, Sixarms's deep voice ordered, "Let them go. I say it. Let them go to their ship. Cena, do you live?"

"I live, you oak-knot! It's no gratitude I owe your hospitality for the fact! Come down here and let me take off your head."

"You are alive," Sixarms agreed. Then he added something strange. "Smell the air."

"What?"

"Smell the air."

Cena cursed shakily. "You are determined to get my life one way or another, aren't you? Smell the air! There are dead Freths down here, you porridge-eating clown."

They retreated through the tunnel-like thickness of wall before the Revolving Fortress trapped them again. High above, on the rim of his vitrified tower, Sixarms bent his head and turned his attention to his shoulder wound.

Morning broke clouded and wan over a leaden sea. The Revolving Fortress looked sinister in the overcast dawn. Waves beat mournfully on the jumble of rocks which was its shore, while the lengths of six-sided basalt left over from building the unique defence suffered their endless washing in the surf, where they did duty as a pier. A shimmering metal hull rode the water, well out from shore.

Sixarms led a procession to that uneven wharf. Two women painted for mourning paddled him out to the anchored ship. Every Danan in her held weapons, except Cena. She had no need to wear paint. All her hot grief and anger showed in her face. Her arm had been splinted.

"I left a dozen of my people with you," she said, without preamble or greeting. "Are any alive?"

Sixarms said as directly, "No."

"Then this ends it! Never will we be wed or allied, never will the Danans make peace with you! Hither we came as your guests, Sixarms—a good name for you, and a hidden weapon in every hand. Let it—"

"*Wait.*"

The one word, spoken in Sixarms's deep voice, dropped like a stone into the midst of Cena's tirade. It stopped the surge of words at their source, for the moment.

"My people have died, too. They were mad with the strongest drink you brew. Did you not smell it, last night?"

Cena had. Her nose remembered it now, strongly and unmistakably. Among the odors of sweat, blood, meat, and the sea, there had been the reek of distilled drink in the liss, strong upon all the warriors she fought.

Only Danans in all the sacred island of Tirtangir distilled their liquor.

"Where did they get it?" she breathed.

"From your ship. The captain brought it."

There had been casks in the liss. Cena remembered seeing them.

"What's that you say?" Valf strode to the rail, an accused innocent. "Me? I took barley beer ashore. Freths can drink that, you make it yourselves. If there was water-of-life handed around, your warriors had it hidden. Accuse me, you ugly miscarriage, and I will have you in pieces."

"There was none in the fortress."

"Excuses," Cena said bitterly. "What does it matter? Your warriors got drunk and started the slaughter. What use were you in stopping it? Send me my dead, Sixarms. I'd depart from here."

"Are you the Rhi?"

"What does that mean?"

"A Rhi judges. I have seen you do it. She does not run because her heart is sick. If your captain or anyone else brought the water-of-life into my fortress, you should want to know about it."

More tangled things to unravel. Cena's broken arm hurt. But Sixarms was right. If the fiery liquor had come to this place in her own ship, and been deliberately smuggled to the Freths, it meant something. She had been betrayed by one of her own party, perhaps one of her own nobles at home. She thought of Gui.

It was wearisome to pick over matters like that until the pattern could be discerned. Far sweeter to be angry, and break what didn't please her. Unfortunately, as Sixarms said, she was the Rhi.

"Last night twelve of my people were slain while we sat in council," she said. "You can't undo that. Neither can I enter your fortress in trust again."

"Then I'll come aboard," the giant Freth said grimly. "Throw me a rope."

"No, Sixarms. I'll search out the truth among my folk, you do the same among yours. Then maybe we can meet. Until then, it's little we can do save argue whose fault it was." Her control broke. She suddenly screamed, "Send me my dead and get out of my sight!"

Sixarms raised a huge hand in acknowledgement. He spoke,

and the women paddled him back to his stone quayside. Others awaited him in the dark forests of the mainland, women who would speak for war because of this. It was proof indisputable that Danans could never be trusted, they would say.

Perhaps they were right, and he mistaken. Cena had mocked him at Sen Mag; now her guesting with him had become a weapon-bathing. How many lessons should he need? Three of his own folk had been slain. She had not asked about that. She too was a Danan; however she desired to live at peace in Tirtangir—or perhaps that was a lie.

Must it be war after all? The haughty Danans did not believe his race could win one; Sixarms knew that it could. The trees of the forest would fight with the Freths.

Cena also looked at the possibility of war, which now seemed so much more like certainty. Something in her welcomed it. There would be an end to groping in the dark, finding ways to make her proud people accept what they did not truly want. Weapons would settle the question one way or another. She would hurl herself into that with the fury of one battle-woman, fighting and fighting until all of Tirtangir belonged to the Danans, as Gui and Sanhu wanted, with so many others.

And Sixarms, honest, patient Sixarms, so gentle and so mighty, lay food for crows? With all the Freths and Danans who deserved to live equally?

Cena used the disciplines of a sorceress until she was calmer. There were questions to ask. Gathering the remnant of her embassy behind her, she spoke to the mariners one by one, asking them what they knew of that deadly cask of the water-of-life. She had reigned for years, despite her youth, and had learned to recognize liars, clumsy or adroit.

The mariners satisfied her that they were innocent. All of them would have found it difficult to hide liquor in a ship where there was no privacy even for a Rhi or a captain. All of them would have enjoyed finding it. Oh, doubtless there were ways, like suspending the little keg, weighted, from a rope below the stern, until it was wanted. But that would attract attention, hiding it and retrieving it.

Then she spoke to Valf.

She had liked the man. Sea-wise, convivial, he had talked to her freely on the journey, not as some seamen did, making it plain that they regarded any landsman as a nuisance aboard, and a passenger as something to be endured. Now, though, she sensed wary resistance under his amiable surface. Well, after the events of last night, that was natural enough.

"How soon can we get away from here, lady?" he asked abruptly. "I'd leave with the tide, before those ugly demons beswarm us in their canoes. We've no more reason to stay."

"We have, captain. I think the Freths were purposely made drunken by one of us."

"I guessed it by the questions you have asked. Lady, I can't say yes or no to that, and it's no concern of mine. This ship is. The prince will hold me to blame if it's lost. Not that I'd be caring, if I had an axe in my body, but I owe him faith."

"Faith," Cena repeated. "Yes. Do you like Freths, captain?"

"I think they're dirt," he answered bluntly.

"So? Then why did you bring them good barley beer last night, and spend time drinking with them in the liss? You were very friendly then, captain—as you were friendly to us on the voyage, friendly with Shaui. Yet you departed before the worms began to writhe in their brains, and left us to face their madness. That was no friendly act. And one swallow of that beer must have told you it had water-of-life in it. One swallow? One sniff!"

"So it would, if there had been any mixed. There was none. You accuse me of treachery!"

"Treachery. Murder. Yes, you false cur! I do! You expected none of us to leave the fortress alive. But for Sixarms, we would indeed have been slain. Oh, and you were so very affable to us, all the way from our own harbors. I thought you true!"

"You change opinions fast!"

"When I have cause! You wanted to raise sail and leave us last night, when the racket began. This your sailors have told me—and they would not, as they aren't part of your scheme, they would not abandon us!" Cena looked at the captain with open loathing, and more of anger. "For whom did you do this?"

Valf's glance shifted back and forth. He found no refuge anywhere, but he had known when he accepted the wages of his treachery that it would be perilous. He stopped searching for a way out and grinned insolently in Cena's eyes.

"Tell me," he said, "why I should be telling you?"

Cena stared at him with her sorceress's eyes. The grin stayed in place, but any bravado had gone from it; now it was a lifeless fixture, hanging there, which Valf had forgotten to remove.

His shoulders began to hunch, his knees to bend. He went down to his hands and knees, fighting the compulsion every inch of the way, yet he went down. The Rhi's voice seemed to reach his ears from a long way off.

"Men, even enemies, stand before me. Curs, betrayers, knives in my back—they do not. Unwise were you, Valf, to ask me for a reason. You might have known I would give you one."

She threw her green silk cloak over him as he crouched on the deck. "Transform," she said, and he shrivelled and shrank. A fish the size of a child struggled on the deck, ugly, leathery, pop-eyed. Even as her people stared at it, Cena rose, hooked her fingers in its gills, and threw it over the side. It circled the ship several times, staring at the woman piteously.

"Come to me by my own shores when you are ready to speak the name," she said. "Until then, never approach me, or worse may happen."

Her people watched this harsh justice with approval. Not even Valf's own sailors objected. His guilt had been plain enough.

Garanowy looked seaward. "Maybe that was unwise, sister. Who now will guide the ship home?"

"I will, little brother. A dolphin or an eagle can do as well as a captain, and no captain at all is better than a treacherous one. Once I have spoken with Sixarms again, then we can depart."

Chapter
Three

The Rhi of the Danans parted from Sixarms with tears, knowing what the future was likely to hold. However, the mighty Freth was the only one who saw those tears. On the voyage home, Cena's eyes were dry as two blue jewels. Racing through the water in the shape of a dolphin, or winging far above as a she-eagle, Cena may have found both a glorious relief from being human—while the transformations lasted. Always, though, she had to return to the sleek metal ship of Prince Nemed's lending.

As she had promised, she guided it safely home, and there she had to report utter failure. The brothers she had left behind were the first to know. Oghmal of the long blue eyes and long lethal hands sighed deeply.

"It wasn't to be," he said.

"Sister, if you failed, it's in my mind that any other would not have succeeded," Carbri told her. His gold-strung harp gave forth strong, hopeful music under his fingers.

"We won't muster for war just yet," Cena vowed. "I'm not

one to give up so easily. Let us see what the Freths do. Meanwhile, tell every fisherman on the coast that if any ugly green fish appears, let them in no way harm it, but bring me the news quickly."

"At such a time as this, you take an interest in fish?" Carbri shook his curly head. "Beware, Cena. You could be deposed for losing your wits if there is much more of this."

"This particular fish," Cena said patiently, "is named Valf."

"Ah."

"Ah, truly. Instruct the heralds for me, will you, brother? And where is Diancet?"

The healer came to her directly. A little man with tufted seal-brown hair, he examined her arm and wrought healing spells over it, so that it mended more swiftly than nature allowed. Each day the bones knitted more strongly. At the end of nine the arm was wholly sound.

In the west, huge Freth drums thundered from lake to hidden grove. The many chiefs gathered in a dozen conclaves. Freth women, aged very young, talked in their own councils. Sixarms was heard with respect; nonetheless, his voice did not prevail.

His promise to send a thousand cattle to the relief of Danan hunger was honored. A demand came with them. The Danans were no longer safe to let walk free in Tirtangir. They must depart, go back to Alba or the more distant northlands, or even the stars if the story of their long exile there held truth; that, or accept the lordship of the Freths. If they did, Sixarms would be their Rhi henceforward, and they would find him a good one.

The laughter of the Danans filled the land. They didn't feel offended; the notion was too funny. Sanhu herself smiled.

The herds of unkempt black cattle which streamed bawling into their country caused no laughter. In more than one place they were greeted with tears of joy. More Danan cattle had sickened each day, and a rain of blood had devastated the wheat. Beasts escaped the hunters and even seemed to be leaving the land. The Freth herds, on the other hand, proved as rich to milk as Sixarms had promised.

But the price of them was too high.

Cena could not have paid it had she wished to. She would have been removed from her apple-wood throne in a day. Nor did she wish to. Peace on an equal footing was one thing. To the demand for subjection she answered a single word: "Never."

The Freths had expected it.

Distracted by these events, Cena allowed the fish which had been Valf to slide from her mind. She trusted her fishermen to report any such matter to her, turning her sorcerous watch westward, and finding enough there to concern her. But Sanhu looked to the rocky, white-sanded coast.

One evening a pop-eyed, hideous fish an ell long wallowed tiredly in the shallows. It moved to swift activity when it felt the splashing riders exercising their horses in the surf. Hope stirred in its dim brain, with memories of firelight, dryness, legs, and arms. Its lumpy tail drove it towards the noises as swiftly as might be.

Gui saw it coming. A triumphant grin split his beard. With a sudden motion of his arm, he hurled a nine-barbed javelin into the fish's side. A thin cord stronger than most heavy rope linked the spear to his wrist.

The wounded fish's flurry nigh pulled Gui from his horse. Gripping its flanks hard with his knees, he hauled on the cord while two of his riders also speared it. Others closed in to hew it apart with swords.

Dying, the fish spoke.

"My curse on you and your evil dam, Gui of Lost Star Lake! You and she will not live ten years. Your son will be taken from you—"

A downward cut split its head, ending its maledictions. The fragments became parts of a human corpse, tumbling in the waves. Gui's men collected them and gave them swift burial among the rocks.

"I do not think your curse will have any great effect, my back-stabbing friend," Gui said to himself as he rode to his camp. "You were no sort of enchanter in life. I've doubts that you learned anything flopping about in the sea."

To his mother, when next he greeted her, he said that Valf was silent. "The Rhi never saw him."

"Indeed that's well. His word could have been the end of us both."

"That will never occur now. Yes, and soon we will master the Freths." Gui's coldly handsome face lit with anticipation. "I will pile a cairn of their heads as a memorial to my uncle."

"There speaks the true son I bred. How tall a cairn?"

"Taller than I!" Gui laughed. "We will grow strong on the milk and cheese of their own cattle. What fools they were to send them!"

He uttered a mistake. With the Danan refusal, the black cattle proved a weapon. Their milk swiftly dried up, and they became dangerous. Even the cows would gore an unwary herdsman, and many a time they banded together with uncanny purpose to stampede through an orchard or house. The shaggy little bulls were wicked, and raged through the land on nimble feet, killing horses and men indiscriminately. Within a month, the thousand cattle had become such a menace in Danan lands that there was no choice but to destroy them.

"Sixarms said that if they were killed, the place where they died would be barren for years," Cena told her people, remembering. "Years, not a single summer; and all else he warned us of has come true."

"I am not for meekly driving them back to him!" Garanowy said hotly. "What, after the harm he has done us? No. Kill the brutes."

"My lord Garanowy says well," Gui said, rising. With Nemed and Oghmal, he was among the greatest fighters present. "No curse which comes with killing these beasts can be worse than the plague they are to us, living. But if there is one, let the sea take it, for the seashore is barren already."

The other lords applauded that suggestion, even Oghmal, who felt small liking for Gui. Then each went forth to gather horses, dogs, and men for the cattle-drive, while there was yet a house standing or a woman or child uninjured in all their lands. They scattered to the ends of their borders, and gradually converged again with their hundreds of bawling cattle, holding the vast herd together with droving skill supported by magic. Even so, saddles were emptied and graves were filled before that drive came in sight of the ocean-cliffs.

The wild beasts from the western forests milled about on the grass, muddy and smeared with foaming slaver. They liked neither the nimble, beautiful horses, the white dogs, or the constant pricking with spears which urged them on. Then a great half-circle of illusory flame sprang from the ground behind them. Its crackling heat drove them to terror where before they had felt rage and sullen resistance. They ran madly before it.

The fire moved at their heels, converging, though nothing appeared to feed it. Indeed, nothing did, except the will of the sorcerers whose minds were the source of its mirage. Yet the cattle were helpless in the face of it, and rushed blindly to a real doom in attempting to escape what was unreal.

The first beasts raced over the verge, to topple through thirty fathoms of air and be destroyed among the rocks at the base. Others fell into clear water, and if they were not stunned, began feebly to swim. But their plunging fellows struck them, smashing their bones, driving them below the water, until the sea was filled with careasses and lowing, drowning beasts. Only a very few strong ones swam around the cliffs and staggered ashore on an open beach, to be speared to death there by waiting Danans. They had suffered much from these cattle, the children of the Earth-Goddess.

"And now, it seems, we're to starve except for what fowlers and fishermen provide," Carbri remarked with understandable sourness. "It's as well that the Freths are not likely to provide us with much of a war."

"If you'd seen the Revolving Fortress, brother, you'd be less sure of that," Garanowy told him, airing his greater knowledge. "I can't believe Sixarms built it himself, as he claims; still, it makes me wonder what else they have that we don't know about."

"A seasoned traveller we have here now," Carbri said. The chords he drew from his harp expressed gentle derision. "Surely they'll have surprises here and there. It's likely they'll outnumber us. But we'd have to make a mighty effort to lose."

Garanowy made a rude gesture. They were so evidently two birds of the same nest, with their tall, lean-waisted build, copper-red hair, and likeness of feature. Oghmal, Carbri's twin, had more the look of an intruder in the nest, with his straight brown hair and quiet stillness. He never blazed or raged outwardly; his flame was an inward one, though when he released it in battle, the hottest of all.

Now he said, "Sixarms is no fool. War may not be entirely of his choosing, but he wouldn't fight it at all if he didn't think he could carry the day. It's for us to show he's wrong. We had better make that mighty effort to *win*. With everything we have."

He held five javelins in one hand, bunched together, and sent them flashing to a target eighty feet away. They flicked from his left hand to the right, and were launched, in such quick succession that they all seemed to fly at once. All five stuck out of the target's center, a space no bigger than a wolf's head.

Word went forth, carried by lean men on horses as yet well-fed, by sorcerers self-transformed to birds, and by naked spirits who ventured even into grave-mounds to summon the Danan dead to arms. Spears were sharpened on many a farmstead where children wailed with hunger, and men thought longingly of chances to shed the blood of those they blamed for the famine. Their hearts shouted the word Freth! Freth! *Freth!*

But they went to the hosting with lean bellies.

"The narrower targets we'll make, then," Carbri laughed. "Your Freth, now, is too wide to miss."

Cena appreciated the spirit behind the joke, but a bitter joke it remained. All available food must go to the war-host. There was little enough of it. The earth itself seemed to have turned against them. The sea still offered its bounty, but fish were not enough to give strength to warriors—or to sustain a family through the winter, if it should prove sharp.

Cena had established granaries, deep and soundly lined, for such lean times, and had them magically protected against mildew. She had also sent to Alba for more. The needed wheat came, obtained through Prince Nemed's kin—but after it came a plague of mice, on a million tiny feet. They gnawed and spoiled. All the spellcraft of Cena's magicians could not keep them out of the wheat, or save horse-harness or the lacings of armor from their indefatigable teeth.

The Freths had their own ways to fight a war.

"When they come out to face us, we will requite them for all this," said Bava, who led the Danan battle-women. Very tall and lean, she fought with two short swords which she called her talons. An intricate tattooed pattern representing crow's feathers covered her body. Male warriors called her the War Crow, and not as an insult.

"Yes, there is surely some repaying to be done," Nemed said. "At least the Firbolgs at home do not fight us with sorcery. They have none."

"We are also the masters there." It was Loredan, his once-round face now lean. "I will make poems that will hearten the host to strike nine blows to the Freths' one. I will summon the dead of all our generations who lie in the earth of Tirtangir to come and fight for us.''

''I'll satirize them so that the strength goes out of their noisome bodies,'' Carbri promised.

Oghmal, whose phenomenal skill with weapons was his one real talent, swore that he would slay whichever enemy dared stand before him, and not flinch from any sending of theirs.

''I will transform them into toads and weasels as I meet them,'' Cena said. ''It will be a fair recompense for their mice.''

Meanwhile the leaves were falling. As forest cover grew thinner and winter approached, the Freth forces gathered. The thick-bodied men with their bludgeons, spears, and polished flint war-axes came in dugouts by river and on foot through the forest trails. Packs of grey wolves trotted with them, like brothers, and bears had postponed their winter sleep to join the fight. Numbers of gigantic deer, with antlers ten feet across, which few Danans had seen, gathered with the rest; and the trees drew their branches aside to avoid entangling them.

They entered the Danan lands through a waste moor with rugged boulders scattered across it; not the best of places for a charge by horses. For that reason the Freths camped there. They feared the Danan riders, as all who met them feared them. No other people had yet bred horses which could carry a man on their backs all day.

Sixarms walked across the moor, a rowan stick in his hand, waiting for it to twitch. It never stirred. The channels of force which ran beneath the skin of the earth, from place to place, did not flow here, and so the Danans would not be able to use their floatwains to bring in supplies. Nor could they carry their wounded out that way.

The huge chief returned to the sprawling camp of his host. Besides men and beasts, it contained folk less canny; horned, goat-footed urisks, holly trees transformed into warriors, creatures fashioned from mistletoe to creep and strangle, a few oaks which had not succumbed to winter's torpor and whose strength was greater than even a Freth's. A group of old women, painted half red, half white, sat around an ancient stone chanting an invocation by turns. None went near them.

On a hearth by a slow·fire, a great earthenware pot bubbled.

This was Undry, Sixarms's inexhaustible cauldron. Two women approached it with armfuls of rubbish; bones, dead leaves, grass, and mangy hides. They threw it in. Briefly, the pot gave off an uninviting smell, but it soon became an aroma of pleasing savor. Men came with their bowls and fed well.

Sixarms ate in his turn, sharing his food with a bear and a gnarled, stunted warrior from the southern coasts. The man smacked his lips over it.

"Good. What are these Danans like, Sixarms? I've never known any."

"To look at? Pale, and smooth, and soft."

"Like grubs?"

Sixarms snorted. "Not so very like grubs. No. They wear clothes made of strange pretty stuff, and their weapons kill better than ours. You have come a long way to meet them."

"From what I've heard, I want them to stay away from my parts."

"It's a good reason. They will spread even to the western sea if we let them. Never will it happen, though. We stop them here."

"If they fight on Winter's day, that's unchancy."

"They mean to do it. They are a folk who will do anything, and not mind." Sixarms sighed deeply. "Unless they receive some taming, they will destroy the Mother in the end."

"They cannot!"

"No? Well, they can injure her." Sixarms turned his heavy-browed gaze to the east again. "And there they are."

The gnarly fisherman squinted across the waste. Sunlight glinted orange from bronze spearheads, brooches, and buckles, white from silver ornaments, emerald green from armor and shields of the magic metal, findrina. Shining cloaks flowed indigo as dusk or yellow as the crocus. The glorious horses which only Danans could ride pranced and gambolled, jewels on their brows.

"The Mother never brought them out of her womb!"

"You're wrong. She did, but they have forgotten her."

"Who's that one with a skin that glitters blue-white, like a fish's scales?"

"Nemed of Alba, a sea lord. If you meet him, strike at his legs or arms. The tunic on his body protects it from all harm. Now do you see the man in red cloth, with brown hair? He

scorns such protection, but don't think to fight him. That is
Oghmal, their champion. The one beside him with the orange
and blue cloak, on the dun mare, is his sister Cena. She rules
them. The one there in black leather, with the white stars on his
shield, is Gui, among the worst of them. His mother will be
somewhere among the host.''

"Who are those others in rusty black?''

"Bava and her fighting women, the War Crows. When they
kill a man, they add his strength to their own, until the battle is
over. Be careful of them, and stand fast. Remember! They're
bright as fire, but they burn out quicker than we do. It's for us to
stand and hold until they break.''

The Danans camped half a mile away, across the rocky waste.
Dismounting, they formed their lines and tethered their horses,
feeding them the last spare handfuls of grain. Cena pitched her
tent in the center, with her troop of fifty household warriors
about her. The host numbered four hundred horsemen, with a
thousand warriors following afoot, behind their various chiefs.

The Freths were sixfold more numerous, not counting their
allies of beast and tree.

"There's glory enough here to go around, that's certain,''
Garanowy said. "We must kill eight enemies apiece.''

"Oh, I'd not be certain of that,'' Carbri argued. "If you feel
lazy, you can hope they break and run at three. It's thoughtful of
them to bring so many bear, elk, and pigs. We'll have our bellies
full of rich meat after the fight.''

Garanowy's mouth watered. "That's worth fighting for! I
swear by the goddess, I could roast a Freth this minute.''

"As could Sanhu,'' Carbri said, "and she would truly do it,
devouring their livers.'' He glanced towards the circle of snowy
wands the sorceress of Lost Star Lake had thrust into the
ground. "We require the help she is calling, but—I think she's
the only one here who could take pleasure in it.''

Sanhu's son stood within the circle, gripping the horns of a
tethered white bull. She leaned forward, peering for the right
place to strike, and drove home a spear precisely behind the left
shoulder. The bull sank down, bawling again and again before it
died with a final shudder.

Sanhu wrenched the spear free. Catching the flowing blood in a bowl, she sprinkled it around the circle while Gui skinned the bull. A ball of phantom white fire blossomed at the top of every wand.

Working like a man demon-possessed, Gui finished his arduous task in minutes. Then he set to work dismembering the bull, while Sanhu lay down, wrapping herself in the gory hide. She let her spirit depart from her body and hover in the air.

"*Ahe*, Danans of Tirtangir, I call you to fight for your tribe on this coming day! Now, on the night between summer and winter, between life and death, the portals stand open for you. The feast of welcome is spread. You who bred us, you who built our houses, sowed our fields, made the Danan race in this island, I call you to return. Fight for your children, and for our children's children! Come, Shival the Seafarer, Hu Longbeard, Lucal, Moraidh the She-Wolf . . ." Her harsh voice quivered. "Come, Mahon, my brother! Come from your graves and drink blood, come from your graves and eat flesh! Come and fight with your descendants again! Danan warriors, come!"

Within the circle, the air shimmered. Pale riders with a silver phosphorescence about them appeared from nowhere, outside the wands. Their horses looked gaunt, with legs and necks too long, heads too small, and teeth meant for eating flesh. Mildew spotted their garments; tarnish lay on their shields and lances. Their faces showed no traces of decay, though, nor their supple limbs, and a high sweet ringing came from the metal they carried. As they appeared, they saluted the pair within the circle, then turned away to seek their own places within the war-camp. Alive or dead, they were Danans.

Sanhu had spoken the truth. On cloaks and cowhides, a meal had been spread for the revenants, food the living Danans could hardly spare, set out to welcome their ancestors. The specters ate and drank with fine delicacy, while their mounts left only bones of the sacrificed bull.

The sun rose to illuminate the battle.

Freth sorcery, too, had been at work in the night. Although no rain had fallen, moisture had welled from within the earth, turning the high, hard ground into a morass. Men squelched when they walked. Even the light-footed horses of Cena's host sank to the fetlocks, as though into glue.

The dead riders Sanhu had summoned were not hampered by

the bog the field had become. They looked eagerly towards the Freth lines, and mounted with the sweet, remote chiming that accompanied them. Their leader touched spurs to his mount.

They moved in a mass, like one windblown cloud, all silver and grey. Their silent onrush was more frightening than a war-shout, yet the Freths in their great, sprawling camp stood fast.

The deep, vibrating roar of their drums crashed out. It broke the unity of the dead men's charge as wind tears a cloud to pieces. They came on, but in plunging twos and threes, their eerie horses touched by fear. As for the living horses pounding through the mud behind them, they panicked.

Freth missiles tore through the ranks of the dead. They crumpled like tinsel, their airy bones crackling, but were swift to recover. When spears tore through them, they lurched, felt pain, and swayed to the impact, yet their wounds closed at once. Then they were in among the Freths.

Their lances thrust and their swords bit. Yet they drew no more blood from their foes than those had been able to draw from them. The phantom weapons caused icy, numbing hurt, and many a jut-browed warrior fell beneath the hooves of the horses, fighting for control of his limbs.

The horses were not invulnerable, either. Sixarms devastated three with a looping swing of his great club, smashing a skull, a jaw, and a chest at the same fearful stroke. Ghostly swords pierced his chest and shoulder even as their wielders toppled slowly earthward. Sixarms jerked in agony, but continued to stand. The Grinder rose and fell, feebly by his standards, yet it crushed the revenants into the mud. They seemed fragile as birds' nests.

The Freth drums bellowed on. Those live horses that were not fleeing uncontrollably reared and screamed. The riders, impatient to reach their enemies, dropped from their backs and let them go where they would, slogging forward through the mire with their long shields lifted. They rushed as single warriors; attacks in close formation had not yet been dreamed of.

Many a Freth proved easy prey, in that first confused struggle, numbed by the touch of dead men's weapons. Sixarms resisted, shook off the effects, and fought more fiercely. He had discovered that they could be beaten. Not destroyed, since they had died once—but thrust violently out of the living world, back to the sphere whence Sanhu had summoned them.

Their spears and swords broke on his heavy shield, which would have dragged down a lesser arm than his. The Grinder hurled them flying with the dreamlike slowness of their insubstantial bodies, to lie crumpled on the ground, where they either renewed their forms or faded from mortal sight. Five times their phantom weapons touched him, sapping his strength until the blood crawled through his veins like concentrated poison, and even he foundered to his knees. There he nearly died as two battle-furious live Danans rushed upon him, dripping spears a-thirst still; but a forest pig like a short log of muscle with tusks and bristles charged over him, to rend his attackers. Sixarms crawled away, his club leaving a track in the soggy ground as he dragged it.

Gui, handsome as a god and fierce as a wildcat, fought to reach the great Freth and end his life, for he was jealous. But a real wildcat from the forest leapt snarling at his face, to cling with its claws until Gui ripped it away and hurled it against a rock. Blinded by his own blood, he lost sight of Sixarms and raged about, barely seeing, while his war-band protected him.

They retreated then, catching as many of their horses as they could while they crossed the quagmire the plain had become. Each man felt that he carried the weight of a stone in clinging mud on each foot, and his lungs burned. The phantoms of their ancestors, whose bones were buried in the land, ran fleetly beside them and turned to guard their backs when pursuit came close. The Freths did not pursue them far, though. They retreated behind crescent-shaped pits and barriers of stakes to await the next Danan onslaught.

Cena looked across the trodden morass to the Freth defences, sprawling but arranged in depth.

"If we charge that on our horses, we do no less than murder them," she said. "It may not be."

"Bava's women can become a flock of crows and fly above them," Oghmal said. "They grow impatient."

"They must wait. Only for this one day can the dead riders fight beside us; then they will return to their own place. While they can fight beside us, let them do it. They must attack again, with you and your band afoot behind them, and two others of your choosing. Not mine, brother; I have decided to lead the last attack of the day. Will you go?''

"Sister, you could not restrain me.''

"My band goes with you,'' Carbri said definitely. "I'd take it ill if you refuse, brother.''

The darker twin nodded. "We two, and Hol.''

Hol was a chieftain of middle rank, but in terms of cattle and followers, one of the strongest in the Danan lands of Tirtangir. A thick-necked, corpulent man, he welcomed the chance Cena's brothers offered. "You the two horns to hook, my band the head to crush, hey?'' he said happily. "And the riders from the mounds to hurl them into confusion ahead of us. I am ready.''

Then Cena watched her brothers and Hol advance behind the trotting dead riders, whose snowy flesh and floating, mist-grey hair proclaimed their origins. They quickened their pace to an eerie, floating gallop, while the living men rushed the gaps in the Freth defences. High over the water-filled pits and slanting stakes they sprang, to spread weakness and terror through the Freth lines. Yet the Freths outnumbered even five generations of Danan horsemen.

Slingstones brought them down. Fang and claw shattered their brittle substance. Against the Freths, Sanhu's dead riders were like fire and mist against rock. They could surround, blind, and even crack it, but not break it except through days or even seasons.

Carbri and Oghmal slid through the gaps behind them. The harper fought laughing, his bronze sword, the Dancer, whirling and lunging in the way that justified its name. More than one Freth felt the long ribbed blade enter his bowels or throat, and fell into the dark with his greater strength no use to him. But the champion was wind and lightning. Oghmal, the dark one, who among the multitalented Danans could make no graceful poems, play no instrument other than poorly, knotted his brow over games of skill, and was lost in the realms of sorcery—this same man defeated seasoned warriors five at a time in battle. His tall body contained the strength of a Freth without the ponderous width; although the mud slowed him, still he moved swifter than any of them. His long-handled axe rose and fell, streaming, sending a racket of shattered wood and bone through all the Freth lines.

Yet he could not be everywhere. The Freth host absorbed his

onslaught at last and hurled him back. A wolf brought him down; he strangled it with his hands while Freth spears penetrated his thigh and belly, and a club smashed his shoulder. His brother guarded the retreat while five warriors carried Oghmal away. Carbri himself streamed from eleven wounds by the time he returned, some light, others worth noting, two serious. He refused even to strip and have them examined until he knew how Oghmal fared.

"He will live and be whole," Diancet told him. "Do you not know me yet? I can heal any wound, child, short of a severed part, or a direct injury to the brain, or the marrow of the spine. Oghmal has none of these. His disrupted guts will digest campaign fare again; his shoulder I can mend, although no other could. No other!" the healer repeated, and strutted. Carbri felt a hot delicious impulse to throw the arrogant fellow over a treetop. His own wounds, and the knowledge that his strange but loved brother was in Diancet's care, prevented that. It remained a pleasant dream.

"But he will fight no more in this battle," the healer concluded.

"Goddess! That is good news for the Freths."

Carbri was tended by Avan and Rhobrun, two of Diancet's children, who had a measure of their sire's healing gift without his self-satisfaction. Their mother's brother and their foster-parents had had more to do with their upbringing than Diancet had, anyhow, as was usual in Danan families.

"You will fight again before your brother," they assured him, "but that is the most we can promise."

Carbri, feeling like something which had passed through a mad dog's entrails, did not greatly care just then if he never entered battle again.

Cena's attack at the head of her own troop likewise failed to break the Freths' stubborn resistance. Then the sun set, and the remaining dead riders departed like smoke, unable to stay. Sanhu mourned her brother anew, and many a Danan who had recognized some kinsman among the dead riders sorrowed for the chasm between them.

Until then, many more had died on Sixarms's side than on Cena's; but on hers, they could less well afford their losses. More than a hundred Danans lay still in the mud; thrice that number could not fight again immediately, if ever. Thus far the

Freths had taken all the punishment the Danans, their bellies growling with hunger, could give. For the first time Cena thought seriously of defeat.

On the second day, the Freths held fast again. They remained steady despite the rain of fire Cena's sorcerers hurled on them from a sky darkened by the wings of Bava's transformed battle-women. They resisted the attack led by Cena and Nemed in concert, a driving spearhead of flesh and metal it had seemed to her nothing could withstand. They had fallen back once more, those who were able, choking on failure, tormented by the smells which blew their way from Sixarms's cauldron of plenty.

"If you yield," he told them, "you may eat your fill."

Cena, who had not claimed so much as a mouthful eaten out of turn with the meanest of her warriors, felt dizzy and tempted. For a moment. Then she felt hot anger that Sixarms should make such a defaming offer to her. It was like the business of the cattle, which had proved a weapon against her people, not a mercy.

"No," she said fiercely. "We are going to beat you yet."

They did not do it that day.

Grey, drizzling rain fell all that night. Towards the dawn it became hail. The Danans tended their horses in improvised stables of leather awning while the Freths huddled close to one another and their beasts, finding warmth.

In the morning, Sixarms spoke to his fellow chiefs and warriors. Fine steam rose from the pelts of beasts and men alike. The transformed holly trees, lean and malicious, twirled their barbed spears. The powerful oaks with their beards of moss leaned on thick staffs, while water bubbled up around their feet.

"Yonder they wait, the ones who have stolen our land and would steal our lives," Sixarms said. "Even the body of the Mother is only a thing to grow grain and give power, for them. We must overcome them now, or in the time of our children—in your own time, you who are trees—we will be the ones a-hungered, waiting to be overwhelmed. You will feel their axes, and they will not even ask pardon for felling you, or give you the proper rites, as we do. Unless we defeat them, they will leave us nothing.

"Their defences are not as strong or deep as ours. They

believe in attack, and it has wearied them. They are hungry; we are not.''

"You know the plan. If any does not, or if he questions it, or wishes to go, let him say now. It's late, but not too late.''

None moved, man, woman, beast, or tree. Sixarms rested a hand on the rim of his bubbling pot and raised his enormous club with the other.

"Then let us take back what is ours!''

This time the Freths were the ones who advanced through mud. They carried long timber ramps to help them cross the Danans' hasty earthworks and brush barricades, and logs hung from ropes to swing into their ranks. They numbered thousands.

"There's more honor in this for us than for them,'' Nemed of Alba said, his blue armor shining like the sea once more.

"Aye!'' Cena answered, and thought, *But there won't be a victory*.

She killed that thought. With two brothers wounded behind her and the youngest at her side, brash and brave, she couldn't weaken. With a smile she called out, "Now they come to us, my comrades, and it's ours to play the hosts! Remember how they received us before, and do not stint your giving now! Give them bronze in their gizzards and bellies, lead in their thick pates, and shame to take home.''

They roared, none louder than Gui of Lost Star Lake. As the Freths came on, pressing doggedly through the slowly draining mire, Cena saw Sixarms, his face painted with the orange zigzags of his tribe, his limbs too. A bear's face laughed wide-mouthed from his chest. His thick shield was painted yellow.

"*Ahe*, my love!'' she shouted caustically, out of her pain and fury. "Welcome!''

The ramps rose, impelled by the Freths' cracking muscles, and dropped on the Danan barricades. Big muddy feet thudded upon them. Leaden sling-missiles whistled into the charging Formors, smashing heads and limbs. The Danan's remaining darts sought flesh, and entered it. Then they met with a reverberating impact.

Cena screamed like a hawk, and some distance away, Sixarms vented a bear's roar. Bare-headed, her red-gold hair piled and knotted like a crown, Cena forgot her wounds of the previous day. Her sword flickered, struck, bit right and left over clumsy Freth guards, ever striking home before they could strike her. Anything she wanted, she could do. Opening the front of a head—so!—was easy. Driving her point into a hairy throat—so!—was simpler yet, and the Freth's beard reddened as he stumbled. Getting past the next man's axe and shield to lay open his stomach took a little more time, but that too she could do, and performed. He collapsed with an unbelieving look on his face, his bass war-shout turned to a high, thin screaming.

Then the Rhi met a warrior of the holly race, his black eyes glinting, his body sheathed in close armor of waxy green leaves. His poisoned spear darted at her thigh. She turned the point with her shield, cut partway through the shaft, then struck at his slender neck. It proved tough as wood. She fought him, and he seemed unkillable. At last he bore her down and began strangling her with the inexorable strength of the forest. Cena had nigh surrendered when Hol, the chief who had supported her brothers the day before, grabbed the holly-man's head from behind.

Growling, he lifted and dragged, levering the head backward on its partly cut neck until it broke with a splintering moist crack. That wasn't enough; to sever the head after that took two strokes of his heavy sword. Cena came back through a whirling purple haze to see the headless shape stagger blindly away. She would have laughed, but her throat would not pass the sound.

Hol was saying, "Get up and lead us. They are turning. If we follow, we have them, and it's now or not at all!"

Cena stood, choking. Hol was right. The Freths and their allies were falling back from her battle-host's resistance at every point, fleeing across the waste. If they were allowed to return, she couldn't resist another such onslaught.

"Mount and follow them!" she said, or tried to say. The words came from her throat as a dumb whistling. She conveyed it by gesture, and Hol supplied the spoken words with a king stag's volume. Oghmal, on his convalescent's couch, heard the orders and demanded the tent be opened so that he could see.

Through spatters of flying mud, he saw the horsemen depart. Over wrecked barricades festooned with the dying, he beheld the Freth retreat. But they did not retreat far. With the sureness of pre-arrangement, they gathered in clusters about the many large rocks in the waste, grounded their spears and presented a circle of points, so that the Danans now had to take a score of instant strongholds. Their horses shied from the spear-points, and the great Freth drums boomed again from the rear, terrifying them.

Nor was that the end. Much of Sixarms's force had streamed away into the woods on either side of the Danan positions, circled through them, and come in from the flanks. The first Oghmal knew of this, he learned from a Freth war-cry and a loping wolf which menaced him. Then their camp was filled with Freths.

The champion dragged himself up from his couch. He would have painted his own body anew before he died, had he time, but there was none. There was barely time for him to take a spear and set his back against a tent-pole, to support the weight his quivering legs could not uphold. The wolf snarled; Oghmal snarled back.

A little band of gnarled enemies came towards him, yelling their triumph, and Oghmal readied himself to take at least one with him, or the wolf, if it sprang first. Then the leading Freth halted, and flung his arms wide to halt the others.

"It's Oghmal, their champion! Brother to the Rhi! You are our hostage now, champion. Give up."

Oghmal said nothing, only looked at them and waited.

Then he felt a grip he knew slide around his body, to hold him immobile against the post. It pinioned his arms, and strive though he did, he could not tear free. He could always overcome his brother before.

"Yes, brother," Carbri said, bitterly gay. "Give up. You can always die, you know, maybe not as gloriously as here, but maybe more so."

Despite his wounds, and at the risk of opening them again, Oghmal broke away from his brother's hold. So strongly did he do it that he fell forward, into the stronger arms of the Freths, which received him almost gently. But there was no breaking loose from their embrace; not then. Oghmal stood still, with a face like carved wood, eagle's talons sunk in his heart.

He didn't speak to his brother.

Other Freths brought Cena back, bloody but walking. She held her head proudly, and strode as though she had never heard of hunger or exhaustion. She halted dead when she saw her two brothers, and whispered, "So. If we three are left, maybe something can be saved . . . maybe . . ."

"Where's Garanowy?" Oghmal asked.

"They slew him," Cena said, in the same shaking whisper, trying as she spoke to control it. "Oh, goddess, goddess, Oghmal, he was young!"

"And better than we." The champion turned his head slowly, to look at his twin. "I will not forgive you this."

Carbri did not care to justify himself. Garanowy was dead. The reckless young brother who had exasperated him, vied with him, copied him, hunted and fought with him, dead in this dismal conflict. And perhaps, as Oghmal said, he was better than the survivors.

In this rocky waste, the Danan power in Tirtangir had been broken. What the Freths might leave unfinished, the coming winter would do. What terms they received would be those the Freths chose to give them. Carbri looked at the muddy, chunky forms, hardly to be distinguished from his own people now, because of the mire which covered both. For the first time, he felt actual hatred for them.

It grew deeper each mile of his journey home.

Chapter
Four

"Fifty bronze cauldrons, with hooks and chains. Three hundred long measures of linen, blue, purple, scarlet, and green. Three hundred cowhides. Eighty cows from each canton . . ."

The itinerary went on and on. Most of it could be paid. Sixarms had said he would be reasonable about the rest. Cena sat on the rug among her lords and advisors, facing the Freth embassy, remembering Garanowy's horseplay and her own joke with the porridge-vat. It might have been a thousand years ago.

"And each year, one-third of all Danan children as they reach seven years, to be fostered among the Freths for seven years more."

Cena heard it with unbelief. It could not be true. One-third of their children, from the ages of seven to fourteen—no! Not for one day!

"We will never do that!" It was Gui, of course, no less arrogant than he had always been, but alive and furious now with an anger all his fellows shared. "You are mad to think of it, and by the goddess, we will start the war anew before we agree!"

"With what will you fight it?" asked a Freth named Bog Treader. "How will you eat?"

Gui ignored that question. "Rhi," he said to Cena, "I have a child, and so have you! Shall they leave here alive? All of you! Where is your manhood, your pride?"

"If there is one blow struck," Sixarms said, the words coming like flat, aimed beats of a hammer, "no Danan will be left alive in Tirtangir by the winter's end."

He meant it, as Loredan could tell. Cena knew also. She had not the least skepticism, either, that he possessed the power. Loredan and Gui did not yet believe. Neither of them had seen the Revolving Fortress.

The master-poet spoke in a tone which none but a sorcerer could resist. "Be seated again. If there's to be killing, let it not happen in the council circle; and let it not happen at all, unless a gathering of all the free men consent to it. You go too far, Gui."

It was Gui he meant to quell, and did. With an ill grace, the lord returned to his place. Loredan spoke on, linking their ears to his tongue with tiny silver chains, as his contemporaries said.

"Why do you ask this thing, chieftain? You will earn nothing thereby except hate."

"I tried to win honorable liking," Sixarms growled. "We know what happened. For the children, I mean no harm. *We* do not fight infants." He sent a smoldering stare at Gui, whose raids had caused more than one Freth to die very young. "By your customs, they would be fostered anyhow. We know this makes bonds of love stronger than blood, and that is what we would forge. Besides—we would teach your race what none of your men and women freely learn, to respect the Mother. You call yourselves her children, but will not own the beasts as your brothers. They fought with us. Even the trees that were still awake fought with us. Does that say nothing to you?"

"Sixarms, you do not understand," Cena nigh-pleaded. "We foster our children to those of our own race. They do not even speak your language."

"They will learn."

"Before they cough out their lungs in your dank forests, or fall prey to the bog-men?" Gui demanded. "I say again, you are mad."

A murmur of bitter agreement went around the circle, from Danan to Danan. Some of the Freths made sounds of doubt, too. They were not all content with the arrangement, it seemed.

"We care for our children, fostered or bred," Sixarms answered. He folded his massive arms. "This winter, for certain, they will eat better than those you keep. Do not speak so lightly of renewed war with us. This time you escaped with small harm. The next time . . ." He paused. "I said you do not respect the Mother enough. She has other children besides bears and oak trees. Some are so fearful that we do not speak of them in daylight—but we can unleash them. You have been pricked thus far with tiny nuisances like drums, quagmires, and mice. Do not ask for more."

The debate went back and forth, in fury, in anguish. In the end the Danans submitted. It took a gathering of all free men and women to agree to a thing so huge, and see it ratified as law. Still, it was done. Then the lots were cast to decide which children should go.

Gui's son Mahon, the shy boy named for his grandam's brother, was among those chosen. His father raged against luck, the gods, and the Freths. He counselled unending hate for all the breed to his child, by way of parting comfort.

"This may not be so ill," Sanhu said, while Gui laughed harshly and sought forgetfulness in water-of-life. "Nothing else could cause so much hate, as Cena whimpered. Goddess! How did such a one ever become our Rhi? She has not even great beauty to explain it."

Gui didn't agree.

"I know you are mad for her," Sanhu sneered. "Well, then, you may have a chance now, if you want it. She has some pride, or she could not lead in war. This will curdle her stomach, too, in time. She has a daughter who will reach her seventh year soon enough. I doubt she has *that* much love for Freths."

"Sa-ha!" Gui commented, insightfully.

"Sa-ha, as you say, my son. Stay close to her and be her strong right arm. Her brothers may not like it. You must deal with that. But even she will hardly wed Sixarms now."

"Meanwhile my only son becomes a Freth, barefoot, with twigs in his hair!"

"You can beget others, with Cena." The thin sorceress's face was like iron. "For now you can do little but wait. When the time comes, though, be ready to seize the chance—and for that you must be in the right place, at Cena's side.''

Others had no such patience, or no such need to exercise it. Prince Nemed was an exile from his own land still, and had no wish to remain in Tirtangir now that his hosts were conquered. He had lands and two wives at home, he said. He could keep himself amused as a pirate until the time of his outlawry was over, and he could return to them. Bidding Cena and her kinsmen farewell, he sailed away.

Others whose loyalties should have been stronger behaved as Nemed had done. Appalled by their defeat, many proud Danans fell to fighting among themselves. Ambush, foray, and feud became as common as eating, and no common farmer slept with the certainty that his roof would be unburnt in the morning.

Gui came to Cena with a plan to control this. He had many good horses; more, in truth, than he could afford to maintain, and a war-band of hard riders. He offered to place these at the Rhi's disposal, and lead them in pursuit of such robbers. They would maintain themselves by hunting in the summer, and could be quartered on the people through the winter. They could also receive a part of such plunder as they recovered, and if the band was successful, it might grow into several troops. So Gui modestly expressed it.

Cena found nothing wrong in the idea. She allowed Gui to try it, and after a year's practice he showed himself successful indeed.

"There are not many raider's tricks I don't know," he said cheerfully. "But the payment in kind must be yours, Cena. It's you who must ever be making generous gifts, and I—I've solved the constant problem of maintaining my horses. It's enough for me."

Cena wasn't fooled. Gui wanted something, and by the bold manner he assumed with her, she knew what it was, as she had always known. However, his "Ranging Band" gave good service. He was worth something to her at last, a help, not a supercilious trouble-maker. If she hadn't looked upon him more favorably because of that, she would not have been human.

Year by year, too, she came to share one of his attitudes; a dislike of Freths. It was not in nature for any strong, spirited people to like being dominated by another. Cena hated it as much as Gui and Sanhu. Thus, like most Danans, she discovered things in common with them that she had not suspected. She lived for the day when they would be their own masters again.

The Freths did make bad rulers. They soon grew too fond of their new subjects' cloth, leather, woodcraft, and, first of all, the fiery water-of-life. A Freth reeling along a hedgerow, drunk in a richly embroidered cloak, was a sight it pleased the Danans to despise. And nothing could be done to stop it. The Freths had conquered; now they were gorging on the fruits of conquest until they grew distempered. Some clever, malicious ones like Gui saw this, and did all they could to encourage it.

One child in three of the proper age vanished into the western forests each year. Of all things this made the Freths most hated, and the name Sixarms was a curse. Stories were told of how he ate infants, or used their blood to mortar his stonework when he built. Cena, knowing better, smiled at such nonsense, but sadly. Then she would look at her daughter Macha and feel burning, furious rebellion.

Yet—they had to have time.

Macha's seventh year came and passed. Her mother, with an aching heart, had her endure the lots like the other children, and shivered with dear relief when the drawing exempted her.

Mahon, in the forest, had long since accepted his lot. Although he had been frightened at first by his new surroundings, he had never greatly missed Gui or Sanhu. The deerhide leggings and wolfskin tunic he now wore, cured to warm softness between the teeth of Freth women, were warm and comfortable. He played with their children, romped with bear and wolf cubs, learned to conceal his true name like a Freth and answer to a sobriquet—in his case, Stagshanks, because his playmates found his legs comically thin, and because he could run more swiftly than any of them.

He learned to know the earth, her fruitful, kindly side, and also her shadows and decay. He learned that trees in their own way were as alive as he. While the Freths did not see it as a crime to fell them for many uses—since trees themselves fought and killed each other for the sunlight they needed—still they were wary of cutting too many, and of neglecting to placate the spirits of the trees they did kill. In the same way they asked pardon of the beasts they hunted, and buried their skeletons whole so that they might be reborn; even of the cattle and pigs they butchered. Many a time did Mahon, now Stagshanks, snuggle warmly to the side of a huge, grunting sow among her piglets, and sleep soundly, fighting for his position every so often.

He learned to ride the wicked black bulls for sport, and to use a sling or throwing-net so well that no bird was safe, no rabbit secure. He learned to give wary respect to the old women of the household, and not indulge his quick, avid curiosity by spying on their rites. That lesson had been most firmly driven into him before he left Lost Star Lake, in any event; it did not have to be repeated more than once in the forest.

He lived happily, and learned to love his foster-clan, the group whose stockade of sunken-floored huts had become home. He spoke their language, now, better than his own. When his new mother, Badger Stripe, reminded him that he would have to return to his own folk one day, he thought of the house on the lake as something in another world. Not a very good one.

Sixarms travelled into that world each year or two. On his third visit, he found Gui of Lost Star Lake at Cena's side. Once he became their conqueror, she had told him that he would never be her man now; that Danans gave freely or not at all. But he had not expected her to take this man instead. Sixarms remembered him too well.

On a later visit, he saw Gui's Ranging Bands at practice on a field. Now they were known as the Rainbow Men, because he had organized them in seven bands of fifty, each band wearing a different color. They might be fewer, but never numbered more, and they were the best horsemen and warriors in the land.

From that sight, he went to a meeting with an angry Rhi. Cena and Gui had two children now, but the Freth did not see them. He entered Cena's house, less rich and ornate now than it had been, due to Freth extortions, and ate at her table.

She looked upon him with no more than the ghost of an old fondness. He had not changed. He still wore a hooded leather tunic and horsehide wrappings on his lower legs, in preference to richer garb. There was no false humility in that. He was Sixarms the Freth, take him or leave him, but he would be himself.

The Rhi was not interested in his choice of clothing. She said grimly, "Old friend, your people grow worse each year. Now they tax even our hearth-fires and brewing-vats. They hardly leave us fuel or drink. It is not to be borne. I know your chiefs and your hideous old women are behind it. Can you not curb them?''

''Not when I see so much practice for war in your lands.''

''That is to keep my own people from tearing each other to bits. It has worked, too. Gui's Rainbow Men have stopped the worst of the banditry.''

''You raised no such force to stop his raids against us. If he decides to begin again, all six of my arms will reach out for him, and they will not be gentle. Where is he, Cena? I should tell him these things in his own ear.''

''Away. He doesn't care to meet you, Sixarms. You can guess why.''

''He's a jealous man. I would think that was reason for him to stay, not leave.''

''Not when I am the Rhi.''

Sixarms still did not wholly understand Danan hospitality. Whenever he came to Ridai, he slept in Cena's bed, but since the Battle of the Waste, they had done no more than sleep. There were many reasons: Gui alive, Garanowy dead, the conquest, and the subjugation that had followed. All of it hung between them like a drawn sword—or a poisoned spear.

And each time Sixarms came into the land, Gui was there to rage for hours against the Freths to Cena—after Sixarms had gone. The grievances were many. Sixarms could check or redress his people's worst abuses, but never wholly prevent them.

The seventh year ended. The first of the children taken to be fostered—the Danans called it tribute, with red hatred—had now to return. All over the land, mothers cut notches on sticks as the days grew fewer, and thought of their chicks as they had seen them last. They added the years of growth and difference as they had tried to do in their minds since the children had gone, into a realm almost unknown, which might for them have been one of the Otherworlds.

In households all over the land, the last notch was cut, and the appointed day dawned.

Chapter
Five

Gui rode to the borders on a splendid sorrel which had not been foaled when Mahon departed. He led a black mare, and behind him rode seven warriors from each band of his force. All wore tough leather war-tunics of their distinctive color, with flowing cloaks in a lighter shade, and appropriate jewels from the amethyst to the garnet.

"Things have changed, lord," one of the purple riders remarked, looking at the carved oak pillars which marked the border. Beyond it a cleared grassy road ran into the Freth lands, marking a channel of earth power. "We'd know which paths to follow now. They've kindly marked them out for us."

"True for you," Gui said. "The blotches would not take our floatwains as a gift before; now they cannot get enough, and so they must clear the right paths, even if it does mean felling more of their precious trees! One day—"

He clamped his teeth shut on the words. One day. Not yet. Looking at the wide, inviting road west, floatwains behind them laden with supplies: food, blankets, kettles, and spare weapons. It would be full war then, not a raid. The border would vanish;

he would take fire, dread, and death into Freth territories again, on a wider scale than before, until they grovelled. The child-tribute would be the first thing he ended—but not yet, he reminded himself, working hard to be patient. Not yet.

He could not have sat more proudly upright when the long procession appeared, but his attention sharpened. Two hundred children were coming home, the first of the missing. For what that meant, there were no words. The crowd of expectant parents around him talked, and wondered, and hoped, and feared, and fell silent again, while the procession drew closer. Many would have run to meet it, but did not. They were Danans, and their conquerors were with that long parade. Long-limbed children walked with heavy Freth arms about their shoulders, the characteristic red or brown hair so tangled, so dirty its shade could not be distinguished. Although healthy, amply fed, and clear-eyed, they had dirt ingrained in their skins and scratched happily at the fleas hopping upon them. The youths carried polished flint hatchets and spears, the rowdy, unkempt maidens, digging sticks, and they walked apart from each other. Their garments were hides cured with the hair on and coarse, undyed linen, filthy past Danan credence.

Among them here and there were goat-footed men, creatures with horses' ears and manes down their spines, spirits of yew, hazel, and thorn, and one large creature whose shape altered in ways difficult to define.

To the returning foster-children, their mothers and kindred looked nearly as strange, like earthbound birds in their brilliantly hued cloth and leather. Their ornate, beautiful jewellery sparkled and their hair shone every shade of red and brown, the men's if anything more carefully dressed than the women's.

Mahon looked for his father, and although he hardly recognized him anymore, knew him at once by the troop of mounted warriors he led. He had heard much from the Freths of the bloody horse lord Gui. The story from their side made ugly telling, yet the adult Freths had never made him pay for his father's deeds. Many of the young ones had been a different matter.

The long-limbed boy walked forward. His companions were making farewells to their friends and foster-kindred, but Mahon had said all his before he set out on this journey.

The men on their gem-harnessed horses looked threatening to him, and none more foreboding than their leader in his shining cloak. Gui's first words were not unkindly meant, yet they were scarcely gentle either.

"Mahon! What has that scum done to you?"

"They haven't done anything to me . . ." The youth hesitated, stumbling in the grammar of a tongue he had not used much of late, uncertain also of just how to address this man. He settled upon, "Sir."

"Have they not? You talk like a bear cub and look like what is cleaned out of a feasting-hall in the spring! They have done enough that can be seen. As for what can't be seen—no doubt I'll find out." Gui led the black mare closer. "You never were much of a rider. Can you mount this, at least?"

Mahon looked doubtfully at the tall mare. She looked at him with equal uncertainty, snorted, and rolled her eyes. Unwilling to admit that he would sooner walk, the youth edged forward. The black mare shied. Bridle and saddle pendants rang together sweetly.

Mahon sprang, caught the mare's mane, and threw a leg clumsily over her. Lacking stirrups to help him, he clung to mane and bridle, riding like a sack of grain. The skittish mare bucked a dozen jumps while Mahon gripped with everything save his teeth. Those were clenched hard. Then he came off, to land with a jolt on the grass. The mare's hoofs flew near his head as she pranced. Gui exhaled a hard outward breath of impatience.

Catching the mare, he brought her under control and gave the reins to Mahon once more. "Try again," he said curtly, "and stay on her back this time."

Mahon went completely over, to fall on the mare's far side as she reared.

"By the goddess!" Gui said. "Are you trying to disgrace me in front of the best men in Tirtangir? Once more, and if you cannot manage it this time, you may go to Ridai in a wain with the girls."

Had Mahon been reared to his full heritage, he would have found that gibe milder. Because he was partly Freth by now, it moved him to reckless anger. Jumping astride the mare, he clamped his legs hard to her sides and pulled on the jointed bit. When she caught it between her teeth and began to run, he beat her about the head with his clenched fist. The blows were hard ones, from a strong young arm. Rather than subduing the mare, they provoked her to strenuous bucking which hurled Mahon perilously through the air. This time he landed harder than he had before, and lay stunned.

Finding no bones broken, Gui didn't look further. In disgust he said, "Toss him in one of the floatwains, as I said, and take him to Ridai. I don't want him at Lost Star Lake. I'll take oath those ugly lobs have exchanged my son for something else. This can't be he."

Mahon recovered his senses on something which looked like a heavy wooden boat, but moved far too smoothly. Many aches and bruises distracted him from thought. His head ached worst of all. Had he fallen asleep on the sea? There was no slap of water or squeal of flexing wood. Land, then. He was in one of the wheelless carts of the Danans, which rode above the ground. This one was drawn by a pair of oxen. He smelled them.

All this laborious deduction was done with double vision and a throbbing head. By the time he reached Cena's royal house at Ridai, his sight was again normal; he'd suffered only a mild concussion, in which he was lucky. His legs trembled a little as he crossed the grassy liss, hesitating to enter the place. With its height, breadth, and roof of patterned feather-shingles, it seemed like an enchanted dwelling to him. Dogs loped towards him, snarling.

A short man with the face of a pugnacious squirrel called them back. They returned unwillingly, and the youth's unknown friend looked him over critically.

"You've had a testing return to your own, haven't you? Or did the Freths do that?"

"No," Mahon answered. "A horse did." He made himself grin. "I hope to see her again."

"Mmpf." The short man quirked his mouth. "Make sure you smell like a Danan first. That was probably half the trouble. You're not from here, are you?"

"No. My mother died before I went to, to the Freths' lands." He took care not to stammer again. "The lord Gui of Lost Star Lake sired me. I'm called—Stagshanks."

He couldn't bring himself to speak his true name to a stranger.

"Stagshanks, eh?" The short man grinned. "I'm Driat, the houndmaster, and my lady Cena will be wanting to see you, but you'll need a little cleaning first. The Powers only know why I should take it on myself to do that, but you are one of our own. Come on with me.''

Driat presented the boy to Cena two hours later, scrubbed, brushed, in clean garments. She paused in the board game she was playing with Oghmal, and smiled warmly at the awkward youth.

"It's strange, is it not? We met once, when you were little, and I welcomed you to Ridai then, too. You came with your father's mother, though you may not remember. Among the Freths, did you ever know Sixarms?''

"Sixarms? No . . . lady. My tribe is a different one.''

"It was different," she said firmly. "Was. You were Danan bred and must learn to be Danan again. Not all at once," she added, as the youth's mouth set stubbornly. "You look as though you've attempted that already, with no great success.'' She considered his bruises. "I'll ask Diancet to look at you. He is our healer, the best of our best.'' With a swishing of her cerise gown, she stood and pressed his shoulder. "Welcome home— Stagshanks," she said, using the name with which he felt comfortable. "This is your home, though you may feel now that you haven't one.''

"Touch what you please," Oghmal said formally; but he meant it. He felt sure the lad would learn better ways here than at Lost Star Lake. "I am Oghmal, the lady Cena's brother, and tonight you will meet Carbri—her other one. He'll be the one with the harp who stops everything when he plays.''

"You are Oghmal, sir?" Mahon had heard of the Danan champion, who slew whatever dared face him, and had killed nine noted Freth warriors at the Battle of the Waste. This controlled, deliberate man with the somber voice did not match the picture in Mahon's mind.

"Oh, yes. But I'm taking a rest from carnage this day.''

When Mahon had gone, Cena said angrily, "Why did you make that remark about Carbri? You are the champion; you saw that boy gasp at your name! Why must you envy our brother so?''

"I do not. I begrudge him nothing. He gibes at me, and I at him. Cena, if you think there's anything amiss between us, your judgement has rotted.''

"I know you, brother mine. You always desired to be the master of several crafts at once, and never were. Carbri, now, he has at least the knowledge of a few, but you—who but yourself is stopping you? When you can throw up an apple, then slice it in four with your sword before it strikes the ground, or see the weakness in a foeman's shield and pare it at your pleasure, you can surely carpenter wood. When you can do the shield-leaping feat, and the nine spears' feat, you could entertain any company as an acrobat.''

"And so forth. Cena, that gnawed on me when I was little older than that youth. No longer. What gnaws on you?''

"That youth. He gnaws on me, for he's Gui's son, and he has lost all his training, all his manners, all his birthright skills. Worse it will be for him than ever it was for you, and for all the others like him! Seeing him brought it home to me. Oghmal, it is not to be endured for longer!''

"We have been enduring it for seven years. I would fight to free us if I thought we could win, but we have been brought too low. Our numbers are still too few.''

"Then let us find allies!''

"We had them before. And—even the trees and the moles whisper things to our masters. Sister, do you think it pleases me? I've bred children, I'm certain. I'm uncle to yours, and that's a closer bond. Sometime we must dare to fight, yes, but not without a better chance than we had last time—and so far we have a worse one.'' Oghmal's long eyes took on a brooding look. "Yet the longer we wait the worse it may be. I marked that lad too, Cena. He talks and even moves like a Freth. Who can say, if it comes to war, that he'll be fighting with us?''

"His blood says it. Oghmal, you and Carbri can teach him what he's been cheated of! Oh, I can do something too, but at that age it is uncles he needs, not a mother.''

"Aye, it's sad his mother left no brothers living. Her sisters, though, they all have men. They might do something, and it is in my mind that Gui should . . .''

"Gui cannot be what he is not. If Mahon doesn't please him, is not what Gui would desire him to be, then Gui won't heed him.''

"I'll do what I can to train him, sister. So will Carbri and Loredan. What he's good for, or what he wants himself, I do not know yet—but with his blood he must have the makings of something.''

"Do not dismiss what the Freths may have taught him. That

is a thing I should like to know, and never will, wholly. But remember what else I said, brother. This cannot go on."

"It will wait," the champion said, "long enough for you and I to finish this game."

He mulled over the pieces on the board, threw his enamelled bronze dice, and moved. Cena beat him.

That evening he sat between the crystal pillars in her hall, his place of honor fitting the champion, and wondered who would challenge him for the champion's meal tonight. He remembered the giant from undersea who had done it one night. Now the giant's skull occupied a niche in Oghmal's house. The tribe's champion must defeat the enemies of his tribe, or cease to merit the honors he received.

The Freths were those enemies now. That Sixarms had intended well by enforcing the child-tribute, Oghmal did not doubt, but when war came again—and it would, as surely as winter—it would mean cousin against cousin, uncle against nephew, even mother against son. That last was the worst thing Oghmal could think of. Had the situation been even, and Freth children been sent to the Danans for fostering in exchange for the Danans who went to Sixarm's people, then perhaps it could have been borne. Although Oghmal's harsh honesty made him concede to himself that his haughty race would not have welcomed Freth children into their homes.

Curious thoughts, these, for the battle-champion. It was as well that none but his twin suspected he had them. He did not mind Carbri knowing.

Lifting a joint of venison, he ate the rich smoking meat so skillfully that his chin was innocent of its juices when he had finished, and his fingers almost so. He'd long taken that delicacy for granted, forgetting that it was one of the many things he had learned when he was fostered—in a Danan household. Young Mahon was going to have trouble; he couldn't help but appear loutish.

Still, the Freths must have taught him something. Oghmal knew they were far from the animals Gui, for instance, considered them. They cultivated barley, lived in houses, and herded cattle. They even practiced sorcery, in their own way; and by Danan standards, if you couldn't do that, you were scarcely human.

Oghmal couldn't. The simplest transformation was beyond

him. He experienced a certain fellow-feeling for Mahon, and wondered again where his loyalties would be when Danan fought Freth once more.

He was important, he and all the other tribute-children. They must know so much about the Freths, from living with them. Maybe enough to make the difference between winning and losing.

After the feast, Oghmal found Mahon having his hair trimmed by the Rhi's own serving-woman. Her little bronze shears cheeped, the shaggy tufts fell, and Mahon flushed under the champion's gaze.

"He'll be handsome yet, lord," Eren predicted, using a comb. "Grow it longer, braid it in an eight-knot just above your ear, and before you are much older you will have every girl you meet in a bother."

"I don't want fancy hair," Mahon said. "If it stays out of my eyes when I'm hunting, I'll be satisfied."

"But few others will," Oghmal declared. "I'm a very plain man, yet I go groomed and finely clad because it matters to look well. All you will gain by scorning that is scorn yourself. And fancy? Tell him, Eren, if one little eight-knot is fancy."

"You will see heads of hair in arrangements as fancy as the rigging of a ship," Eren promised, "your own father's among them. Yet I never heard him called a poor hunter."

"From the back of a horse, with dogs to do his tracking," Mahon said in disgust. "Is that hunting?"

"Be still, or I'll take off your ear. How do you hunt, then, since you know so much?"

"Stalking afoot, the way Whitethorn taught me. You get close enough to throw a spear, all by yourself—and if you miss, you go hungry. You give the deer a good burial, too, so that its spirit won't hate you, or walk in rage. That's where your ghost stags and bears all come from. We have one haunting Lost Star Lake. I saw it, years ago."

"Before or after your grandam told you about it?" Eren teased.

Mahon looked stubborn again. "Ride a horse through our forests and a branch would knock you from the saddle before you'd gone a mile. You can't do any real hunting that way."

"Come out with me and I'll show you that you can," Oghmal said. "And I'll tell you something, boy. Being too sure that we knew everything brought us to the predicament we are in now, so do not make the same mistake. Can you even ride? No? That is something else you will need to do, here. You can show me how to stalk on foot first, though. I'd like to learn that.''

Oghmal could track with the best and sit patient, without moving, for as long as he needed to. However, he thought he would let the boy learn that after bragging a little more. He seemed to have a share of his father's arrogance, and it was showing after he had been home for one day.

It was as though Mahon read his thoughts. The youth said slowly, ''I'd like that—to go with you, sir. But it's true, what I said. The beasts are angry if they're killed without care. It's why they fought against you that day. The old women's magic wasn't the reason. I'll learn to ride.''

''Yes. And you'll show me some things, too.''

From elsewhere in the hall came the sound of Carbri's harp, cooling as a draught of spring water. Mahon cocked his head to listen, and Eren's shears caught a pinch of skin. He looked at her furiously; she glared back.

''I told you.''

''You did,'' Oghmal agreed. ''The improvement is worth it.''

He found to his pleasure that Mahon could handle a spear and shield passably well. He'd never had a sword in his hand, though, and as one of the land's greatest lords, he would need to. Since descent was reckoned through the female line, he rightly belonged to his mother's sept; and that large, noisy household would have been better for him, especially since it had two tribute-children in it already. But they would not take Mahon, and Gui would not let him go, even though displeased with him, for they were the last of their line. His children by Cena were Cena's, and he had no sister whose children he might help rear. Fatherhood was not the strongest relationship among the Danans, or any of the tribes they knew. Sometimes it was all but ignored.

Learning new skills was not a great difficulty. Mahon saw the need and applied himself. No matter how many bruising tumbles he took from a horse, he returned to its back at once, unless he couldn't move. He never flinched when Oghmal or Carbri, or even his father, led him in weapon-drill and their swords flamed at him as though to kill. A slow pupil, he yet learned thoroughly and well.

Hardest of all was for him to learn manners. To him they were like elaborate rules with no purpose, except to allow other youngsters to sneer at him—and his was not a nature to accept that gracefully. The timid boy of long ago had survived years in the wild forest, faced a manhood initiation which the ritual scars on his chest commemorated, and killed a boar. When he carved a side of beef clumsily, and someone mocked him for it, or tripped him as he carried a platter to the table, he was ready to fight over it against four or five lads, but not so ready to forgive them or let the matter be past. That Gui hardly acknowledged him was ironic, since in some ways Mahon was very much his son.

Carbri and Oghmal were his particular mentors. The champion showed him Danan hunting, as he promised, and followed Mahon into the woods to be shown the Freth way, as he'd also promised. Follow was the word. Mahon heard things before he did, and would often silently point to a sign or print which Oghmal could not see, but which was always there.

He felt footsteps through the earth, even at a far distance. He did not have to place his ear to the ground as Oghmal did, only to stand and sense the faintest of impacts through his bare soles. The skin of the earth to him was like the skin of a drumhead; he knew if a pea fell upon it. Nor had his declaration that he could stalk a deer and spear it been false. Oghmal saw him do it. Once he even saw Mahon spear a hart without using his eyes. Hearing its heart beat on the other side of a screen of bushes, he flung his spear at the sound, and hit so tellingly that they had only to track it a furlong. Yet Mahon was crestfallen later, not exuberant.

"Whitethorn would have beaten me for that," he said.

"Why, and again why?"

"I could have hit it anywhere, or crippled it to die slowly. And for nothing but to show off. Men have been changed into deer for that. Some of the part-beasts you have seen, lord, neither one thing nor the other, they came to be for such reasons."

"You think so? I'm no sorcerer, but this I know. Some have put on the skin of a beast, and through their own mistakes found they could not take it off."

"No doubt. They may be why the Freths don't do it, lord."

"You needn't," Oghmal said, "call me lord oftener than once or twice a day, and never when we are like this." His gesture encompassed his own rough garb and Mahon's, bloody from dressing out the carcass, and the sun-dappled woods. "Your own blood is so high that any children you father may be the Rhi, Mahon." He saw the youth grimace. "What is it now?"

"Sir—Oghmal—would you not call me Mahon? I know it's my name, but—"

"But Freths don't share their true names freely, lest some enemy learn them and so get power over them. You're a Danan, and we're not so fearful. It takes more than knowing our names to give power over us."

"Are you sure? The Freths knew all your names, and they rule you now."

Sudden wild anger glittered in Oghmal's eyes. "With some help from their weapon-arms! Are you glad they rule?"

"No!"

"I think you lie. But tell the same lie if another asks. You'd be slain for the truth."

"Would *you* slay me?"

"Hmm." Oghmal thought over that wholly serious question without smiling. "Never lightly. Were you spying for the Freths, I would indeed."

"They are not your enemies!"

"But they are. I have scars which say so, as you carry scars which say as loudly that they are your friends. They made you one of them. Listen to me, Mahon . . . Do not scowl so darkly; it is your name, and no secret. Be known as Mahon Stagshanks if you like. It's a good enough name. Stagshanks alone, though, fits a buffoon. Are you wishing to be one?"

"No."

"Then I'll return to the subject, if I can remember it."

"Yes. The Freths are my enemies, for they are my people's. You will see soon enough what they are doing here. We're taxed of metal, cloth, kine, and even the fuel for our fires. We'd be taxed of our horses if the Freths had any use for them. We *are* taxed of our children, for that is what it amounts to. Once we were promised that if we submitted to them, Sixarms would rule us well. He does not."

"You didn't submit."

"Horvo's hot red lightning, you take some chances! Put a bridle and bit on that tongue of yours until I finish. He could still do better than this. His lesser chieftains swagger in here as they wish, and they're all too fond of the water-of-life, which the wise Freths call *thri vasagn*.'' He almost pronounced the slurred, coughing words aright. ''Tawny ruin. They will do anything when it is in them. You know what happened at the Revolving Fortress.''

Mahon did. He knew, besides, whose treachery had been to blame, but this time he kept silent, as advised. Oghmal was telling him, not listening to him.

''More than one woman has been ravaged, more than one man slain,'' Oghmal went on. ''It's true that Sixarms punishes such things, but avenging them after they happen mends nothing, and a Freth when he's drunken does not care. They don't belong in our lands. Until they are back where they do belong, and it's ours again to choose which ones we will have as guests—why, they are my enemies, Mahon.''

Mahon did not know where he found the courage. ''They are my friends.''

Oghmal struck him, once.

''Friends!'' he insisted.

This time the champion struck the earth, in exasperation. ''Goddess, you are stubborn! Or are you trying to provoke me? I just advised you not to be saying things like that.

''It doesn't matter. Cena and Sixarms were friends, may still be, and rather more than friends. It didn't help them when war came. They fought where their loyalty was.

''If war comes again, you will have to decide where yours is. Whether *this* is the badge of where you belong,'' he continued, ruffling Mahon's hair, ''or this,'' touching with a fingertip the raised scars of his initiation rite. ''Until you do, learn to wear your mouth closed. You still don't believe how easily it can flap you into trouble.''

Silence.

''But not now. You can say what you will, here with me now, and it will go no further than me.''

''It is unfair!''

''It was unfair that we had to send you away in the first place. You will be spending time at Lost Star Lake with your sire and grandam. I shouldn't bleat about what is 'fair' to them. They hate Freths so much that they would kill you as a traitor, and swifter than others would.''

"Do I have to go there?"

"You can't avoid it. Like playing the harp and playing Raven, you must at least be able to put up an appearance."

"An appearance is all I'll ever put up. I still ride like a crane perched on a saddle, and I can't tell one harpstring from another no matter how Carbri—the lord Carbri—instructs me."

"Practice."

Gui and Sanhu were better pleased with life in those days than they had been for long. The air of oppression and hatred was one they could breathe better than most. Gui had become powerful, honored, and the lover of the Rhi, all as his mother had advised.

She was unchanged. Thin, grey of hair, with bitter age in her eyes and youth in her skin, she considered what to do next.

"Sorcery must win for us," she told her son. "You have never known enough of that, while the accursed Freths know more than I ever dreamed."

"They?" Gui scoffed. "They used little enough at the Battle of the Waste. We rained fire upon them, changed shape, even brought home the dead to fight beside us—and still we were beaten!" He spat forth the word as though it were filth on his tongue. "Little use was all our sorcery to us then. Now our wealth and power have gone, except in horses. Our numbers are no greater than they were. It is allies we must have, allies and weapons—and the spirit to fight!"

"Save such ranting for your Rainbow Men, son of mine. They are fools enough to be impressed by it. I have spied on the wilderness in the shapes of owl, wolf, and beaver. The old women of the Freths wield greater powers than anyone suspects, and I have studied them while you played with your horse-warriors. They did not do much in the battle that defeated us because they did not have to. Ah, but had they wished! They might have summoned their own dead from the grave-mounds in the hard-fleshed body, not to be destroyed or halted, instead of calling their fragile spirit-selves. They could summon monsters of a kind even Oghmal would flee before, things of the inner earth, things no Danan has beheld.

"Believe me. And believe this, too. I have learned how to give protection against such beings. That is the first step. The next is to discover how to raise them myself."

"You rant too, my mother! This is the heart of the matter; our people will fight. They grow desperate, but desperation will not win. We must have allies, and for that Cena must act to win them. Only she is the Rhi.''

"Then work upon her!"

"What else have I done for years? She will do it, I know. She will lead the Danans to war again.''

"And I, when she does, will know enough to protect our councils from betrayal. Today even the leaves whisper secrets to the Freths. It's well that they are often too drunk to hear. That is our strongest weapon, Gui. Given another few years, the whole sodden race will be ready to fall to our hands.''

"Given another few years, half our race will be spoiled by those animals, like Mahon! Forget your plotting, your talk of magic. I'm sick of it. I want my spears to drink Freth blood, and the children I got with Cena to grow as Danans!''

"As they will. Yet even children spoiled by the Freths have their uses.''

"Like the sly-faced vixens you have installed in the bower to spin and back-bite? What use are they?''

"That is something you had better, much better, not ask. The Freths have men's magic, and women's magic, the second sort being the stronger. These girls are all steeped in it from their seventh year. I lead them, I teach them—and I learn from them. More you need not know. It isn't a matter for men.''

With that at least Gui agreed. It seemed to him that his mother was losing her wits in their lonely house, mumbling of imagined secret powers. He wanted her away from there, and would have liked to dismiss her coven of cunning-faced girls. But Sanhu had too firm a grasp on his household.

"Invite her to Ridai more often," he requested of Cena.

"I?" The Rhi was no less direct than she had been. "You can do that, Gui. You are her son, and Ridai is like a second home. She's welcome here.''

"If the invitations come from me, she will know why I send them. We've had words about this, she and I. She's webbed like a spider into that place, with little to do but rage at the servants, brood over the mirages in the lake, and dream of making the earth swallow Freth war-hosts. That coven of little brats she has gathered flatters her, and practices some kind of small nasty magic they keep secret, but which I suspect is not much. Never will we be free that way.''

Cena nodded slowly. "She is your mother. Well, my man,

suppose that instead of asking her here, I ride to Lost Star Lake
with a party of *my* young women and children? Lively, healthy
ones who will bring a little cheer to the place and lessen the
gloom? Sanhu will not like it if she sits there spinning darkness
as you say, but I am a woman too; I'll make a better judge, of
her heart and her sorcery, than all your Rainbow Men!''

"If you'd do that, I would be grateful," Gui said, meaning it.
"But ask her here, too."

"That I shall see. Gui, she has been a recluse there for years.
Surely there is no hurry for the next day or two!"

Cena had grown from the fiery, warlike young Rhi of that
losing battle with the Freths, to a more patient woman. Her
children had much to do with that; she sometimes had to learn
patience or strangle them. Nothing was safe from their fingers,
their curiosity, or their demands—and they were growing
inexorably towards the age of seven. Macha, her mother's
image, now riding and playing with toy spears, had safely
passed that age. The others might not. When Cena thought of
them drawing the red pebbles and passing from her sight in a
wain with the other tribute-children, her own fingers ached for a
spear again. She had not forgotten how to use one. Her brother
Oghmal was as mighty as ever; Gui had grown mightier.

The dream she had shared with Sixarms of blending their
races in one realm was dead. War must decide the issue. But
how? The Freths held the strength.

Some days later, she rode to Lost Star Lake. The lurid sheen
of the water looked more baleful than she remembered, the
reflected stars where no stars existed in the sky above, more
sinister, the house's roof and pillars, more drab.

One of her attendants frowned in distaste. "The stables look
better kept," she said.

The stables were extensive, and very fine. That was characteristic of Gui, to set a higher value on his horses than his
mother—although she had her share in allowing the place to
become what it was.

It startled Cena to meet her. Sanhu's hair had grown odorous
with neglect, and she was drably clothed, even though she had
known the Rhi was coming. The servants had done a poor job of
preparing the house. Sanhu's own attendants impressed her
poorly. Knowing they were tribute-girls, she had been prepared
to find them raw, slovenly, untrained, though the Sanhu she

remembered would soon have changed that. Their air of furtive
secretiveness jarred on her more.

"My lady," she said. "Sanhu, we have seen too little of you
at Ridai."

The words tasted insincere in her mouth. The sorceress
sneered openly.

"I doubt that. Why pretend that you are eager to have me
there? We have been well enough pleased to avoid each other
since Gui found his way into your bed."

"So we have. Yet your son's children are there, and I do not
think you would avoid them."

"And how long will it be until they go to the Freth stockades
and bury their heritage in dirt? Do not bring me my son's
children and expect me to coo at them while that overlordship
presses upon them! I have Mahon before me often enough,
useless lout that he is!"

"He's more often before me," Cena said sharply, "and I
have not found him useless. Nor have my brothers. Had I begun
as he did, I'd learn what I must more slowly than he is doing."

"He's ruined, and will never make a man, nor any of the
tribute-children! Cattle-herding or slavery is all they will ever be
fitted for."

"Yet you let them attend you, I see."

"I can get nothing better, in these evil times."

Cena choked on that claim of pathetic helplessness from
Sanhu, of all people. The sorceress had always been well able to
get what she wanted. There was force in her yet, unchanged,
unabated. If she had ceased to care for her person and
surroundings, it was because she had focussed her energies on
something else. Gui had told her what it was. Cena wondered,
though, if it was as meager and harmless as Gui believed.

"You can dismiss them all tomorrow, and I will see that you
have the young women of half the cantons parade before you!
They will bring some air and cheer into the house."

"You find it a cave, do you? How long are our children to live
in caves for the sake of your desire for a half-beast?"

Sanhu's attendants sucked in their breaths. Their mouths
fairly watered, the taste of scandal delicious.

"You have gone too far, Sanhu," her guest said in the voice
of a Rhi. "Do you wish to try your strength against mine in a
sorcerers' duel?"

Not yet.

"No . . . lady," Sanhu said.

"Then come out into the light and enjoy your son's children! You have not troubled to see them since they were babes, only Mahon, the one who doesn't please you. Now you shall go to a little effort to please me, and I will have no more insults. Come."

Cena's retinue ate, drank, and played in the open with a merriment in contrast to their hostess's manner. She behaved with courtesy, forced though it was; but she and her attendants seemed like so many moths dragged into the sunlight by their powdery wings. Cena had paid more rewarding visits.

Riding homeward, she thought that Gui sadly underestimated his grim dam. Perhaps he wished to. Still the old woman was right. The child-tribute had to end, and if there was no way to end it but war, then let swords do the deciding.

She sent a message to Sixarms.

Chapter
Six

Now the Freths rode to their destination in a floatwain, those who had not mounted their shaggy ponies in imitation of Danan horsemen. Now their weapons were of bronze, though disfigured by a green tarnish such as Oghmal never allowed to defile one of his weapons, even for a day. Gui, scanning them, wanted to vomit.

Sixarms had not changed. He paced ahead of the slow-moving wain with the Grinder on his blocky shoulder, as grizzled and powerful as on the day Cena had first seen him. A buried feeling stirred in her now, but not strongly. Too many years had accumulated over it for the affection to struggle to the surface. Too much hate and wrong hung in the air.

That which emanated from Gui might have left deep, splintered scars on a war-shield. He did not glare. He held himself well, and gave the loping chief a greeting of punctiliously correct politeness, but not a fingernail's width more. His heart said, *Die and rot, you foulness* . . .

His children and Cena's played on the grassy liss. Dar chased a parade of geese, whooping as they scattered, their witless dignity gone to tatters. Mailin tried solemnly to stand on her head, and fell sideways at each attempt. She stood up gamely to try again.

Gui had wanted them to be here. Not from pride in their beauty or health, not because he felt a patriarch's intense share in their being, but as a way of saying to Sixarms: You wanted her, and she considered you, but she chose me instead. You conquered her but never possessed her. She bore my children, not yours.

It didn't work. The sight of them playing on the grass stung Gui, not Sixarms. He was reminded, himself, too strongly, that they might have been Sixarms's offspring there; his spawn, by bright, long-limbed Cena, had events gone as Cena herself wanted them. Gui writhed within, remembering what he was able to comfortably forget, most of the time. His schemes and his mother's had thwarted Cena, might even have been her death, yet without them, Gui never would have obtained her. She must wonder yet why the treacherous captain she had transformed to a fish had never come to her, and received his human form again; wonder, and shrewdly guess. There were those riders among his Rainbow Men who could tell her.

Sixarms might have his own ways of finding out. Gui yearned to remove his great, distorted shadow from their lives. He looked as indestructible as ever, though.

Cena greeted the Bear Tribe's chief without smiling. "Welcome, Sixarms. You came swiftly to oblige me. I am grateful."

In his deep, slow voice, Sixarms said, "When you ask with your brother as a messenger, it must be important, Rhi of all the Danans. I am here. It has been long since I guested with you."

"Too long. Still, we have felt your presence." Cena's bitterness came through those words like vinegar seeping through cloth. "Will you rest and bathe, lord?"

Sixarms agreed, and his party removed the grime of travel. Later, they ate in the open, under the stars. Cena wore orange, russet, and white, with gold seashells dangling from her ears and gold double-spiral bracelets on her arms. The warriors attending her were those of her own household, more individually clad than the Rainbow Men. Their shoulder-capes, tasselled belts, and enamelled bronze collars shone in the light of the yellow orbs which dangled from stands. Moths flitted and swooped. The standard of the Bear Tribe stood in its honored place at the center of the trestle tables. More than one of the young men present would joyfully have thrown it down.

Sixarms interpreted their looks aright; still, he had seldom feasted so richly. The dishes included salmon cooked in honey, herbs, and cream; spiced pork, apples, and beans; venison, roast ducks, and swans, bowls of pears and nuts, whole boards of cheeses, milk, and curds; almost everything except porridge. Sweet ale and bitter, with flowing rivers of milk, washed it down.

His capacious belly satisfied, Sixarms listened to Carbri playing his gold-strung harp and watched a trio of tumblers in striped breeches. They spun, somersaulted, lifted, and tossed one another, springing as though they could almost fly.

"The entertainment is always fine when I visit you, lady," Sixarms said, "but what is truly in your mind tonight?"

"The rule you hold over us, lord," Cena said frankly, "it has lasted too long."

"We earned it with our blood."

"Yes, and in some ways it has not been to our cost. Each season has been plentiful, each harvest rich. There have been no plagues of beast or man. Two things only are unbearable, Sixarms; the heavy taxes on everything, even our winter fires, and the child-tribute."

"Tax gatherers are a pest I would sooner do without," Sixarms agreed. "Your people are too ready to fight, though; if we left you spare wealth to use, it is for warlike purposes you would be spending it. The child-tribute is the quickest means to make you understand our ways and follow them."

"And that's your greatest mistake! You are wise, Sixarms, but you do not really understand us, any more than we do you. The children who come home split families apart. There are mothers who swear that their own sons and daughters have been eaten in your country, and enchanted half-beings sent back in their room. A new word has come into use for them—*changeling*."

"And do you believe that?" Sixarms guffawed. "What silly women they must be!"

"It is no joke!" Cena's strong hand clamped on the Freth's hairy wrist. "Some women have killed their own children in the belief. That has never happened among Danans before, Sixarms. We do not even have legends about it—and now, in this generation, it is real. It must stop."

"It must, I know. But it's best stopped by punishing the women who do it, with deaths as cruel as the ones they deal. Tell them such stories are sea-foam. Make them know!"

"How?" Cena demanded. "By saying to them, 'It isn't so?' Is that some of your vaunted wisdom? The mothers are wrong beyond measure, yes, and what they do must be ended, but where do you stand in the reckoning?"

"Where you would stand if you had conquered us," Sixarms said. "If these killings are known, the children's Freth foster-parents and sibs will come to avenge them, and I will support them because it's right. You have brothers by fosterage; are they less to you than those of the blood?"

"Is that all you have to say?"

"You want me to remit the tribute for your people's sake. For the sake of my own, I will not. Too long did we think upon it before deciding."

"Not as long as seven years! Those have shown it to be a hideous mistake. You can call another council, a series of them, take a year. Then remit it. Of all the things which drive us to desperation and fury, this is the worst."

"Are you threatening war again, Cena? You lost the first one. You have less to fight with, this time."

"And one-third of our children are in your hands, as hostages."

"You said that, not I."

"Still it is the truth."

"We don't fight through children," Sixarms growled. "If war comes again, we will meet it."

"You are stubborn. Hasn't the tribute served its purpose? One-third of all Danans now growing will come back to leaven our race with your ways—and weaken our unity in the face of any trouble with yours. Don't continue taking them each year. Let those with you now be fostered for the full seven, and return them to us as their time ends. A deal of hate will burn less hotly for that, here among my folk. You will have more time, and so will I."

"When the last of them come back, what then?"

"The first of them will be past the age of twenty, and more will reach it each year. There will be no war then. It will grow less likely, the more time passes."

"I'll take your word to the tribes. Mine is not the only one,

Cena. The Wolves, the Kingfishers, the Red Deer, the Foxes; they all have fostered Danans among them, and none will lightly give them up."

"I'm not expecting them all home on the morrow! But what example will the Bear Tribe set? Sixarms, will you place your word in favor of this? It's the word which counts for most."

The giant mulled the question for a long time, turning it over, looking at it from all sides. At last he said, "No."

The hot flame of Cena's anger blazed forth. "No? Then leave! Go from my house while you can! I'm no longer your host. You are not welcome; we're friends no more! When next your ugly beasts come for our children, they will need weapons to take them. Get out!"

Her household warriors cried out in her support. Gui laughed aloud for joy. Cena had risen, her eating-knife held like a weapon, blue eyes burning like sulfur-flames.

Sixarms rose also, looking like a shaggy, dangerous bear. He rumbled, "Never will I stay where my host grudges me room. Yet beware, Cena. Once it comes to war it is too late to turn back."

"You had better go."

Sixarms glanced at Gui. The man was eagerly ready to add his word to hers, and enforce it. Never before had the Freth chieftain seen him so happy.

"Yes. But since I'm your guest no longer, I want sureties that we will be allowed to depart. Coming in through your gate, I saw that it was guarded by men in yellow. The lord Gui's own Rainbow Men. It might seem better to them that we be taken captive, or die."

"What?" Gui reacted with the false amazement of one who had been thinking just that. "I'll meet you and have your head for that."

"You will do no such thing at all, Gui." Oghmal had remained seated, relaxed like a cat amid all the vehement upstanding and shouting. "I'll go with you, Sixarms. A little ride to settle my meal is about what I need. My honor as a pledge, none shall molest you. If the Rainbow Men *should* forget themselves, knowing that, I'll take the matter . . . as an affront." He looked coldly at Gui while he said it.

Oghmal saw the Freths out of Ridai and safely to the borders. As they parted, he said, "Your feasts and councils with Cena seem always to go ill. She's right, though, about the tribute. It's a great harm and may not be borne. It even makes me glad I have no children. Have it remitted, Sixarms, and let the trouble work itself out.''

"Until the next incursions by your folk? No, Oghmal, those must be stopped forever, not for as long as it takes the weather to change. My thanks for your word at the feast.''

"It was nothing," the champion said. "I do not like Gui. But he's become one of the greatest among us since your tribute began. Think on that.''

He reined in his marvellous grey with a chiming of gold bridle-ornaments.

"Farewell," Sixarms said.

"Oh, we'll meet again," Oghmal promised. "May we both like it when we do.''

Gui had made the most of his opportunities while Oghmal was gone, not that Cena would have needed his persuasion. The fire of her sudden rage was banked now. She was only determined.

"If the child-tribute is not stopped, we must fight," she said, "and with everything we have, even the Wailing Spear.''

"We'll need allies from Alba," Gui said. "Nemed might come back with his ships if we call upon him, and there is Manahu of Falga. On the ocean, he's the most powerful sorcerer alive.''

"I will visit them," Cena said, "and no Freth shall know I've done it. *They must not know,* until we are ready to strike. Their old women could bring hunger on the land again, if they had warning. We will hold no war councils at Ridai, or in any place which is not guarded by sorcery against our words being carried west. We will continue pleading for the tribute to end, and seem to do nothing else. Freth magic is strong, but it has this disadvantage; it's slower than our own.''

"When we strike, it must be like the hot red lightning," Oghmal said. "We cannot afford to fail; let us all remember that.''

"I am not likely to forget," Cena assured him. "Now, someone must take my appearance so that it will seem that I am still here—or something, if not someone.''

Changing into a simple long tunic and sandals, she took a bundle of her sorceress's adjuncts down to the shore. There she gathered seaweed, driftwood, and shells, shaping them into a pile, and worked her arts over them on that beach where, if she had known it, Valf had died at Gui's hand those years ago. But she did not know it, and her mind looked to the future now, not the past.

When she had finished, a figure as like her as anything could be stood before her, from white feet to the tumbling wealth of red-gold hair. The difference lay behind the face, not in it, for the illusion had none of Cena's individual fire. It did not even move or speak of its own will, and if she remained away too long it would become still and mute—in which case the dullest person at Ridai would know it was not truly Cena. She expected to be back before that occurred, though, and Gui would remain close by the illusion's side lest there should be mishaps. Freth magic, so far as she knew, did not extend to the sea or its shores. The risk was a safer one than most others they must take.

Her similitude walked up from the pebbled beach, away inland, while a white dolphin with a bundle fastened to her back by a harness of cords frolicked in the waves offshore. Then she turned her nose eastward, under the moon.

She paused in the waters around Falga, which sparkled with enchantment, heady and dangerous. Seldom was anything twice the same in Manahu's realm. If she attempted to go ashore there, she might reach it within a mile, or find herself swimming through an endless emptiness of sea towards land which always receded. She might encounter storms intense enough to drown her, though no watchers in Alba or Tirtangir would perceive a sign of them; and if she did reach the shore, she could well find that one day in Falga equalled generations anywhere else. She could not afford that. Swimming wide of the sea lord's isle, she raced southward, uttering the squeals and croaks which echoed back to her as pictures. She sought one of Nemed's metal-hulled ships, none of which she would mistake at a range of miles. The tone of the echoes had a tinny sweetness no wood could duplicate.

She found three of them at last, in a harbor on a long peninsula craggy with mountains; Nemed's home, of which he had spoken so often. Seeking privacy, she swam into a wooded cove and there, in the shallows, put off her dolphin's skin. In changing to a woman she became entangled in the harness she had worn, and was helpless for a while until she had untied some sea-hardened knots. She cursed them inventively before she was free.

The bundle she had carried contained her wands, a cloak of eagle feathers, and a doeskin. For everything else, she would have to rely on herself. Creating the illusory appearance of a wall-eyed pedlar, with a pack of goods conjured from flowers and leaves, she began walking. By the time she had reached Nemed's house in the mountains, her unreal goods had been traded for a distinctly real skirt and blouse, some welcome food, and a pair of strong wooden shoes. Behind her lay a number of Nemed's subjects who would discover they had not made such good bargains as they thought, when the pedlar's silks turned back to leaves.

Gaining entry to Nemed's house and talking with him in secret was a business less easy than it looked. His time of exile over, he was back in his own land, with the wives who had waited for him and ruled the land while he was absent. They would not like it that a foreign queen—and a splendid one, Cena added happily to herself—came seeking him to draw him back to her own country. If she tried to reach the prince through them, she doubted that he would even hear of her.

Laughing, she changed her appearance again. Now she was taller, heavier, with thick, scarred arms, a beard, and the war-trail garb of one of Gui's warriors; a yellow tunic with a brown leather vest above it, and a cloak like a patch of daffodils, all badly sea-stained. She would have to explain her innocence of weapons, since she did not care to go about with illusory ones. They wouldn't help her if she was challenged.

Nemed's mansion stood at the upper end of a mountain valley, beyond a long narrow lake. Unlike Ridai, it was octagonal, with gables facing outward around the tiered roof, and three sun-porches at the front instead of a single balcony above. Barns and other outbuildings occupied the valley floor, while a little stone fort commanded the heights. Cena thought it confining; she preferred the open lea around Ridai, where horses could race and an enemy could be seen coming. Far above, a scarlet flash which was surely one of the Alban dragons crossed the sky.

"I would say," the doorkeeper declared, "that you are not much good as a warrior, if you come here without jewels or weapons, and your clothes so shabby and dilapidated. You should not be seeking to enter this house, but asking for food at the dairy, and clean straw to sleep on. My lord, Nemed, is particular about his guests.''

"No more than he should be," Cena returned. "Yet I am one of the best warriors of Tirtangir, for I belonged to the Rainbow Men before I killed a chief in a quarrel and had to flee. I am Drudo, son of Linsa, and with the barbed spears there was not my better except Oghmal the Champion and Gui, son of Sanhu. This I'll demonstrate with any fighting man in your narrow little valley, the prince included, if someone will lend me the weapons.''

Several warriors had gathered to listen to his boasts. One asked doubtfully, "Then how did you come to lose your own?"

"Because foul winds drove our boat into a fleet of curraghs manned by Firbolgs, and they swarmed us as fleas swarm a dog. We shook them off. They came again. I, Drudo, leapt into one of their play-boats and stove its bottom with my axe, then made a leap to the next before the first began to settle. Eight of them I sunk that way. The ninth was too far even for me, and I fell short, in the sea, though I kept hold of my weapons.

"The Firbolgs paddled close to me then, and began to strike me where I clung to my shield. I fought back, so that their corpses floated around me, making the waves red, and when I saw my chance I slashed open the leather side of their boat. The others surrounded me at a distance and began to cast their spears. Ten, then twenty, I struck aside with my axe-head, but at last the Biter was knocked from my hand.

"Then I, Drudo, stood on my shield where it floated, and spread my wet cloak to the wind. It carried me skipping and dancing like a leaf over the waves, leaving the Firbolg boats far behind, but I grew careless and fell off it when I had come within sight of land. Thus I had to swim the rest of the way, dry my clothes, and walk. Now I'm here, to ask a return of the hospitality your lord enjoyed in Tirtangir for years, and to prove myself worth it if I must. Though I don't recall that our Rhi asked any proofs of him.''

The warriors and the doorkeeper were laughing openly by this time. They accepted the most basic elements of "his" story; that he had left Tirtangir because of some crime, encountered a band of sea-going Firbolgs in their leather-covered boats, and finished in the water without his weapons or ornaments. The details he gave made amusing hearing, blatant impossibilities though they were.

"You will prove your worth if you must, eh? How about against we two?" The warrior who spoke, a black-haired veteran with a greying moustache, nodded to one of his companions, a more typical brown Danan, younger and light on his feet. "A game only, to see what you are worth."

"If it's a game, there should be stakes," said the egregious "Drudo." "Lend me the weapons for the bout, and if I win I will keep them. If I don't win—a ridiculous supposition, to be sure, but supposing I do not—I'll work as a herdsman until I have equalled the worth of the weapons. Is that fair?"

"I'm willing," the older warrior said, with a derisive chuckle. "Are you, Oban?"

"Indeed. I'll even put up my best spear, so that our friend will be with us for some time."

They faced each other on the small training ground by the lake. Cena found the balance of her borrowed spear a little too far forward for her liking, and her oval wicker shield somewhat large, but they would do. These warriors seemed good ones; however, she had often fought against Carbri and Oghmal together, the twins complementing each other like one pair of hands. Although she had never won, she had so increased her skill that she felt sure of herself against these lesser men.

They came at her from different sides. She feinted quickly at Oban, voicing a wild shriek which would have done credit to Bava the War Crow, and bounced quickly in the other man's direction. Her darting spear-tip forced him to lift his shield quickly. With another cry, from the bottom of her lungs, she reversed the weapon, striking a hard blow to the outside of his knee with its weighted end. He stumbled, and she turned to face Oban again, more swiftly than he expected. Her illusion of bulk made her seem slower than she was.

With a crash of colliding shields she bore him backward, jamming her spear between his shins and tumbling him down. From the corner of her eye she beheld the black-haired wight rushing at her, feet moving in wide sweeps so that he could halt at any instant in a solid, well-balanced stance. He was the better man of the two.

Cena drove a short, hard thrust towards Oban's stomach, "killing" him. If they had been fighting in earnest it would have reached its target. The black-haired warrior thrust his point at her seemingly oblivious back, only to have her spin and knock the spear aside with the edge of her shield. Letting out a third ear-splitting cry, she sprang her own height in the air without warning, from a standing start, and stabbed downward at an angle as she rose. The black-haired man felt nothing, and closed with her as she touched the earth again.

"Wait!" she panted. "I won."

"No, indeed! You'd have slain Oban yonder, but you never touched me."

"Look at your throat."

The black-haired man frowned, feeling a tiny sting now that Cena mentioned it. Her point had left a graze above his collarbone. If she had thrust a little harder, he'd have been a dead man.

"I'm sorry for that," she said, meaning it. "That could have gone deeper than I meant. It was too serious for play. Still, I have shown that I'm fit to enter your prince's hall, have I not?"

"You have for me," the other replied. "Drudo, son of Linsa? Some of the men within were in exile with Nemed, and I have not heard that name spoken."

"None of them will know me," Cena said. "I won my way into the yellow ranks after they left Tirtangir."

She passed through the hall's bronze-hinged doors, and announced herself to the prince's second wife, Siranal, a happy brown jay of a woman. She chattered and exclaimed, but inspected the disguised Rhi shrewdly and assigned her a place in the hall without wasting time. She seemed to accept Cena in her assumed character of a loud, outrageous boaster who nonetheless was a good fighter.

Nemed was out in the farther fields, inspecting his herds. He returned that evening, driving the yearlings up the valley, along the margin of the lake. Cena did not announce herself to him then; she waited for him to bathe away the dust and cattle slavers, and hear the story of the stranger from Tirtangir who had bested two warriors at once. Cena was pleased with herself for having been able to do it, and remaining so agile after bearing two children through long years of enforced peace. It came naturally to her to strut a little.

Nemed sought her out, as she had hoped he would, to ask for news of the place where he had spent part of his exile. His indolent, predatory grace was the same, and the hungry cast to his mouth, though his hair had perhaps thinned a little more, and his waist grown. He might become outright fat with a few more years of ease.

"And how fares Tirtangir under the louse-bitten Freths?" he asked.

"Worse each year, lord. They demand more, they are never satisfied, and the children they foster are no longer Danans when they return. War is coming soon, or I do not know my people."

"And do you know them?" Nemed asked.

"I should," she answered in a low voice, dropping the rough baritone she had assumed with a warrior's appearance, and using her own rich contralto. "I am Cena. Who but Cena and Oghmal do you know who can perform that salmon-leaping trick, now that Garanowy is dead? Have you heard my true voice long enough, lord?"

Years as an exiled pirate make a man quick-witted or lifeless. Nemed blinked and stared, but said only, "Cena?" He did not raise his voice when he uttered her name, either, she heard with relief. "How came you here?"

"I swam as a dolphin. Do you not remember that about me?"

"Spittle of dragons, yes! I remember too that you changed my captain, Valf, to a fish, and he has not been seen since! It's danger you have courted by coming here."

"You won't harm me, Nemed. My brothers would come for your heart, and my foster-brothers with them. Besides, Valf deserved his fate."

"Never was I certain of that."

"You were not at the Revolving Fortress. May I speak with you in secret, as myself?"

"I've two wives in this house; how? No, much though I prefer you as yourself, you had better remain as Drudo the swaggerer while you are here. We will have a drinking bout later, and talk of old times in Tirtangir until Vivha and Siranal both are too bored to pay heed to a word. Then we can speak of what truly brings you here."

That Nemed's course was wisest, Cena couldn't deny. Still, it disappointed her. She liked herself better in her own semblance, as well, and surely he could have arranged it, in his own household.

When she saw his first wife, she understood. If Siranal was a jay, then Vivha resembled a golden pheasant, and the strength of her gift for sorcery could be scented across the wide hall. If she grew curious enough to look at Cena closely, she would see through her disguise of illusion as deeply as Cena's dolphin senses penetrated the sea. Her attendant, a short Coranian with ears huge as a bat's, doubtless knew most of what happened in the valley himself.

Much later, when the household had gone to bed, leaving Nemed and Cena to yarn endlessly of cattle-raids and sea-fights and warriors they had both known, the prince said quietly, "Now. What upwelling of waters from the pits of the Otherworld has made you come here alone? You said things go ill in Tirtangir. How ill, Cena?"

"So ill that we mean to fight, and this time to win. You left something unfinished when you departed, Nemed. Will you bring your fleet across the sea again, and complete it?"

"Demons! You haven't lost any of your impetuosity! I was an outlaw then, with no certainty that the ban would ever be lifted. Now it has been, and I am a princely farmer with a family to care for. Why should I rush to Tirtangir to fight a war that was lost once?"

"For honor, perhaps. We welcomed you then. Now we are the ones in need, and that comes hard to my lips."

"Yes. And besides honor? Once I hoped to take new land, but now I don't have to win it."

"Surely some of your kinsmen do! The Firbolgs ravage Alba as the Freths oppress us in Tirtangir. There must be landless princes with their war-bands seeking a place."

"Many. Indeed, I've had to fight some of them to stop them from taking mine. I'd be pleased to see them all in your land, fighting for a better cause . . . so pleased that I'd carry them across in my ships, for a moderate share of the plunder . . ."

He paused, and smiled like a fox dreaming of unguarded hens. "It's difficult to quit thinking like a pirate when you have lived as one. You may find that out, if you fail this time."

"I couldn't turn pirate with three children clutching my skirts. No, Nemed, I am going to win."

"Your strength is less."

"That's why I am here—to increase it. Besides, the Freths have changed since they overwhelmed us. Once, the only ways to the heart of their country lay through forest and river, impassable bog. You needed boats or Danan horses to go through. Now, the courses of earth power have been divined, and there are wide roads founded on logs and stones which follow them. The Freths cut those roads themselves, Nemed! Before their conquest, they would have perished before they allowed it.''

"Oho! Your airwains could follow those roads as easily as theirs, and you can still move faster, strike swifter than they . . . I suppose they have forbidden you to breed horses?''

"That is one of the few things they have not done.''

"Their grave error, then. I suppose they never thought of it. Best you move before they do. Even here, we have heard of the Rainbow Men. Thoughts of what they might do will stir even in Freth skulls before long.''

"Will you aid us? Nemed, I have it in mind to destroy their strength so that they cannot come against us another time—burn or throw down their fortresses, wreck their dams, plunder their storehouses! We'd be doing little but take back our own, and the Freths owe us much. We need you to accomplish a particular thing, so that Sixarms will not control the western seaways any longer.

"I want you to destroy the Revolving Fortress!''

Nemed drew in a long, patronizing breath. "Is that all? Nothing easy, like sailing to the Sea at the Center of the World and overthrowing Crete. I'm even told you have been to that place—''

"You know I have.''

"Then what makes you think it can be taken at all?''

"A troop of women known as the War Crows, whom you may remember.''

Nemed shuddered a little. "I do. May I never be their enemy and fall into their taloned hands alive! How many of them are left? I'd think they would pine and die without war.''

"They are eighty strong. They could fly over the turning walls and wreck Sixarms's war engines while you came from the sea.''

"Faced with those walls, there would be little I could do. Are they as mighty as they're said to be?''

"Stronger, if anything, built of upright columns of stone. The foundations they are built on turn three times an hour; that's as often as you can get in or out, unless Sixarms changes the rate for you, and trying to scale the walls—'' She shrugged. ''There's another name for that stronghold. The Mill of Red Corn.''

''You do not fill me with hope.''

''You would have the War Crows to throw ropes to you from the tops of the walls. There is something else, too, Nemed, a thing we have devised which can bring down even the Revolving Fortress. I won't speak of it here. But I swear the oath of my people that it's so.''

''That suffices. If I come to Tirtangir I will have to know more.''

''I'll tell you more, then—if you should come. Can you find enough footloose war-bands? We will need all we can muster, with their gear and food stocks. The last is important, Nemed. Food and pasture are our worst hobbles. The Freths take too much. Sixarms once threatened to make us eat our horses in desperation, and it could come true, unless we do something now.''

''It would be glorious,'' Nemed said, tasting it, ''to overthrow the Turning Fortress. All the western coasts would lie open, once that was done. The sorcery you have in mind had best succeed, though. I remember that summoning the dead to your aid was of little use, the last time.''

''We won't be fighting on Winter's Day, so they would not answer our call, but all other weapons we have, we will use. Oghmal is to bring the Wailing Spear, and we have sorceries prepared which will shake the Freths for a thousand years. We spy on them constantly in the shapes of bird and fish; we know what they are doing.''

''I'd hope so,'' Nemed said good-humoredly. ''What other allies do you have?''

''None as yet. I'm seeking the aid of Manahu of Falga; my uncle will go there as my ambassador when I return home. Through him, we can perhaps enlist the Lyrans, and there is a chieftain called Shaui I can make one of us, by reminding him of a bet he once made.'' She looked at the prince with eyes of blue flame. ''This is no gamester's bet now, Nemed. I have to win. I ask again, can you find the free war-bands you need, with their supplies?''

"Easily. Cena, the Firbolgs have left so many Danan tribes landless here that the seaways are choked with them. Haven't you had trouble with their raids?"

"We have surely. It's because of that, and our own squabbles, that the Freths haven't demanded we give up our weapons. I should thank those foreign raiders—and if they deliver us, I'll thank them with Freth land!"

"It's how they would prefer to be thanked. Well, I understand enough for now. Mind, after this thing is achieved, it's your aid against the Firbolgs I may be calling upon, in some future year."

"And you will have it! It's a strange thing. All tribes, all peoples, rise in the east like the sun. Then they move westward and set at last. The Freths are setting now, I think."

"Aye. But we will flourish for a long time yet."

They sat together for a while, drinking their wine. Nemed looked at the scarred, burly figure of his guest and reflected on what lay behind that surface appearance. The Danans had a special gift for illusion, for making pebbles seem to be gold nuggets. He wondered if all they had talked of tonight would seem like a wine dream in the morning. The Freths were surely not dreamers—and neither were Nemed's wives.

"She's most beautiful," Cena said, "that first wife of yours, Vivha. She must be strong, to have held this land for you while you were exiled. Is she a sorceress, too? She seems to be."

"She is indeed. She knows illusion as you do; it's luck that she hasn't penetrated your disguise. You had better stay out of her way, Cena."

Nemed seemed almost afraid of her. Cena said, "How will she like your faring off to outland adventures again?"

"She won't mind that. It wasn't yesterday that I came home; I've been here all of three years now, and the outlaw I used to be is fretting idle. She will forgive me, so long as I succeed. What have the Freths, besides what they have taken from you?"

"Gold, furs, and hides. Copper ingots in store-houses. They have become shrewd traders since they conquered us—or supposed they conquered us. And the men who receive land in Tirtangir can become your clients to repay you. We can hammer all that out later. You won't lose by it, my lord. And if ever this place is threatened, you have only to say a word in Tirtangir. May it never be needed!"

"Never, indeed. My clan has been here since before the sea broke through and made Alba an island. There was only lichen and stunted birch here then—and the ice, and the dragons. They held the valley with spells that made time flow more swiftly here than elsewhere. They knew the Freths, too—but they were mere savages, then, and avoided the valley for fear."

"Did they have the metal ships then?"

"Of course. We're the only Danans who still have some, save Manahu. It's said that he possesses the last of the ships that travels where its owner wills, without sail or oar, but so many other things are said about him. You'll have to go to Falga to learn. I hope he allows your approach; rather would I have him beside me in an attack on the Revolving Fortress than ten of your Shauis!"

He laughed, "I've gone back to talking of war."

"It's good to know you will aid us. Warn your chieftains that their preparations must seem like a great raid against us, their cousins. We can deceive the Freths that we are raising our forces to fight you. Then, when you land, we turn on them together."

"Good. You might even ask Sixarms for help against this war-fleet, and enchant or slaughter the warriors he sends."

"No," Cena said. "That would be more than trickery, it would be stealthy murder. I'm only desperate as yet."

"They are your lands."

"And Sixarms is no fool. You should be glad I will not do this thing. If I did, I'd be as likely to betray you."

"So? Are you criticizing my honor?"

"No, Nemed. But Sixarms has a claim on mine."

"I'm glad to hear it. By the goddess, I cannot see that you owe honorable treatment to such brutes anyhow, and least of all when they steal your children year by year!"

"It goes back to days before that vile tribute began. Let's not quarrel, Nemed. I see you have children of your own, born since you came back here. It surprises me that you can leave them while they are changing so fast."

Nemed shrugged. "They are pretty, but they aren't my sister's children. For that matter, my first son and a brace of nephews are old enough now to come on this expedition. They'd fight for the chance."

"There's room for all; bring them! But do not promise them passage home on my account, only that they may settle in

Tirtangir if they wish. And—I've heard of your enemies, the Firbolgs. They have strange weapons others cannot use, and great numbers. Would any of them join our fight?"

"The Firbolgs!" Now it was Nemed's turn to look askance. "You do not want one of them setting foot in your sacred island, my Rhi. No! I've had experience with both, and I tell you a million Freths are better to deal with than a single Firbolg. Where one makes his footprint, you will soon have a million, anyhow. If you want them, you must do without me."

"Then I will do without *them*," Cena said positively. "You are right. Why should I fetch in still another race to quarrel over the earth of Tirtangir? Now here's another question; how can this brash man Drudo disappear in a way that will cause the least interest? If I remain here long someone is bound to learn who I am, and my semblance at home will not pass scrutiny forever."

"I've been considering that. There's a way, and it will fit the brash character you've assumed as your changing-skins fit your body—without seam or visible join. Listen . . ."

Cena listened, and the next day, "Drudo" boldly asked Prince Nemed to accept him into his personal war-band, in the highest place next to the prince's own. A dozen warriors reached for their spears and trod forward to teach him that their places were not so easily usurped. Nemed ordered them to stand back, and frowned pensively at the stranger in yellow.

"You're a fine fighter and a good drinking companion," he said, "but you seem something of a trouble-maker to me, and any unrest we want in this ice-sculpted valley, we can make ourselves. Take you into my war-band? Maybe I will—in the lowest place, and it will be for you to earn a higher one. You did hear that I said maybe?"

"Yes, lord. Well, what will decide you?" the disguised Rhi asked, still arrogantly.

Nemed smiled wickedly. "There is a client of mine who claims he has paid his full price and is free. He lies, but he issues challenges of single combat to any man I send to dun him for payment, and he wins. His name is Lef. He dwells on a mountain three leagues up the peninsula from us, and his house is surrounded by a maze of dry-stone fortifications. You cannot miss him. Indeed, he won't allow it, if you shout my name and say that you have come to collect my debt."

Nemed's warriors grinned and nudged each other.

"I'll do this task, lord," the stranger said. "Then I will come back to ask some of these fellows why they were laughing, and why they could not achieve it for you."

"Drudo" took his satchel and set out through the mountains. Once she had left the valley behind, she sat on a stone and thought about the mission Nemed had given her. She was expected to don her cloak of feathers and fly to Tirtangir as an eagle, now that she was out of sight of Nemed's mansion, and forget this balky debtor Lef. All would assume that Drudo had been a braggart after all, and departed for regions unknown, rather than do his errand. More charitable folk might suppose he had met his death in the unfamiliar mountains. Whatever they thought, the stranger's disappearance would not be viewed as any baffling mystery.

Cena had intended to do just that. The more she thought of it, though, the less worthy it seemed. It wouldn't reflect much credit on the men of Tirtangir, nor would it impress Nemed. He might reconsider giving her aid if she departed so tamely. Also, she felt curious to see this redoubtable fellow called Lef.

Taking out her eagle's plumage, she stood between two of her sorceress's wands and wrapped herself in golden-brown feathers. Stretching, twisting, in pain and ecstasy, she changed her shape, the real flesh and bone, not simply the appearance. A huge taloned bird sat gripping a rock.

Working clumsily with beak and claws, Cena thrust the pair of wands back into her satchel, then carried it through the air. Soaring high above peaks of crystalline rock, with the sea furling in blue swells on either side of the long jut of land, Cena felt a magnificent soaring drunkenness. Her new eyes saw the finest details even from this height, as she glided on the wind. Once she saw a rabbit, once a fawn. Each time the raptor's nature tempted her to drop the satchel and strike. Each time her human mind refused the distraction. She flew on.

After covering three leagues which would have left her footsore and panting in her own shape, she saw a crag with dry-stone retaining walls built over its sharp ridges. Each wall protected a pocket of soil, which otherwise would soon have been blown or washed away. Drifting on huge wings to the highest point of the crag, Cena perched and watched with the eagle's patience. If none of Nemed's warriors had been able to collect a debt from this man—who apparently was very poor, else he would not live in such a place or toil so hard—then there was a reason she hadn't been told.

Nemed, of course, hadn't expected that she would require to know. He'd underestimated her pride and desire for adventure. The Rhi of an entire people and mother of three had few chances to act without consulting others.

After some hours, she spied a man climbing the mountain with an ewe on his back. Sturdy and brown-limbed, clad in an assortment of blowing tatters, he hardly looked imposing enough to give Nemed pause, or to resist the prince's demands for a debt. Yet Cena had scanned the whole crag for most of a day, and nobody else had moved upon it.

Gliding down from the peak with her satchel gripped hard in her claws, she landed in a cup-shaped corrie and allowed her body to assume its own shape. With a nearby rain-pool to serve as her mirror, she renewed her illusion of being Drudo the warrior. The nose and brow, she thought critically, were not quite the same. Still, it would do.

Walking boldly up the winding rock path after the man she had seen, she cried, "Lef the debtor! Are you there?"

He emerged from his stone hut in a spate of temper. "Another?" he bawled. "Another? Fool, I've paid your master his loan to me several times over, and I'm my own man again. I'll convince him of that if I have to fight all his warriors one after another, and beat them. Do you want to be next? If you do, have at it."

Lef, although weathered and greying, was younger than he looked, by Cena's assessment. There stood no warrior, though, no trained fighter. He neither carried himself nor moved like one, which she found puzzling. Surely any of Nemed's followers could handle such a man . . . yet evidently they couldn't.

"He's not my master," she said, "as yet. If he's treated you unfairly, you can spread that word about, or fast at his gates until he yields for the sake of his good name. As long as you refuse to heed him, though, he will keep sending men to demand what you owe. Do you pay or not?"

"Yes, I pay," Lef answered furiously, "with blows! Wait you there."

"I promise you there was no thought in me of shifting."

The shepherd vanished into his tiny hut, returning in a moment with a battered, leather-bound shield and a flint-headed spear. His method of holding both was ludicrous. He must, he had to be playing the fool.

"What is this?" Cena asked harshly, in her role of Drudo. "If you cannot do better than that, you should pay what you owe now, and save yourself ugly harms. There's no honor for me in fighting a loon who hardly knows which end of a spear to grip."

"Come ahead, then, if I look so easy!" Lef challenged, almost dancing with rage. "I've sent other fighting cocks home with their combs cut and their spurs blunt, aye, better ones than you. They were all the same in one way, though. They each began by trying to beat me with their mouths. Just like you. Do you talk all your victories? Do you, ha?"

"You shall judge that," Cena said angrily. "A man as unskilled as you should be more careful of his words."

She moved towards him, expecting a sudden change to a more expert stance. None eventuated. He held his shield too low, his spear too far from his body, and moved slowly. Cena thrust her own weapon through gaps in his defence—if it could be called that—three times in the first minute. She halted her thrust each time without drawing blood.

"You see?" she said reasonably.

"I see that you haven't the force to reach my skin, you weakly windbag! Ha, you're no better than the others!" Lef grinned nastily. "I lied about paying the prince his debt. I haven't, and won't. None of the fighters he sends up here are man enough to make me . . . and you . . . are surely . . . the weakest and most pitiful yet."

Each pause in his speech was accompanied by a clumsy jab of the flint spear, which Cena evaded with ease. Then she struck him for the first time, a mere flesh wound in the shoulder to teach him manners.

To her amazement, it did not bleed, and closed at once. The nasty grin on Lef's big mouth didn't alter. In quick succession she touched him three more times; over the ribs, in the pad of muscle at his hip, and in the arm. Not a drop of blood fell, yet she knew her point had gone home. She had felt it. She began to see how warriors lost to this ranting tyro.

Now he attacked her. She warded his point from her flesh easily, but striking him brought no advantage. He was invulnerable, though perhaps not over his whole body.

To test that notion, she drew him sideways with a false attack, and slipped nimbly behind him. Her point went into his left buttock, deeply, and again there was no blood when she withdrew it. He turned about then, to face her, doing so more slowly and clumsily than ever. For once he seemed concerned, and he promptly changed his position until he faced the sun. Cena was fully prepared to let him. She did not want its light in her eyes.

It occurred to her that she had enjoyed the advantage of having the sun behind her since their fight began. Lef had never tried to do anything about it, and when he did get the glare briefly out of his eyes, he seemed to want it back. Cena tested the theory by trying to maneuver him around so that his back once again was towards the sun. He stood fast.

Perhaps she had found his secret. One of her own people, Alinet the Sunwitch, had powers which were strongest by day and weakest at night. In that case, she had only to last until sunset for his invulnerability to be gone, and sunset was close. It did not feel like a true solution, though. Lef was unperturbed; he made no attempts to end the fight quickly.

"I'll wear you down if I fight all night!" she boasted, to test him.

He laughed at her. His power wasn't derived from sunlight, then. It must have something to do with his preference for facing the sun and having its light in his eyes, but what? Cena slowed the pace of her attack, giving herself time to think.

Lef had not liked it when she tricked him and dodged behind him. Maybe if she did it again she would discover why. With less swiftness than before, she closed with him, caught him off balance—not hard to do, for he was clumsy—and circled him to place the sun behind him. At once he slowed greatly, as though movement had become an effort. He stopped.

"Come out of there," he said heartily. "You have the sun blinding you. I've advantages enough; I do not need that one as well."

The heartiness rang false to Cena. Her adversary was worried. As yet she didn't know why, but the knowledge that she was close to an answer filled her with fresh energy.

"I'm comfortable where I stand," she said, "and I do not need more advantages than I have, either. Let's fight!"

Now Lef backed away. While trying hard to reverse their positions again, a thing the more agile Cena would not allow, he also performed contortions and prancings which seemed wholly pointless. At other times, he stopped dead as though chained in place. She dealt him several mortal wounds to no effect at all, and yet he was desperate. *Why?*

Cena felt desperate herself. Her own blood was flowing from three wounds. Clumsy though Lef was, he could touch her as he pleased when he did not care about being touched himself, and he was trying for the kill now, in his inconsistent way. He shuttled from side to side, his shadow now falling on her face, now exposing her to the late sun's dazzle.

His shadow!

Cena trampled on it, stamping hard. She heard him gasp. Backing swiftly away from him, she drove her spear into one of the long shadow legs which streamed away, far up the ridge. Blood flowed from Lef's own calf, at last.

"Ahe!" Cena cried. "I have you now!" She stabbed the shadow again. Lef winced, and bled a second time. "Shall I attack your shadow higher, Lef? Shall I try to reach its throat? Or shall I simply go away and tell your secret to all who will listen, beginning with Nemed?"

"No!"

"Then pay him what you owe. Do that, and the knowledge is safe with me. You may not even see me again. I will see him, though, and if you have failed to honor your client-debt—"

She made swift motions with one hand, in a charade of a mouth opening and shutting, chattering everywhere. Lef whitened.

"I'll pay."

"Yes, I know you will. Nonetheless it is good to hear. The prince will be pleased, too." Cena listened to her own words, wondered if she was rubbing in the salt too hard, felt her wounds stinging and decided that she was not. "You must tell him that Drudo sent you; remember that."

"Drudo," Lef repeated. "I won't be forgetting." He sighed, and lowered his weapons. "You beat me fairly. Will you spend the night in my hut, then? It's mutton and leeks to eat, just, but there's a jug of honest beer. A stranger to these mountains shouldn't wander them at night."

Cena accepted with pleasure, though she slept with one eye open and a hand on her knife. After she departed in the morning, Drudo was not seen again. A white dolphin crossed the mild enclosed sea to Tirtangir, leaping in high spirits, and a woman came secretly to her own home at Ridai shortly thereafter. Her brother, the somber champion of their people, took her to her own bedchamber, where her moving image lay seemingly asleep. Cena caused it to rise, touched it, spoke a word, and a trash-pile of kelp and driftwood lay on the floor. The Rhi had returned.

*Chapter
Seven*

Like air from another world, the message went through Danan lands and holdings, headily scented and stronger than thrice-distilled wine. The Rainbow Men called at the houses of refractory lords on the obvious pretexts, and in private bade them be ready to fight Freths instead of their neighbors, since the time was coming. Many a Danan trained in sorcery lay at home in his body, or hers, and flitted through the night in spirit form of hare, bird, or cat, carrying the same message. Alinet the Sunwitch was seen flying by day in her second shape of a golden, fiery bird, a living beacon calling Danans to warm their hands again at the fire of freedom.

They were more than ready. However, caution had been ground into them, their courage and pride given a long diet of evil days. The Danans would be fighting not for amusement or glory now, but starkly to win.

Hol, now balding, heard the message from a wayfarer who stopped at his hall for a night and who looked very like Carbri the bard. He gave the brief answer, "I haven't forgotten the Battle of the Waste."

Oghmal rode to his own estates, which lacked a woman's managing hand and showed it. All was masculine there. Descending to a hidden store-chamber, the champion unbarred a door which had long been shut, and looked without crossing the threshold at the weapon which lay inactive in a vat of icy water. Few but he would dare take it out, and even he used gauntlets with bronze links sewn to the palms. The Wailing Spear was almost as dangerous to its wielder as to those it transfixed, and could never be used lightly.

"Stop dreaming, lady," Oghmal said to it. "Stop dreaming and start to arouse. Your time will be soon."

Loredan his uncle, Siala's brother, made the dangerous journey to Falga, home of the sea lord Manahu. Only the master-poet could have undertaken such a mission with confidence, and even he went without certainty. Manahu seldom had guests in his island; he visited others in his ship or wave-sweeping chariot, and those who went to him did so at their own discretion. Or lack of it. Even by Danan measure, the sea lord could not be predicted.

Yet Loredan, with his round face, comfortable stomach, and generally ink-stained fingers, went to Falga smiling. After riding to the coast and boarding the ship Cena had commanded for him, he set out through the chancy, illusion-filled seas, the sailors in the ship as jumpy as mice in a cat-haunted barn. With another passenger, they might have mutinied, and fled anywhere in the seas of the earth except to Falga. But Loredan's tongue had power over fear. The master had been shown in a tapestry as drawing a multitude of people after him by fine silver chains through their ears, the single terminal chain attached to the poet's tongue. Loredan had laughed to see it, declaring that the clumsy literalness of the fancy was unworthy of the tapestry's craftsmanship. Nonetheless, many thought the fancy apt.

Strange, glass-clear currents spun through the grey seas, as though born in different oceans. The muscular seaman at the rudder-oar labored until his bones cracked to keep the ship on course, and the island of Falga showed nowhere in sight although it was less than a day's sailing to reach it by any normal reckoning. A sea monster rose playfully to the surface, displayed its full awesome size by arching slowly out of the water, and then sank again.

On the second day, the curragh sailed more slowly although the wind still blew. The ship's master thrust a pole into the sea with effort, and drew it forth again with a puzzled, uneasy exclamation.

"The water's as thick as porridge!" he swore. "Lord, see if I lie!"

Loredan gazed mildly at the waterline near the ship's bow where the waves clung and fell away in caked, jellylike lumps, improbably slowly.

"Yes," he said. "It's in my mind that someone wishes us to wait for him, and we haven't much choice but to do so. It's a hindrance, but no monsters will swim after us through water like this."

"You're too calm," the sailor said, perturbed. "We could be dragged down and preserved like oak in a bog for all you know. Or die of thirst. This is *danger*, lord, not a poem you are making!"

"The poems I make can be smoking with danger to those who hear them. I know what I deal with here. See! Our ocean-curdler comes now."

A whirl and glitter showed in the distance, like sparkling gold flakes scattered above the sea. Changing size and form, it came towards them, and none but Loredan saw it as it actually was until it drew within ten spears' lengths.

The chariot blazed with hammered gold and a thousand jewels. Large enough for five, it rolled across the sea on spoked man-tall wheels, drawn by white horses who galloped over flowers and grass. To Loredan it was as though he stood poised between two worlds, with rolling, viscid sea beneath him in one and fertile earth in the other.

The charioteer balanced on his merman's tail. Blue-scaled to the crown of his brutish head, he reined in the horses and goggled coldly at the ship with the eyes of a haddock. His lord stood behind him, one of the tallest men Loredan had ever seen, besides the most comely of proportion. A beard the color of malachite curled on his face, and he tossed up two narrow-bladed spears for show as he greeted them, grave-faced as his gesture was exuberant.

"Is it welcome you wish to be, or to go elsewhere?" he inquired. His spiral arm-rings chimed against his breastplate as he lowered his hand. "Manahu is not entertained by uninvited guests, and I did not send for you, so I suppose your purpose must be weighty."

"Even Manahu," the poet said, "can be entertained by a

visit from Loredan, son of Siala. I'd always thought your illusions and monsters were to frighten away the thievish, the ignorant, and the boring, kinsman. Have you such aversion to Danans?"

The Lyran lord chuckled. "You are Loredan. Honey flows from your mouth in rivers. But kinsman? That's saying more than you ought. We're as distinct as the mountains and the lakes."

"Not entirely. Danan blood flows in the Lyran breed, and the sea penetrates the land also—a long, long way, in some instances. It's on ties of blood that I call now. Must we speak of it here?"

"Ties of blood," Manahu said resignedly. "I know what you are going to say, now, and I'd be just as well pleased if you did not. We have done splendidly without meeting thus far."

"It isn't my vision that we fall on each other's breasts crying beloved." Loredan touched the intricate pendant of a master-poet which hung around his neck. "Though I'd have met you long ere this were you simpler to reach, and it seems you were not irresistibly set on meeting me. No, I wish to guest with you as one high lord with another, and talk of a matter which faces my people."

"But is this matter which faces your people likely to affect mine?"

"One day there may be a matter which concerns yours, kinsman, and leaves the Danans undisturbed. For that matter, I never heard of my mother's mother's brother asking such a question when the breed of your charioteer was plaguing Flaga."

"Nor did he. Well, follow my chariot. You are welcome to tell me your mission, kinsman, and take a friendly parting if we cannot agree."

The viscid sea thinned to the consistency of right water again, and the curragh slipped lightly over it. Following Manahu's chariot, or even keeping it in sight, was less easy than saying the words—and Loredan knew that taking his leave in an amiable way if the sea lord refused aid would also be difficult.

He stayed in the ocean-dim island of Falga for eight days, in surroundings of amber and pearl, fretted wooden screens, walls painted with starfish and crabs, dolphins and twining kelp, merfolk and Lyran men and woman who swam like seals. He poured out the prodigal wealth of his poetry, talked with bitter eloquence for long hours of the ill Freth rule his tribe suffered, never once repeating himself; he described the richness of Danan gratitude, the loyalty of their friendship, the honor of possessing it; he described the glory of winning against such powerful foes as the Freths; he did everything a mortal could save offer a true, compelling reason for the Lyrans to commit themselves in war on the Danan side.

There was not one.

The Freths would never menace the Lyrans. Even more than the Danans, they were a land folk, an earth folk, and far more than Danans were they stolid, unchanging to any great degree. Danans had once aided Manahu's people against their deep enemies, and the poet reminded him of that with fluent passion. But when he had finished he still did not know whether he had convinced his host or not.

Manahu studied the round, unremarkable face before him. The features were nothing unusual; he knew what the tongue and brain could do.

"We don't fight on land-earth in any battle, we children of Lyr," he declared at last. "No, kinsman. But I will bring my ships, my warriors, and the powers of the sea against the Freths in the west, so that those tribes can spare no men or witches to go against you with weapons. Since I've spoken of weapons, I will send you those too, from my armories and hidden places deep under the sea, from many far coasts. The Freths have taken much of your bronze, I know. It's for you to use those weapons."

"Use them we will, kinsman, and thanks beyond measure! Is there more you can do? We fail for want of food when our Freth masters are angry with us. Their old women can make wheat die in flawless weather, and milk dry up in a churn."

"They have no mastery over the sea," Manahu said with pride. "I'll send you whales and fish in multitudes, oysters, seaweed, and strings of birds, until your every eastern landing-place is scented with food. Milk you shall have, too, and oil, if you're not too nice to learn new tastes—and what else you need I can send my captains to get, in foreign harbors. Lyran ships go fast and invisibly, kinsman. Take that word to your sister from me."

"Brother—" Loredan's voice trembled a moment as he

considered the size of this generosity, from a man he could not enchant with his voice. "Brother, this is beyond the openhandedness of Danans."

" 'Brother' is too close a word," the sea lord said realistically. "That mutual father of ours was a poor crossbred fellow whose main claim to be remembered is the women he got to accept him. What we are, we obtained from the womb."

"Little that signifies! I would gladly be known as your brother. Have you a reason why you do not care to be known as mine?"

"You are touchy, and your skin has all the thickness of a cranesbill petal," Manahu laughed, "which is to say that you're like most poets. One day we might be fighting each other, Loredan, or my ships could bring destruction to your seamargins. Where would our brotherhood be then? For now, we are friends—maybe for a long time. Let that be enough, and let it grow if it will."

"Aye," Loredan said slowly, struggling with tides of feeling which had surged out of ordinary bounds. His mission had succeeded; he was taking back word of the sea lord's support, and Manahu knew well that the poet had been sent to him partly because they were half-brothers. In his place Loredan would have been less than completely pleased by that.

They parted with an embrace by the shore, and Loredan returned to Ridai with each detail of Manahu's promises etched finely on the internal surface of his brain. Cena wept for hope and joy when she heard of it. Gui, her ever-present consort, showed the snarling pleasure of a fierce dog which sees its chance to bite.

"This is all that we need!" he exulted. "We'll take them now, and wipe them from the earth of Tirtangir!"

Cena gazed at her man with the troubled mind she had so often now, concerning him. She had never truly believed he loved her, and since their third child had died so young, even their passion in bed was dying. Gui hadn't shown grief over the babe. Granted, his sister's children would have meant more to him, if he had had a sister, just as Macha, Dar, and Mailin were closer to their uncles. But Gui seldom seemed other than cold, except when he scented war and destruction. Her own family was hot-blooded, in all things, even the darkly reserved Oghmal, but none of them killed with malign delight. Cena supposed that his mother accounted for something, that grief-eaten, bitter woman of Lost Star Lake. Siala had been warm as summer earth.

"This time we will unmake their name!" Gui was saying, with a strut.

"Before we do anything of that sort, if it's to be done at all, we must break their collar from around our necks," Carbri said rationally. "Ranting won't break it. Nemed is coming with many a war-band, he promises. Now Manahu has committed his folk to more than that—to every sort of aid but direct battle."

"If we can trust him," sneered Gui. "I have my doubts of folk so furtive they must sail the ocean in glamor-hidden ships."

"I never heard of Manahu dealing treacherously," Loredan said levelly, "nor do I think he will—and I am the one who made the alliance with him. He didn't seem to me, either, the kind who promises and does not fulfill."

"You did exceeding well, mother's brother," Carbri declared. "I'll own now that I never thought he would give us a fishbone."

"We have allies, and that is good," Cena said, bringing an end to the useless rechewing. "We have Freth chiefs here in our lands to take as hostages when we please. Or to kill. Most of them would be the better for it, the brutes."

"No. *We* would be the better for it," Oghmal answered. "There is not much to be feared from them as observers, for they are too drunk to see what's before their eyes, most of the time. If we begin killing more of them than we have formerly, it will show the Freth brains which are not sodden that something has begun."

"They don't spy well." Cena leaned forward in her cushioned nest on the floor. "They scarcely need to, when the leaves of the forest and the field mice carry tales to them. That, none of us must ever forget. If we'd be secret from Sixarms and the Freth hags, talk between walls, not in the fields, and *seven times never when hunting*."

"We too must spy. We must know the strength and the power of every Freth tribe, what enemies it has, what members loafing in our lands, and how dearly they would be missed."

"The changelings, too," Gui interjected. "They are more dangerous spies than a few Freth sots who can never disguise themselves as Danans."

"The tribute-children *are* Danans," Oghmal said. "Short of

slaying them all there is nothing to be done about that risk. And hard it would go with any man of mine who dared suggest such a thing to me.''

"But I am not a man of yours, Oghmal," Gui said, "and I have no fear of suggesting such a thing. I'd do it, and begin with that supposed son of mine, did I think it would help us win. It would not, though. We'd be divided so deeply by it that the Freths would have their next victory as a gift, and . . . *I* . . . *want . . . them . . . howling . . . for . . . loss.*"

"I wasn't imagining it was the plight of the children that moved you." With his customary hard exercise of control, Oghmal refrained from adding, "you abscess of poison," as he felt impelled to do. "No matter. We agree, at least, that it is a poor idea. Now can we study a map?"

The map was a clay model of Tirtangir, in faithful relief and fine scale. The cleared highways into Freth tribal lands were shown as crimson lines, arrow-straight. They talked for half the night of which forts and villages they should level in their first onslaught.

"This isn't feeble revenge," Oghmal said time and again. "We shatter the strongpoints which matter, to lessen their might, and then we win, and *then* we take the revenge we're owed. It can be the sweeter for being delayed, Gui."

"Not beyond so many years," Gui retorted. "If it grows any sweeter for me, my gullet won't pass it."

"That is your sorrow." Oghmal might speak less viciously than Gui, but he knew his own appetite would be hearty when the feast-day came. "I'll clear away everything I find at that banquet."

Cena rose, pointed an arm ringing with bracelets, and said sharply, "Brother, stop bickering with Gui or leave this council. Nay, I want no excuses! It's this sort of thing which gave the Freths their chance to rule us, this which has kept us weak since they won. We stand together or fall separately from this hour."

Oghmal did not feel like the one at fault, and would have argued; then he saw that he had been throwing gibes and pinpricks at Gui. And perhaps Cena had rebuked him because she thought him the more likely to be reasonable. True it was that they could afford no quarrels, and—like it or not—never with Gui, who lay beside Cena and led the Rainbow Men.

The champion bent his dark-brown head briefly. "True for

you, sister. Lord Gui, I spoke what I should not." *The exact and sacred truth, you fighting toad!* "If I gave offence, I ask pardon."

"You did," Gui said arrogantly. He knew how Oghmal disliked speaking those words, because he would have hated it more, and it pleased him to see the champion who disliked him squirming. "I will pardon it so long as there is no more of it."

Carbri played a small two-string sound on his harp which sounded like a chuckle. Gui was such a little man. In Oghmal's place he would not have apologized if the life of the tribe hung upon it.

The other lords present were repelled by Gui's vaunting, but bit on the distasteful portion, chewed it, and swallowed. The promise of hurling the Freths back into their lakes made anything palatable.

A springing excitement had come back into the Danan gait. The child-tribute, more than anything else, had kept their resistance and fury alive when misrule might have crushed it. Cena had told Sixarms it was his greatest mistake.

Weapons began coming to little coves in sailcloth bundles of axe-heads and swords. Danan fishermen made such catches that their nets could scarcely hold them, and several feasts near the coast left nothing but bones of a whale. Manahu had begun keeping his promise.

The Rhi and her lesser judges worked endlessly to heal the many feuds splitting Danan chiefs. Again and again Cena sat in her throne on a mound of green turf, sifting through a tangled history of raiding and two-sided wrong, searching for a judgement which would be fair and yet cause no new enmity.

The feuds were not all evil. Sometimes they served as an excellent excuse to Freth masters, to account for the farings of armed men by night. Former enemies would meet, plan an attack on a train of Freth floatwains, then rattle some weapons and fire a few easily spared bough huts before parting. Later they would raid in earnest, and the Freth wains would drift empty above the ground while thick-bodied corpses lay by the track.

So Danan tribute came back into Danan hands.

Illusion and glamor cloaked their actions. The raiders all looked alike, or their recognized leader would prove to have been at home, feasting a Freth overlord who could witness his innocence. Silver mail, ornate helmets, and white horses were all the survivors of most attacks could remember, and those trappings were false as the smile of a leaping dog. Before the raiders reached home they would have shed their conjured appearances and be riding in simple leather, on horses of common colors.

Without such deeds to stir Danan hearts, there would have been no renewed war, no greater resistance. Yet it also gave hints of their purpose to the Freths, and to the tribute-children. The latter had often suffered from their own people, and mockery, beatings, and sometimes death by ordeal because of the changeling accusation. They were the first ones the Freths asked when they wanted to know who had been robbing by moonlight.

They were also the first ones to die at Danan hands if they told. It was such a slaying, the finding of a Freth chief and a tribute-girl sewn contemptuously together in a cowhide and left dead in a ditch, which finally brought Sixarms to Ridai again.

His old friendship with Cena had faded past their wish to restore. She did not hate him, but he was her overlord, the paramount Freth, and the greatest of all barriers against freedom for her people. She watched him come as he had often come before, mighty and changeless, with all the strength of the forests in his graceless, plodding body, the Grinder on his shoulder. As always, a Freth floatwain came behind him, drawn by oxen and followed by bears. He never failed in the courtesy of bringing gifts, but now that made Cena angry. The giving of presents between host and guest was for equals.

"Greetings, Cena," he said from his tree-bole chest. "How fare your brothers, how your children? How does your life?"

"As my people do," she answered. Her voice was like unsheathed bronze. "Less than well."

Sixarms lumbered on his huge splayed feet. The broad, low-browed face with its many seamed wrinkles frowned barely a yard from Cena's.

"That's true, though maybe not in the way you mean it. There has been killing again in the bogs by their moonlight riders. None can describe them to know them again, and most Danans are skilled enough to cast such illusions. But I cannot believe you know nothing. I think you know much."

"Meaning that I lie. Since that is how you begin, let us not pretend that your visit is friendly, conqueror. Say to your subject what you intend.''

"Within your hall," Sixarms rumbled.

Cena called grooms and attendants. "Our master has spoken. Let him be given what he desires, and do not hold back any good thing; being a Freth, he will take it in any case.''

Sixarms ignored that. Beneath Cena's rooftree, between the red yew pillars of Ridai, he lowered his thick-boned bulk to some cushions and accepted drink without the falsity of thanks.

"Something is forward in your land," he said as a flat statement of fact. "More Freths have their throats cut. More Danans ride into the heartland to make their weapons red. If it continues, Cena, there will be full battle again. Is such your plan?''

"That's a foolish query. My people are at each other's throats more than they slice Freth ones. The only dead forestmen I know of are some who have stolen too much or ravaged a girl. Or that is how their reputations tell me they died.''

"However they died, it's forbidden. The old women can learn from a dead man the manner of his death, and who struck the blow. Henceforward they will. It's an ill thing, to make the dead speak, but we shall do it, to punish the slayers.''

"You sink ever lower, do you not?" Cena said grimly, yet smiling. "Tell me, Sixarms: was it truly your people who won the Battle of the Waste? Are they happier now? Are they more or less free of Danans than they were then?''

"Whose queries are foolish now? We conquered you because you would else have conquered us. You have not even seen anything dreadful yet, that we can do—and you raised your own dead at the Waste, that I remember.''

"To win a battle, not to plague them with idle demands how they died! Excuse your actions to yourself all you will, but not to me, overlord. Only tell me what you plan here today.''

"I'll travel through the Danan lands, bare feet to the earth, and hear what the Mother has to tell me. The lords' houses and the swineherds' huts I will visit alike, and few will know I am coming before I arrive, unless magic works to tell them.''

"You'll take them cunningly by surprise, to trap them. Nothing uncommon in that. Most tyrants do it.''

"If there is nothing dire, they'll receive no harm. Cena, I do not seek piddling failure to pay tribute or even the proof of raids. Nothing less than murder and planned uprising concerns me now.''

"Then go and find it," she challenged.

Hot, furious, and grieved behind her eyes was the thought, *If you do, you may not leave these fields of ours living, Sixarms; not even you. We have borne too much, by the goddess!*

Sixarms went, and searched thoroughly. He followed the green clear roads which marked the channels of pulsing earth power, close below the skin of the land, and the women in the floatwain attended him. Often he turned aside from the roadways to investigate out-of-the-way steadings where much might happen unobserved. Just as often he ignored what would have seemed to most a conspirator's most desired refuge.

Once he disappeared for days, he and his bears, the floatwain, the strong, chunky old women with their jagged faces, and his great club; disappeared despite the most ardent efforts of a hundred Danans to find him, alive or dead, and was seen again only when he appeared at a farmstead twelve leagues away. He walked through the fields, stood beneath a yew tree, sniffed slowly at the exhaled scents of the earth, and dug up a cache of war-weapons after treading once on the spot where they were buried. The men who came running with scythes, mattocks, and spears when Sixarms broke the first sod had never been heard of since.

"Now let us see that place where the four tax-gatherers died," Sixarms said, at which the old women nodded in gleeful unison. He might have offered them a rare morsel of food for their starved yet particular bellies. In a way he had. Their tongues travelled about their long, heavy lips as they rode to the island in the stream, anticipating. They needed little time and no help to find the very place where blood had drenched the ground. For a while they sat there mumbling, with crumbs of the murder-defiled sod in their mouths, and when they spoke clearly again, they could cite all the circumstances of the four men's deaths.

The slayers were dead themselves and suspended in a row before the month had ended, though the Freths who performed the hanging did not long survive. This time the avengers departed the land for a while, promising their kindred that they would return with Prince Nemed. By crossing the sea they drowned any hope the earth witches had of following them. The blue waves retained no trace that the Freth women's senses could discern.

Sixarms's party camped on a hillside for a night, among stones as grey as the clouds in the sky above, and that night the moonlight riders came looking for them, hooves falling noiselessly, lance-tips a-glitter. The illusion of silver trappings and white horses left them unrecognizable.

They found an empty hillside. It might have swallowed the Freth king-priest and builder with all his companions. Neither dogs nor trackers discovered a footprint of a Freth.

"They have to be here!" a baffled, almost frightened voice insisted, over the wind that hooted among the rough stones. "Those misshapen old women couldn't stir from place in the time. Even Sixarms is no swift mover."

"Then you bring me his head."

That nobody could do, and the hunters rode away thwarted. By daylight, Sixarms left as he had come, seeking out other concealed resistance, his bears around him as before, though a little footsore by now. They departed from the same hill-slope their would-be slayers had ridden over the previous night, searching.

The Danans did not know every secret of Tirtangir's earth yet.

When he returned to Ridai, Gui was there, and Cena's surviving brothers. Slowly he looked them over, knowing that if these attacked him, he had no choice but to use the Grinder's whole force and his own. Gui alone would be formidable in destruction.

"So," the handsome trouble-maker said, inevitably speaking first, "the gallows-feeder forces his ugly self into Ridai again. How often is he to do it, Cena, and walk—no, shamble—away unscathed?"

"Not much oftener," Cena said, standing so close to Gui they pressed side to side. "This may be the last time, indeed, but you have this last time, Sixarms the Freth. Go from Ridai unharmed for now. Your porridge-feast was better entertainment than your hangings. I don't care how many times you conquer us! Never come to Ridai again unless you desire to see it burn. Its roof will not shelter you again!"

"I shall not come to Ridai again unless you bring me,"

Sixarms said. "If the presages I found are true ones, you should beware of doing that. A second defeat for you would be worse than the first, children of Siala, and even winning you would find ruinous. Best you control the sort of men I had to hang."

"Better still that you take your departure, Sixarms," Oghmal said. "We haven't yet become the sort of folk you can lightly talk to of control and hanging."

"I stay until my people are rested and fed," Sixarms answered. "That I do not ask as a guest, I claim as lord. A rooftree to shelter us we can easily do without. Tomorrow we will go."

"If you must demand it," Cena said angrily, "have it! I do not think the more of you for enforcing your will. A Danan child would not take so much as space on the ground if it were begrudged."

"I am a chieftain," Sixarms said, "with a far journey to go."

"For so long as he stays here, I will be at Lost Star Lake," Gui said.

Carbri's mouth became wry with utter contempt. Not even an inquiry whether Cena might have need of him at Ridai, now that open defiance had come. Thanks to the goddess, she at least had kinsmen. How she had ever begun sleeping with Gui was more than Carbri could explain. He noticed with approval that she did not call him back.

The leader of the Rainbow Men rode hard for Lost Star Lake through a light summer rain, followed by ten of the Green Band in their moss- and apple-colored garments.

His mother Sanhu welcomed him warmly enough, for her, but grew quickly vituperative when she learned the situation.

"Oh, nine times a fool! To leave at such a time! She quarrelled with the beast, bade him never come back, and you have left her alone with time to consider anew! What if you find him again her guest when you do ride back there?"

"That I doubt. Cena isn't so swift to yield."

"She is not you either, to refuse to yield a step whether reflection shows other courses or not. Son of mine, do you think she is yours forever, because she took you into her bed? If you are never with her, she will take a new consort as a Rhi can. It is in my mind that she keeps you now only because she needs you to fight the Freths."

Gui sneered. "Then you do not know everything, my mother.

It's your own mind you reveal there. That is the single use you have for me. To fight Freths. Well; I do not mind satisfying you in that way, but it is for myself I do it. Let us pour their blood through all the rivers of Tirtangir until the last of it is washed to the sea, and the island is clean.''

''On that we're of one soul.'' Sanhu poured him wine. ''My dear son.''

The sudden fondness made Gui ill. He wondered why he had fled Ridai to come here, for it was fleeing. Cena's warmth, generosity, and open heart were as unlike Sanhu's as Ridai, with its constant presence of guests, was unlike the silence of this mansion, haunted by a dead wife . . . and a living sorceress.

Moodily he said, ''She won't make up to that wart again. She has determined on war. It's too late to turn back, now. By the end of the year we will have left not a Freth east of the lakes, or we will be racing out of Tirtangir for whatever land will shelter us.''

''Perhaps *you* will,'' Sanhu said, ''and if you do, take my malediction with you. I will regain everything, or I will die. If we succeed *and* die I will reckon it well worth the cost. No half-measures here.''

Gui half closed his eyes, feeling weary. He should not be tired when all he had worked, schemed, and fought for was so close within his grasp. It must be that he had ridden a long way . . .

The noise lashed through the growing fog in his head. Slight though it was, it drew him rushing to the door, his hands ready to seize and tear. Mahon stood outside, Gui's only son, the Freth-reared disgrace. He looked steadily at the horse lord, with no silly pretence that he hadn't been listening.

''Sssoo,'' Gui breathed, with a kind of relishing pleasure. ''The Freth spy caught. How much did you hear?''

Mahon walked past him into the room. The spoiled beauty of his grandmother had something wholly malignant in it now. Gui turned from the door. Mahon was a handsome youth, he had to concede, with Danan garments on his body and his hair coiled Danan fashion. His jewels shone like drops of fire.

Then he opened his mouth. The grunting, barking accents of a Freth animal ruined the picture at once. Gui remembered how he had caught the boy.

''I heard it all,'' Mahon said, ''and I'd guessed most before.

Haven't I seen you, sir, galloping out on raiding moons, and haven't I seen the men coming here to talk between sunset and dawn? All with disguising glamor on you. Better if they had come by daylight, though I'd still have been suspicious, and still wondered, for guests are never what you'd call many here.''

"Then now you know." Gui's smile taunted. "Your ugly foster-folk will get nothing more from the Danans except spear-thrusts and baneful magic. Cena has resolved to fight them. I helped persuade her. You are old enough to fight now. Where will you be?''

"He will be making clean bones on the floor of the lake," Sanhu hissed. "Kill him at once."

Mahon stared at his grandmother. Her face was a demon's, corded with stress and glaring. Choked, wasted, poisoned emotion spilled through the bars of her rigidity. Mahon, who by contrast had a warm desire to live and the shoulders of a bull calf, drew on certain memories of Oghmal's lessons in fighting, even as he told himself his father would never do it.

He was almost too slow. Gui had glanced at Sanhu with feigned astonishment, and begun to say, "Mother mine, that's far too drastic . . ." Mahon never paused to learn whether he was dissembling or not. With an ear-splitting wolf howl, he sprang at his grandmother and seized her arms. She felt like a bundle of dry branches wrapped in some fearfully elastic, powerfully twisted stuff which now began to untwist in his grasp, bursting out of his hands. Mahon thrust her violently away, his skin prickling. She collided with Gui, and in that instant Mahon decided on flight.

Bounding on the lean, sinewy legs which were the source of his nickname, he reached the door. Springing, he caught the jamb, swung himself up, and braced himself across the passage outside, just below the ceiling. Glances both ways showed him no warriors in attendance, and he dropped on Gui's shoulders as his father emerged from the room with a knife in his hand.

The lord might have fallen on it. Luckily, he did no more than gash his own side. Mahon dashed down the passage, sickened with ignominy, knowing now how this would appear; Gui wounded, a knife left behind, Mahon fled . . . a plain story.

Caught spying for the Freths.

If caught in the dark he could be slain. Gui and all his warriors were seasoned night riders; also, there was Sanhu's magic. Never would he escape them by stealing a horse. In the open fields they would ride him down at once, if they saw him. *It's night. I know the night as well as they.*

Oghmal would not cringe in fear, or bewail his poor chances. Maybe he would not stand and challenge them at odds of a score to one, either. Mahon took tally of his own abilities and decided they were sufficient. He slipped through the garden, climbed a stone wall, and crossed the earthen ramparts outside. Then he hid in a shallow depression which would barely have concealed a hedgehog, covering his body with grass and flowers.

He lay there virtually in the open, where they would not look for him, and heard the shouts from within the mansion's wall. They went on for a time, intermittently, before they ceased. Then the gates opened and a band of horsemen accompanied by baying dogs rode forth. They were satisfied that he had left the grounds, so they must have searched, and now they would seek him in the open country.

Mahon quietly went back the way he had come, scaled the wall where the shadows were darkest, and lay atop it watching the garden. When he was satisfied, he entered it, found a patch of friendly, unruly earth, and merged himself with it as Freth teachers had shown him. While he did not have the skill of Sixarms, he would have gone unremarked by all but a very few Danans, even if they trod on him.

The tribute-youth waited again. Ants gnawed his flesh, and a moth blundered into his half-concealed face, but none of this tried his patience. It was all as it should be. A very faint smile tilted the corners of his mouth. He had begun to enjoy outwitting the pursuit. If Sanhu didn't find him, he doubted that any would, and even she was more likely to find him if he moved than if he remained still.

Gui's riders harried the country for him the entire day. When they returned at sunset, empty-handed, Gui's anger was combustible, his mother's virulent. Mahon heard some parts of their quarrel even in his hiding place.

She was unlikely to cast any sorceries at such a moment. Mahon stirred, a little at a time to restore his circulation, and crossed the wall a second time, with even greater care. By nightfall he was well on his way to Oghmal's home at Dar. Ridai, although closer, would be watched by the Rainbow Men.

When Mahon appeared sore-footed out of the summer

afternoon, he found Oghmal practicing with his heavy bronze sword against two opponents at once. They had no chance. Skilled though they were, they seemed to aid him lazily in their own defeat, launching their strokes at places his shield already covered, giving him openings through which to insinuate his blade. It was the ease of utter mastery, and Mahon forgot his errand in watching. Then Oghmal saw him.

In that instant of the champion's distraction, the first man tried to smuggle his blunted point over the shield-rim. Oghmal's body fought for his roving mind, then, lifting the shield by instinct for the necessary hand-span while he rapped the other man's shoulder with his blade. His opponent's weapon fell on the trampled grass, and Oghmal had turned on the other warrior in a relentless, eye-blinding continuation of motion before the weapon struck the ground.

The man saved himself from defeat for a moment by retreating. Then his moment ran out, and the blood from his throat would have run with it, if they had been fighting for that. He lowered his weapons in acknowledgement of defeat, a man almost as big as Oghmal. They exchanged a word or two; then the champion excused himself and came striding to Mahon.

"Lad, you have plainly been in some trouble. It will save some time if I tell you that I've heard about it. When his several-hued sworders couldn't find you, Gui let Ridai know you had escaped. *Escaped*. That was his word. He swore you had spied on him to learn his plans for the Freths, then run back to them."

"It was untrue!"

"I can see that the last part was. What of the rest?"

Mahon told him. Oghmal's breathing, which had begun to cool after the practice bout, quickened again. "To talk of such things to Sanhu so freely, knowing you were in the house . . . he's a dolt. I'll tell him so. But you listened?"

"Yes, Oghmal. I listened, and I would again. These are my foster-sibs and parents you plan to overwhelm, my folk."

"Best you do not say that to anyone else. It seems careless tongues are common in your family. But you are here and not there, as you should be if the Freths are so much your folk. Surely you know the decision you have made by coming to me."

"Yes." Mahon's gaze remained steady. "I thought myself

better away from Lost Star Lake, but if I meant to be a Freth I
know the way to go.''

''Ai-hunh. You are right about Lost Star Lake. Gui carries
too much authority at Ridai for you to be safe there—but I rule
Dar. I'll keep you here if you wish, as a prisoner, or as a guest if
you swear to me not to utter a word to any Freth of what you
know.''

''I cannot swear such a thing.''

''That makes it easier, in a way. I'll put hostage-chains on
you, and you'll bide here. Gui cannot claim you. A man is of his
mother's family. I'll make my life the pledge that what you have
learned goes no further than this place, and, Mahon, by the
womb of the fertile earth, I'll see that it does not!''

''I can't give you my word.''

''I heard you. I do not need it. This is no game of words. If I
let you spill this secret so vital to us all, I'd have no other choice
but to die, and as quickly as I might. What's more, if it comes to
that, I'd slay you to prevent it. I'd be more effective about the
deed than Gui and Sanhu, I believe. Maybe, when you think it
over, you will decide you owe it to the Freths to kill me and get
word to them, after all. Do not look so shocked. Of course you
would kill me if you had to. Your chances of succeeding are
about the slimmest ever reckoned, by the way. I am not Gui.''

He did not smile. He hadn't smiled once while he spoke. It
was a guardian and possible executioner who towered above
Mahon now, the champion of his tribe, who would fight to his
utterest limits for it. The youth knew with a sinking heart that he
had less chance of telling Sixarms now than he had ever had at
Lost Star Lake. Oghmal might like him, but liking counted for
nothing in this.

Mahon knew something else, too, suddenly; that he was his
father's son after all. He could not match Oghmal's strength of
purpose, and no shallow trickery would get him away from Dar.
He was fated to ride out this storm on the Danan side. He had
made that fate himself by seeking out the champion—and he
had known what Oghmal would do.

He could have gone to the Freths instead. In a scald of
blinding, bitter pain, he wished that he had.

Chapter
Eight

That summer ended; that winter passed. Mahon remained at Oghmal's dun, wearing the light chains of an honored hostage, but those chains were impossible to break, and held him as though they had been anchor cables. Mardo and Crican, two court magicians, guarded against his passing messages by such couriers as trees or beasts. The Freth-reared youth knew how to speak to them.

"You trust me no more than my father does," he said.

Oghmal grinned at that, for it verged on petulance. Thrusting his long, breeched legs towards his hearth, he poured Mahon a warming cup of the water-of-life and held it towards him.

"Take it like a man," he advised. "For courtesy's sake I could fill my mouth with lily petals and cry, 'Oh, surely I trust you!' I'm a warrior, Mahon, and you may be one yet. Lies are not fitting between us.

"I'll tell you what is in my mind. None of you tribute-children have an easy road to walk. You may be finding yours so hard that you would run back to the bogs and forests like a hare if you could be sure of your welcome." The long, pale blue eyes scanned the boy. "Maybe it means little to you that Freths rule over us, the children of the goddess. Then think on this. If we break the Freth power, there will be no more boys or girls in your predicament. To me that's a thing worth fighting for."

"That is fine," Mahon said, after a moment. He laughed then, impudently, and jingled his chains. "Would you see it in that way, now, if you were the one wearing these?"

"No. But as it happens, I have been a hostage, and worn them, so do not think I have no awareness. Play Raven?"

Mahon assented, and they arranged their pieces on the board. Spring air flowed through the fretted birch shutters. The youth's hostage-chain brushed the table as he threw the dice.

In Alba, the same spring freshness brought sailing weather to the forested bays of Nemed's domain. His golden wife, Vivha the sorceress, looked upon his ships as though they were rivals.

"Last time, they took you from me for many long years," she said. "Beware lest too much use weakens them. They are very old."

"And stronger for each year of it," Nemed answered. "Never fear, darling, they won't keep me from your side longer than a season this time. We had the winter together, did we not? Half the women I know would be glad their men leave them for the summer. They stay lively and come home interesting. Or if they do not, at least the women have been rid of them for a while."

"I am not Siranal." Vivha's eyes flashed. "She would accept that drivel from you, and laugh about it. Nemed, I know where you are faring and what you have agreed to do. Remember, that fortress has powdered the bones of every host that has tried to take it. Do not let the Rhi of Tirtangir use you."

"It will not be she who does the using," Nemed said with a vulpine grin.

"No? She is beautiful, isn't she?"

"A handsome man-killer," Nemed said, "more at home with spears than with a spindle, with horses than other women."

She's attractive to him, Vivha thought.

"Will she be at the Revolving Fortress?"

"Not this time. She leads the Danans by land. With us comes that band of breasted demons they call the War Crows, drinkers of blood and makers of frenzy, for our crimes."

This time the disparagement rang true. Nemed did not care at all for Bava's cult. Vivha combed down her hair, singing, while sails were raised on the smooth blue-metal hulls which had carried Nemed over the many strange seas he had crossed in his exile.

They made short work of crossing that strangest of all between Alba and Tirtangir, which contained Manahu's island. The cult of the War Crows came aboard, led by the lean-fleshed, conspicuously tall Bava, her two short swords tapping her thighs as she walked. Crow-feather tattoos marked her skin in a pattern like scales. Neither she nor any of her sisters wore a trace of armor. They scorned it.

So might I, Nemed thought, *if I could fly.*

Magicians in white, indigo, and crocus-yellow robes came aboard, rolling leather-bound wooden kegs up the gangways. Those were securely stowed, lashed in place, covered, and enspelled against leakage or shattering, for less than any other thing they carried could this substance be spared. The wax sealing the kegs had a light, spicy odor.

"With this we will pull Sixarms's fortress down," gloated Enghan, a squat magician whose chosen powers had compressed his body. He ran his hands over the bindings. "All the warriors on the ridge of the earth are no answer to it."

"You say?" A pug-nosed fighter with sunburnt and freckled red limbs took him up on it. "What are your abilities, greatest of wizards, that no warrior can equal?"

"I can change a woman into a cat."

"So can any man who is allowed near one. Deal with her evilly, that is all it takes."

"And I can raise a storm of black hail from a clear sky."

"I can raise a storm like that myself, by raiding a village of the little dark people of the hollow hills. A black hail of their flint arrow-points."

"I can make a stone sweat blood until it tells me what I wish to know."

"I give you best there," the warrior conceded. "What can you do that is kindly?"

"Asks a man of red weapons. My gifts are not of that sort." The squat magician nodded portentously. "Lore of wizardry changes your soul, mortal."

"And mortal to you. Now, I can eat a meal, laugh, and talk to the woman who made it, build a bower in the forest to keep out the rain, even make a poem which will pass in a merry company, keep my word and grip a man's hand in friendship. I've the skills of a warrior, too. Well, if we bring down the fortress I may come to think better of your powers, but—can you drink cheerfully, at least?''

The warrior produced a glugging leather flask from his satchel.

"Ahh!" The stunted wizard's eyes gleamed. "Let me show you that I can. You have bantered with Enghan Skylock, as it happens.''

"I'm Keir, of Cup-bearer's Dismay. If you saw how the rocks lie tumbled and strewn between the pools in that valley, you'd know why it has the name. When I grew tall enough to look beyond the valley's edge, I had to travel. Now I'm one of Shamo's companions.''

Enghan was barely listening. His hairy throat worked blissfully as he tilted the flask. Keir grew annoyed, then outraged as he saw how the angle of the flask was increasing.

"You perverted toad! I didn't invite you to finish it.''

Enghan took his mouth away, shook the flask to demonstrate its emptiness, thrust back the stopper, and tossed the vessel casually to Keir, who caught it instinctively. Then he nearly dropped it again. It had the bubbling weight of a full bottle. Astounded, he opened it, and a more heady fragrance than before spilled out to delight his nostrils.

"That's one other thing I can do,'' Enghan said complacently. "It's no illusion; drink and you'll find out. Just do not expect me to do it more than once.''

The blue ships glided like shaped mirrors over the sea, and Nemed put on his armor, which reflected his adversaries in each metal scale, dwindled a thousandfold. They might well meet enemies before they came to the Revolving Fortress.

Two more days passed in peace, and then contrary winds held them back for almost a nine-night. They waited in a long, narrow sea-lough while shrieking demons of the air threw waves like flat slabs of brine up the grinding beach. Spindrift flew. It was more like an autumn gale than the weather of spring.

Most of the warriors camped ashore and hunted their food, watchful for attacks from the forest. They were deep in the Freth coasts here. They knew that an average Freth could rend apart a normally strong Danan, since the Freth had such thick bones to anchor his muscles, and what they did not truly know about Freth sorcery, they imagined.

"Never let them get close to you," the chieftain Shamo declared. "With axe or club, they will separate your limbs, and if you smite them with anything less, they will hardly know they have been touched. Javelins and sling-stones, they are the food that can quell their hunger for trouble if you catch them in open country. This beach, now."

Shamo had fought Freths from his childhood, when farmsteads still burned in the night and were called "Blackmarl's Beacons." Now Blackmarl was dead and other Freth chieftains had advanced to the fore, though Sixarms remained the paramount chief he had been in Blackmarl's time, and long before that.

Sixarms was nowhere near the lough. Had he been, he would have led the onslaught which eventuated there, and it would have been better timed. Because he was not, the Freths who broke from the forest's edge and raced roaring along the driftwood-strewn shores of the lough caught only a few Danans away from their main force.

The wide, wrinkle-browed faces were painted in contrasting halves, yellow and black, and with their stone axes the Freths could chop a man almost in two. Keir saw a bounding demon in a wolfskin kilt rush towards him. Not caring to waste his spear, the only long weapon he had, he bent for a stone and hurled it. The rock slammed into his enemy's belly with an impact Keir imagined *he* felt. The Freth dropped, writhing, wrapped around the stone.

Two more came running after him. When they picked up stones of their own, Keir retreated, dashing in short zigzags to make himself a harder target. The Freths threw with accuracy and frightful power. His sides pounding, the raw wind spiking his ears and teeth, the yells of encouragement from his own side like Otherworldly whispers to him, Keir caught a stone in his leather-clad side.

The impact knocked him down and out. Although he struggled to rise, he could barely crawl, and his hands kept a baby's grip on the shaft. He lurched to his knees in a nightmare. The Freths were coming.

Slender javelins of his own folk flashed over his head, to skewer the heavy chests of the attackers. Light Danan feet hurled up spurts of sand as they sped in his direction to hold shields above him. A heavy rock thudded off the protecting wood, and a man's arm snapped. Keir pressed himself up from the sand, feeling a furlong tall with his joints all working backward. He staggered down the beach. If only he could find the strength for one cast, so that he need not say his only work here had been done with a lucky stone. He lifted his spear.

"Into the ships," a Danan with chestnut hair said, supporting him as he stumbled. "Go. There may be more of them around these shores! You couldn't throw your skewer hard enough to hurt a sparrow, now."

Keir mumbled something. Strength had returned, in a measure, though a beast with a hundred teeth still gnawed his side. His arms were a child's instead of an infant's, and his legs at least could lift him inboard of a ship.

He blinked through the running spray. No more Freths were to be seen, yet their war paint showed that they had not come this way by chance. He twirled his spear experimentally. The chestnut-haired warrior who had shoved him along was right; more could be lurking.

A man might hope.

"I'm in your debt," he said painfully. "Who . . . are you?"

"Varl, son of Liorm, from Harvest Song Valley in Alba. One day I'll go back there. Meanwhile, there are beaches to clean. Are you recovered?"

Keir's wind would not allow him to take part in a pursuit. Some of his ribs were probably cracked. "No."

"Then bide."

With that, Varl ran to join the band which was about to beat up the woods seeking other Freths. The ships could not depart at once, and they must know. Those who found the truth might have to fight hard if they wished to live to tell anyone. Keir felt his side. It let him know that it was too sore to feel with a definiteness which set his head ringing.

Through wind and blowing spray, across a waste of running water, Keir saw his fellow Danans enter a forest which might conceal anything. Waiting for them to come out was a long business, and Keir expected new outcries at any moment. Another of Shamo's men bound his ribs while they sat idle. Keir winced, and made valiant conversation to take his mind off his discomfort.

"How many were there? I did not see much before I was hit."

"Thirty or forty, as I heard. If that is all, they cannot have been waiting for us. Maybe someone else they do not like has been using this lough as a stopping place." The other tugged his ear and frowned. "Maybe the forest told them we were here, and forty was the most they could gather at once."

Either was possible. They would not learn unless Varl's party captured a Freth alive, but it seemed to Keir that even that might be profitless. Their true business was at the Revolving Fortress.

Little to Keir's surprise, the band returned with nothing. It was impossible to find a Freth hiding among trees. Doubtless they would bear the news of their encounter to Sixarms, or to their own tribal chief, as quickly as they might.

Away in the forest, a Freth drum began to speak in heavy reverberations. Others, more distant, answered it and carried the message farther. Even above wind-noise and sea-noise, the bullhide drums talked with distinct voices.

"My ships cannot outsail that," Nemed said, his mouth wry. "We must be ready to do some brisk burning and sinking when we arrive, else we will be beswarmed by all the canoes in the northwest. A good thing no canoe paddled by half-beasts can come near us."

The wind died. They rowed out of the lough. They were still rowing when they reached the stronghold of Shaui, the pirate, who owed Cena his head over a drunken wager and anticipated the day she might come to collect it. He and Nemed knew each other from the prince's outlaw days.

They might have been cousins, with their height and similar reddish hair, though Shaui's betrayed a green tinge in the proper light, and he was burly and exuberant while Nemed behaved more coolly. He was direct enough with Shaui, though.

"If you understand the Freth drum-gibberish, you will know by now why we are here," he said. "Cena has decided that the Turning Fortress should not stand any longer, after what befell in it. I'm here to level it. Why don't you come with me and share the plunder, Shaui? There should be enough for all."

Shaui hooted. "Oh! Oh! The fool you are, dear man! I warned Cena against that quern for men's bones, and she would not listen. She got no joy of it. I will not go near the Revolving Fortress, and there's an end."

"Yes, I thought you would say that." Nemed's eyes drooped

farther at the corners, increasing his look of foxy, indolent calculation. "I've one thing to say to you in return. *Don't*. You know what I mean by that, old comrade."

Shaui knew precisely what he meant. He said blandly, "So. Now, shall I leave the rest politely unsaid, or shall we make all clear? The Rhi has not decided to smash this fortress because of a wrong years old, not with the Freths ruling her tribe. She goes to war, to hurl off the Freth lordship for all time, or she would never touch the Revolving Fortress. Brought you back from Alba, didn't she, to help? The same reason you were here last time, prince. I'm not blind and deaf on this little island, and it's maybe not as remote as you are thinking. I hear news."

"Then join in the war. Are you not a Danan?"

Shaui guffawed. His broad belly shook with it. "Danan? What should that mean? Danans have been cutting other Danan throats since the Sun was born! Who knows that better than you? We're a fickle, restless breed, prince, and I do not even belong to it wholly. As for you—you are a greater pirate than I am! You're getting rich recompense for this raid, if it succeeds. If you fail there is a snug harbor waiting for you across the sea. I should make war for the love of my tribe? Are you, prince, are you?"

"If loot is what you want, there is loot to be had. The Revolving Fortress isn't poor."

"It isn't far from my isle, either. No. This is too much of a losing fight for me. Cena fought her war years ago, and she lost it. If she couldn't win then, when the Danans were free and all the might and sorcery of the tribe backed her, how can she be victorious now?"

"Maybe that is why she has been waiting," Nemed suggested, his armor chiming softly. "To rebuild her people's strength and undermine the Freths. If you fail her, she won't be kind to you. What does your Lyran blood tell you these days? No tidings from that quarter?"

Shaui grinned. "I feasted with a second cousin of late. No talk of war then. Are you saying the sea-people are part of this? I will believe it when they tell me themselves."

Manahu was being discreet, then, or gulling the Danans. In any case Shaui meant to hold himself aloof. Since he did not absolutely need the man, Nemed said, "Tell me of the feast. I never knew the sea-people invited outsiders."

"It's not often they do. They make exceptions for me, and it isn't for my blood. They hate that mixture. No, it's because I am useful to them, and they to me. And their feasts are worth it. You are lucky you found me here at all, prince, for I'd still be under an overturned couch on the sea-bed if I had my way, with a jade-haired darling as playful as a seal and as limber."

Nemed let the talk run on such careless lines, for he had the answer he came for. Shaui was in close accord, or at any rate communication, with his Lyran kin, and he had heard nothing, so he said. The question was what to do about it. Sailing on to Sixarms's fortress and leaving Shaui at large behind him would be a mistake, if he intended treachery. But wasting strength on a minor pirate chieftain with the Revolving Fortress before them might be a far greater one. They could not take time to battle every meager force they encountered.

The metal-hulled ships set forth on the final stage of their journey the next day. With a fair wind on their quarters, they cut through the sea like frictionless knives, leaving the mainland coast unseen beyond the southern horizon.

Then they heard it, the wild growling of the fortress as it turned on its stone foundations. Nemed lifted his head, and covered his balding brows with a helmet.

"Here we have arrived!" he called across the sea. "War Crows, are you ready to fly?"

"Yea!" Bava answered. "Our wings are strong and our beaks hard!"

"Shamo's men, are you ready? Ean's war-band, and Grivlet's? All you sorcerers, are you prepared and strong with magic?"

"We are!"

"Our weapons are hungry!"

"All is waiting, lord. Our cantrips have the power of dragons!"

"And my men!" Nemed thundered, swinging to face the warriors on his own deck. "Sons of Alba! Are you ready to fight the Freths? Are you with me?"

They shouted like wild men and threw up their weapons, then crashed the butts of them on the oak planking, then twice again. The name they cried was his, and he laughed.

"Victory, then!" he said. "Shake their fortress down!"

The mirror-blue ships raced on, and the island grew ever

more near. Grey crags withstood the shock of the crashing, sounding sea and upheld the six-sided natural pillars from the Giants' Cliffs, fitted exactly together as immense turning walls on enchanted foundations, fed by earth power and gyrating slowly. The whole island trembled with the forces employed there.

By a crude jetty of discarded pillar-fragments, a hundred log dugouts and skin boats were moored, their paddles drying in the sun. Such vessels supplied the fortress and acted as its eyes upon the sea, warning of Danans, hostile Freths, Lyrans, blue men from the northern islands, and sometimes the furred Alfhirns from the north, relentless beyond all. Against every such foe the Revolving Fortress stood guard, and because of its siting no raider from east or north could easily avoid it.

The heavy catapults on the ramparts began to whang. Big, lumpish stones rose on counterweighted beams, flew out to sea in beautiful arcs, and made white blossoms of foam. Well aimed, they came far too close to the ships, which a direct hit would have crushed like foil. Nemed's own vessel bucked on a surge of gold-tinged water as a young boulder struck within a spear's length of his hull.

"Against them, you fierce War Crows, before they improve!" he ordered, standing straight and maintaining course.

The battle-women lifted from the decks in a dark cloud, their arms changing to wings, their weapons to beaks. Harsh crying presaged their arrival as they swooped over the ramparts. Their talons ripped the Freths' faces from their heads, so that they dropped screaming and blinded. Some fell off the stone ledges or rolled under catapult frames, but others caught their attackers and doggedly stabbed or throttled them. One vast crow received a full-arm blow from a club which hurled her from the ramparts completely. She plunged to the waiting sea trailing a broken wing.

Other battle-women landed on the inner walls with a heavy flapping. At once they became human again. Their feathers shrank into their tattooed skin, and their weapons fell into their hands almost before their faces changed. Catching them expertly, they darted among the catapult teams, swift and vicious.

They chose the mighty engines over human victims, at first. Their blades bit into leg-thick ropes, torsion skeins, and the leather pouches for missiles, until each was useless. One young girl slashed at the triple layer of oxhides until a spear transfixed her through. Eyes and mouth wide in her agony, she clung to the war engine. With her last strength, she slashed the pouch apart.

Her slayer swung her above his head like an impaled fish, grunting with effort, and gave a twist to send her plunging into the grassy space below. As he released her and her body began to fall, a black-feathered demon with knives on its feet slammed into him, sinking talons into his back, dealing great buffets with its wings. The Freth staggered, tripped, and pitched after the youngest of the War Crows, his hoarse yell ending suddenly as he struck the turf.

With Bava leading, the women slashed their way to the rampart above the inner gateway. Burly Freths smashed them down with clubs like thick saplings, and paid as the War Crows expertly drove spears past their shields. A shrieking and roaring mingled with the racket of weapons as the embattled groups fought on.

"There is the signal!" Nemed barked, seeing an orange cloak flutter like a flag from the rampart. "In!"

In the ships went, driving sleekly ahead under the strokes of their oars, past the crude jetty and up to the shore. Men dropped into waist-deep water with small kegs held over their heads, and waded ashore in the teeth of Freth resistance. More appeared as though from nowhere, with toothed war clubs and mattocks. Danans came dripping out of the sea and closed with them. Again murder seethed.

Movement showed among the island's grey crags. Cairns of loose rock curtsied and fell as levers were thrust into prepared holes. The stones rebounded, fell, and bounced again. Bigger rocks with men's backs thrusting against them first toppled, then dropped ponderously, rolling, leaping, smashing. All the way to the water's edge and beyond they cleared their way, leaving splashes of crimson among wailing wretches. One stone, making a longer final leap than the rest, burst through the side of a ship. Lesser rocks came down on open decks to maim and kill with their impact.

The surviving War Crows changed again to birds, lifting from the ramparts to fly around the fortress with unnerving cries. Danans in bright tunics began to climb the unmoving outer wall, seeking holds like lizards. Others lay dead at the bottom, alone or in mortal embrace with Freths. Keir of Cup-bearer's Dismay was among those who survived to climb.

Freth guards in cumbersome wooden breastplates pushed half-bridges out across the gap between the inner and outer walls. Since one moved while the other did not, the bridges could not rest on both ends at once. The Freths had to jump the last couple of feet across the gap. One poor wight fell, to roll down the steeply inward-sloping ditch at the bottom and slip under the foot of the turning wall. A long, bubbling scream arose, a sound like that of acorns being crushed, and a crimson smear was left on the stones.

Keir gained the top of the outer wall, unaware of that accident. On his back in a web of rope was one of the kegs they had spent blood to bring ashore. Taking it off, he swung it by rope loops and made it boom on the shield of a Freth who was charging him. The shield cracked, as did a stave of the keg, and some of its yellow contents oozed out as the Freth clung desperately to the top of the outer wall.

Keir tossed his keg accurately into the gutter at the base of the inner wall, where it met the foundation. The keg jammed there. Under that enormous pressure, the keg burst. Its contents spread like butter along the grinding rock surfaces, which swiftly ripped the wood of the cask to fiber. Other warriors who reached the wall flung other such kegs, or drew them from below by ropes, while their comrades fought the Freths.

Nemed had made his orders clear; use all the kegs, then retreat to the ships and save their own lives if possible. He was there himself, in his shining armor, setting the example with two accurate pitches and a number of sword-slain enemies. Now he began sliding back down the wall by a rope, and Keir followed him.

As he descended, he passed a wounded Danan clinging to the wall while blood pumped out of him. Swiftly he crossed to the helpless warrior and supported him, while continuing down the wall. The wounded man's dead weight became like an oak's in seconds. He fumbled, putting his feet in the wrong places and slipping badly. Keir had to brace himself more than once to prevent the mumbling, bleeding automaton from taking them both to the ground by the swiftest way.

Keir had almost reached the bottom with his unknown

comrade when a deadly tremor ran through the wall. A basalt
slab tilted outward from the top and sledded insanely down the
battered outer surface of the wall, straight towards Keir and his
burden. The pug-nosed warrior saw it coming, flung himself
desperately sideways with an arm about his wounded fellow, and
hit the rocks rolling, entangled with his burden.

The basalt slab hit the grass, spun end over end, and thudded
against the ground. Keir winced at the nearness of that impact.
Another foot or two, and it would have crushed their bodies flat
where they lay together. Then he knew glorious exultation. He'd
done it! They were safely down!

"Come, fellow," he gasped. "We are leaving this place, and
you can have bandages, white and clean, with salve for your
wounds. First let me stop your bleeding, though—"

Then the other's head lolled towards him, and he saw the
front instead of the intact back. An edge of the bounding basalt
slab had, barely clipping him, ripped away his skull from the
eyes upward. Keir choked at the sight. Leaving the dead man, he
slid down a rock slope into the sea. His limbs quivered with
stress as he swam for the nearest vessel.

Dragging himself aboard, he sagged over the side-railing,
gripping it with his hands. For a bitter while he cursed fate, the
gods, and all men who went to war. Then he looked at the
Revolving Fortress.

Something seemed wrong with the endless grinding as it
turned. Now he heard, and saw too, that it had begun to shake
apart. Some of the basalt pillars had split from their mates,
while several together had jammed their bases in the foundations and were acting as groaning, suffering brakes to the whole
circular wall. It was not turning as one integrated piece any
longer.

Swiftly, the stuff in the kegs did its work. Stone had softened
at its touch to the texture of clay. It continued to soften,
inexorably, hour after hour, at a dozen places throughout the
base of the wall. No longer did its vast mass revolve as one
integrated circle, but hopped, stuck, and split in many different
segments. As the night wore on, it began to break.

Soon the Freth garrison was trapped within an unsafe
defence. Pieces did not fall out of the impossibly strained inner
wall; they split as an ice-bound tree splits in winter, shooting
bits of stone across the inner yard like arrows. Whole groups of

tall pillars, pushed out of place by the groaning advance of others behind them, toppled either inward or outward, shattering slowly. The earth power which drove them could not be stopped; it must find release. Sixarms's fortress slowly rent itself asunder.

Nemed heard the great inner walls crash down. Like jammed logs, like splintering tree-trunks, the stone pillars fell, criss-crossed, broke, and formed new masses as the turning foundations on which they piled jumbled them anew. A section of the unmoving outer wall came down after some hours, the pillars spreading outward in a fanlike delta. Only the double-walled tower at the center of the fortress remained intact.

"Goddess!" Nemed said, awed despite himself. "They must be trapped in there. They cannot get out through that—that madness, and we cannot get in! I'd thought we should at least have a fight and some booty for our trouble. Take us out of the harbor, pilot, before the fortress falls into the sea and crushes us all!"

"Aye, lord," the pilot answered, in no way reluctant.

One by one, the metal ships moved back from the crags of the island where the Revolving Fortress stood. Still gyrating, still devouring itself with the energies which fed it, it filled the night with its long, agonized roar.

"All that from some herbs and leaves," Keir said, astounded. "That magicians can do much, I knew—but turn stone into lard?"

Enghan Skylock chuckled harshly. "Even that. It's not a thing you see daily, Keir, because the potion takes three years to brew and can be ruined by one mistake. It's rarely worth the trouble."

"No question that it was worthwhile this time!" Varl stared with fascination at the falling citadel. "I wish this Sixarms monster who built it could be in there."

"And why?" Keir asked. "What is he to you but a name?"

"I fought some of his mangy breed by the sea-lough, did I not? I don't like them." The Alban warrior continued to stare at the fortress. A new section of wall was displaced outward as he watched, and slid down the crag, dissolving thunderously into its component parts. They crashed over the stone jetty and sank in the harbor, a storm of bubbles marking their grave. "That's the right stuff for them."

"Spoken like a right hater," Enghan laughed. The squat magician was enjoying the fortress's destruction himself. "As for Sixarms," he went on, dangling his short legs from the thwart where he sat, "be glad he is not here. Yon creation of his would never be swallowing itself thus. He'd control it."

"Not with his severed head in a bucket of salt."

"It may happen, so, but not here. The great Sixarms's bane is going to find him in the east, if anywhere. The master of my college predicted it."

"Oh, then that assures it will happen. But if you happen to know where my bane will be, keep it for your own secret," Keir said, and stretched. "Too many of us met their ends here today."

Varl shrugged. "Victory has its cost. We won. Now we'll go to the final victory, and break the Freth grip."

"So we will," Keir said intensely. "There will be plenty of room in Tirtangir, afterward, for those who aided. Have you farming appetites, Varl?"

"I have, but not to be sated here. There's only one place fit to farm, and it lies in Alba. I told you."

"What made you leave it?"

"A dog barked at me. They said it was an omen."

Keir understood that he was not to be told. Prince Nemed at least did not care who knew he had been outlawed; but perhaps Varl's story was worse. He let it go.

"When we have won, I'll return to *my* home," he boasted, "and take presents to all my kindred, stolen back from Freth thieves. I'll clear the Freths out of our fields as well. Those who survive will go back to their bogs with their heads shorn and backsides naked! None rules Danans in the last truth of it, except Danans."

He had learned that fine talk through listening to Nemed and Cena. Enghan gave his raucous laugh, seeing through the young warrior. "You want to keep Freth bailiffs off your farm girls and out of your hen-runs, Keir. Aside from that, it's little to you whether your Rhi is Cena—a glorious ripe peach, agreed—or a caterpillar from a beech leaf."

Keir would have answered this hotly, had not the island shuddered. The foundations of the Revolving Fortress split across, the sound going up like stony thunder to the sky, and molten stone oozed out of the cleft as it squeezed shut, liquefied by the energies released. Glowing red, it flowed into the sea, and enormous volumes of steam rose hissing like dragons. Within the warm fog, the wrecked walls stopped turning altogether, and the central tower came down with a crash.

Enghan was silent for once, daunted by what he had witnessed. All three had the same thought; not many could have survived such a collapse.

The night wore on. Red flames crowned the wreckage of Sixarms's great fortress. All the western coasts were now exposed to Manahu's raiders, and any lesser sea-thieves who might care to try their luck, such as Shaui. He would hear of it soon. The Danans danced their victory on Nemed's decks. The magicians had bought it for them, little fighting having been done by any save the War Crows.

Then morning came, and the tide for them to depart, and with it there was ample fighting for everybody.

A fleet of dugout canoes rode the water, thirty paddles in each, all driven by the powerful arms and shoulders of angry Freths. Leather boats accompanied them in greater numbers still. A few heavy rafts bore small stone-throwers, more of Sixarms's work.

"Demons!" Varl swore, and lifted his shield. "We earn our way out of here, it seems."

The prince's eyes narrowed as he studied the sea-host coming against him. Numerous yet clumsy, it could be left far behind if he broke through it, and break he would. One ship might have to be abandoned, the one whose side had been split open and which now had a spare sail warped around the damage, but he vowed to lose no others.

"Around the isle to windward, and away!" he commanded. "They have no chance if we are swift!"

The voice of the experienced pirate spoke there. His mariners sprang to their work, hauling on lines, bending to the oars, and sounding the water. The leading ship rounded the grey rocks, where foam seethed dangerously on kelp-skirted granite. The damaged vessel lumbered after it, sluggishly rolling. Freths raised a bass shout at the sight of its lameness, and they paddled like men racing for the islands of the blessed to catch it. Keir and Varl looked at each other grimly, saying without words that they were mightily glad not to be in *that* ship.

Their own, the prince's, and another vessel fell back to guard the leaking ship's rear by fighting off the Freth boats. There was a simple way to disable the curraghs; leap into the sea with a knife, swim under water until the air sacs in your lungs began to rupture one by one, and slash open the boat's leather side between its light timber ribs. The dugouts, far stronger and excellently seaworthy, had the weakness of capsizing easily if dragged side-on to the waves. Using bronze hooks on the ends of ropes, the Danans set about capsizing them. The more Freths left struggling in the water, of course, the more of their friends had to spend effort to save them instead of slaying Danans.

There were enough to perform both tasks. Keir and Varl did not swim well enough to take the glory-filled but deadly work of holing curraghs, at which a man might live to sabotage three if his gods were with him. They took swords instead, and stood by the longship's rail with the rowers' heads nodding level with their knees. The curraghs raced through the water more swiftly than Nemed's longships, their greased leather hulls skimming over the waves. Short-nosed Freth faces glared at them, breath panting between big even teeth, heavy muscles bulging as they drove the paddles.

"I'll sneeze and blow over your pig-boats!" Keir yelled.

The leather boat began to fill as though his gibe had been heard by a whimsical water-god. Two Freths sprang overboard with hatchets, looking for the real reason, and a wet Danan head broke the surface behind the curragh for a breath. Then he duck-dived again, two burly figures kicking through green dimness after him. They caught him, what was more, and left him floating with his belly split, but not before he had torn open another curragh himself; not before he had inflicted a mortal wound on one of his slayers. Keir cheered him.

Then he was wholly occupied in raising a tally of slain enemies to pay his own way through the cauldron of rebirth. A Freth canoe had come alongside, seized their ship with wooden grapples, and spewed its wrinkle-browed complement over their rail. The oak dugout dragged like an anchor. Freth weapons smashed holes in the Danan line; Keir struck back, driving his sword's point into a long-lipped mouth, smashing another with his shield-boss. The impacts jolted his body to the feet. Then he saw his chance to chop loose a grapnel, and did, before a Freth hammer split his shield to send him tumbling among the rowers. His sword clattered somewhere, and he groped after it, swearing. A rower held it out to him, with the terse suggestion that as a fighter he had best learn how to keep hold of it even if it impaled him.

Keir snatched it with a growl, shook loose the split remainder of his shield, and thrust carefully upward into a Freth groin as it appeared over the rail. Then, as that invader voiced a scream, Keir rose to fight at the gunwale again, shoving the maimed man back into his canoe.

The struggle went ferociously on.

A second canoe bound fast to them, was cut adrift, came back for another attempt, and failed. The first hung on tenaciously for a long, dreadful time, but finally dropped astern after every third Freth in it had been wounded or killed. Keir had done his share. His lungs burned, and his nicked sword flung spatters of red as he plied it. The last Freth aboard turned on him suddenly, seized him in fearfully strong arms, and began to break his back, heedless of the spears men drove into his body. Keir felt his spine beginning to crack, and braced his knees against the Freth's belly while butting his nose time after time. He felt it break, but not for that reason had the terrible hold loosened at last; the Freth had become a fleshly sheath for two blades and three spearheads. Keir drew himself out of that dead embrace with a grunt of profound gratitude.

They were clear of the island, beating their way eastward against the wind. Somewhere behind them, the damaged ship lay at the bottom of the sea, where Freths of the Cormorant Tribe had sent her. Nemed had rescued the men in her, but then two other ships had been lost, dragged down like stags assailed by hounds, a bitter shame and loss to the prince, who had been prepared to accept one if he must. When battling the notoriously stubborn Freths, it was rare to escape so lightly.

The prince had succeeded, nonetheless. The Revolving Fortress lay in tumbled ruins which even Sixarms could not restore in less than five years, and which a lesser builder would never rebuild at all. The thing was done. Now to finish it, in the east, where it would have to be finished, in the company of Cena and her brothers—and that rabid dog, Gui of the Rainbow Men.

Someone was assuredly going to pay for the loss of his ships.

*Chapter
Nine*

Invisible Lyran vessels came up from the north and south, bringing sea sorcery with them. The ocean rose hundreds of feet as though the winter gales had returned, to tear down cliffs and burst up through the river estuaries, forcing whole tribes out of their territories and bringing death to others. In the train of the sea-waves came the Lyrans with their tame seals and bone-barbed weapons, to take whatever their roaring green father had spared. They harried in the west as Manahu had promised, making nonsense of Nemed's misgivings, and none of the seacoast tribes could send so much as one man to fight the Danans. That war was left to the Freths of forest, bog, and lake, with the Bear Tribe for their main strength and backbone, and Sixarms for a leader.

Sitting before a council fire, his face painted black and a bear's scalp on his grizzled head, Sixarms thudded his club on the earth and gazed at the chiefs, magicians, and warriors before him. Women were not a part of this council; they held their own, and to be valid under tribal law a decision reached by one council had to be ratified by the other.

"The tale is true," Sixarms said heavily. "The Revolving Fortress is broken. Nemed, the Alban prince, did it at Cena's asking. They have sent the war cloak among their clans. The sea-people feed them! Our women can do nothing against that, nor can I. We know only earth magic."

"Curse the Danan fields and orchards, then," an old man grunted, "and the wombs of woman and beast. Sea bounty or not, the Danans cannot thrive forever unless the earth is good to them."

Murmurs of savage assent came from a score of hairy throats. Eyes set deeply within cavernous orbits glowed like the peat fires.

"That must be talked about with the old women," Sixarms said, his voice deep as a Freth drum. "When we do, I will say: no. The Danans would not move unless they were desperate, or ready in great power. Cursing their fields and cattle will not dissuade them in time. This one says that we must raise swifter evil against them, and set the Despoilers free."

All present had heard of those monsters. Of all men now living, only Sixarms had seen them; he was the hero who had shut them away from the daylight.

"The Despoilers!" a young chieftain said incredulously. "They are a tale."

"No tale."

"Then they are dead. Nothing lives underground for generations of men."

"Hate doesn't die. The Despoilers were born of hate and malignancy. They make their own venom and feed upon it. The story is true; there was once a man with so evil a heart that when he was cut to pieces by the folk he had wronged, three tiny worms hatched from his heart, worms so poisonous that everything they touched or breathed upon died. They grew so huge that they would have wasted the sacred island, perhaps, if they had not been overcome. They will have lived."

Another ancient Freth said from a toothless mouth, "This is a thing worse than the Danans have done. My mother told me of the Despoilers, and of the warrior Ochai who drove them into the earth. If you open their pit now, men will curse you as they blessed you then—and not only Danans. What if they should do as you have done? The Despoilers are not the only foul things in the earth's belly. The Danans know some of them, and they have less wisdom than you.''

''Thorn,'' Sixarms said, ''the decision is not made yet. It faces us. You can refuse; the women can refuse. This one will give his voice to it.''

''Your voice is the heaviest. You lead in war. Even the old women would not go against Sixarms in a matter like this. But you are wrong.''

Sixarms spread his hands on the air in a flat, definite gesture. The destruction of the fortress which guarded his people had provoked him to burning umbrage. The devastation of their western coasts once that protection was removed made him wish the Danans, also, to know the meaning of devastation and terror.

The Danans, in their ignorance, had never heard of the Despoilers. They knew the extent of Freth powers, or thought they did, and knew their own. At a great council at Sen Mag, the First Created Plain, they moved openly to war for the first time since the Battle of the Waste.

''I will lead you,'' Cena said, ''and die before I retreat. In the shape of a bird I will oversee the battle and direct it. As myself I will be where the spears are thickest, and where Sixarms is, there I will seek him. If I should be slain, place my body on a litter and carry it before you so that I may lead you until the fight is won, and never turn back for fire, iron, or dread.''

''I will fight with the Band of Dar,'' Oghmal said, ''and I will carry the Wailing Spear which pierces everything in its path, flying back to my hand, and which kills whatever it strikes. The greatest Freth champions I will encounter, to slay or die and never to withdraw.''

Bava, the War Crow, promised to foretell the deaths of their greatest enemies, and appear to them with the prophecy so that the heart would be drawn from them before they arrived at the battle. She promised as well to spread such fierce carnage in the Freth host that they would cry for peace.

''I will make the blades and rivets for all the weapons you need,'' said Beren, the master bronze-worker, ''and see that they do not break in the battle.''

"With my sorcery, I will lock the urine of the Freths and their beasts within their bodies, so that they will have to withdraw from the fight," Enghan declared.

The nine royal cup-bearers swore to ensure that every fighter on the Danan side had his fill to drink, while their enemies went thirsty. From Luchtan the carpenter to Talvi the master weaver and all the magicians, they offered their skills and their wealth to the Danan cause. When the craftsmen had finished, the lords spoke, describing how many men they would bring to the fight and with what power they would battle. Afterward, the individual warriors had a chance to utter their own boasts, and did so joyfully, with many a quarrel and insult-match over prowess and precedence. There would have been fights to the death had Cena not forbidden them, and enforced the ban with her magic. All killing was to be done against Freths until they were free.

Nemed and Gui, the strongest men there in terms of followers and two of the best warriors, were rivals besides. Gui never chided his men for behaving arrogantly. It increased the fear in which his own name was held. The exiles from Alba, though, had seldom heard of Gui before, and cared little for his reputation. They mocked his supporters' boasts and made more outrageous ones of their own, to provoke them. They would fight as rivals, striving to outdo one another in valor and tenacity, and perhaps they would be friends later.

Supposing that there was a later. Cena knew how much they were all gambling. She looked at young Mahon, now freed from his hostage-chains and acting as her brothers' cup-bearer, grave and trying, but awkward still. She crooked her finger for Hend, one of the nine.

"Give young Mahon some advice in private, Hend," she said, "and suggest that he not try so hard."

She saw the youth afterward.

"You are learning something of how we Danans go to war," she said. "Proudly, Mahon, in our best garments and jewels, leaving nothing behind to grieve over or regret. In this fashion we say to our enemies, 'See, I am worth plundering; come for me! But if you loot me of what I wear, you will earn it.' Now, what of you? You cannot be on both sides in this battle, or on neither, and you no longer have chains. You must know where you stand and make it clear. Will you fight for the Freths, or for us? You should speak to your father as well."

"Lady, you know how we parted."

"As badly as it could be done. That is why you should approach him now. You will have no chance to speak to him again, Mahon, if he dies in this battle. Have you thought that he may regret what was done at Lost Star Lake?"

Mahon's mouth twisted at the idea.

"You and he!" Cena said. "Two demons for pride! Sulk apart, then. Fawn upon Oghmal, who is not of your kindred, and refuse what is difficult. Keep clear of me, though. I do not like to have sullen boys around me."

Mahon thought over those words. Gui was his blood father, not much of one, true, but perhaps he did not have such a splendid son. He could scarcely be happy, living with gossip that his mother had poisoned his wife, and—what stood in the way but resentment?

Mahon took a flask of strengthened wine and two simple cups to his father's seat.

"You are going to be very happy, sir," he said. "The Freths have been struck hard already, and now you are going to strike them harder."

"Don't weep over that to me," Gui snarled. "You accursed little traitor!"

"Traitor be sworded!" Mahon replied. "They fostered me. If I am still here, it is because of Cena and Oghmal. But that is wrong. They are no blood kin of mine. You are. There is nothing I can tell the Freths now that they do not already know."

"Then go to them! I'll be glad to see the last of you."

"Had I decided that, I'd not be here." Mahon looked into his father's eyes. "Have you space for another warrior in your band instead, sir?"

"For other warriors, yes. Not for one who still fights on foot because he falls off a horse."

"That doesn't matter. I am your son, and it's my right to battle in your band, and your right to have me there."

"My right? You arrogant little spy! You say you are doing this for me? I think you wish to feather your nest on the side that will win. Have you in my war-band? You, who ran from one man and a woman when you were caught spying?"

"I listened to you and your lady mother," Mahon agreed, using the title with something of an edge on it. "Well, have you never done a thing that was other than straightforward? What schemes have you carried out that you would not wish the Rhi to know?'' Gui's eyes shifted, then narrowed in anger. Mahon spoke on. ''My choice was made when I went from the lake to Dar, and not westward. My father, one or both of us may die in this fight. It would mean something to me to fight in your band.''

''You who love me so dearly and hate the Freths so much?''

''Let's not talk of love. There is little . . . it may be that there can be more. For now, every weapon-arm helps, and mine knows how to wield a sword or axe. Judge when you have tried me.''

Gui said, ''Very well. I'll try you now. Come outside and have a practice bout.''

They fought for half an hour, and Gui was vicious. Mahon fought back hard, never complaining. Three times his father came near inflicting a severe wound, and each time the youth returned boldly to the practice. The fourth time, he halted the weapon-play.

''You nearly laid my arm open there! Come, you know by now that I can fight.''

''The poorest of my Rainbow Men would laugh at you,'' Gui sneered. ''If you think I will have you among us on foot, swinging like a girl with a grain-hook while we ride carefully around you, think again. You can fight among my clients with a spear.''

Mahon felt angry because of the tone, but he knew he was a poor rider. In any case, not many men did fight well from a horse's back, even among the Danans, who were said to be born twinned with colts and fillies. The youth said:

''It's good company to be in. Your horses may have to withdraw behind our spears for a rest before the day is over.''

Gui laughed again, but this time it was almost an amiable sound. Almost. He said, ''Oghmal has been teaching you some of his own manners, I see. Well. Did you bring that wine only to stare at it, or shall we finish it together?''

They did finish it, and then another like it. Some of Gui's Rainbow Men gathered about them. They sang old drinking songs, and the ancient war songs from beyond the stars, of Shalmiv's Defence and the Poison Warriors. The drink flowed more freely, and brotherhood reigned in the fumes of distilled

wine, as did fatherhood and sonhood. Gui led the singing with
his excellent baritone, one arm about Mahon's wide shoulders
and the other keeping time. Oghmal watched from the shadows,
and for once his hard-boned face was not sardonic. Maybe Gui
could only be like this on the eve of battle and drunken. Still it
made a memory, and Mahon was his only son, and he had no
nephews. Oghmal could be pleased about that, even for a man
he disliked.

The next day, work began. The Rainbow Men ceased to ride
after cattle-lifters and keep order at lawsuits. Now they descended on Freth steadings, twenty or thirty strong, and sent the
masters scurrying for the border, when they did not promptly
hang them from the nearest green trees. Not even the tribute-
children had any tears for them. The Freths who dwelt in Danan
lands and battened on them were the lees of their race, and the
Danans who served them willingly the scourings of theirs. In the
day of reckoning, they shared the same fate.

Old weapons were unearthed and sanded to brightness.
Practice took place in the open daylight. Pipers played the sept
call by a dozen family megaliths, and Danans came to hear the
place and day named for their meeting with the overlords.
Prince with a horse of pride or farm laborer with straw-stuffed
wooden shoes, they were ready; and they knew that after their
years of dominance, too many Freths were not.

Riders cut deeply into Freth territory again, taking the old
foraying tracks through bog and forest, but using the new grassy
roads as well. Fortlets and stockaded store-houses went up in
snickering flames. Floatwains so heavy with loot that they
almost touched the ground were drawn back to Ridai, Dar, Lost
Star Lake, and a dozen other places. Oghmal led a band of
twenty men on foot to a stronghold deep within monster-
haunted bogs, and took it, leaving a pile of ashes, so that Danan
boats could pass that way through stream, bog, and lake to sack
a rich townlet where three rivers joined.

These were thorn-pricks. The true damage was done when a
college of Freth wise women, hundreds strong, was smoked out
like a wasp's nest by Luchtan and their shrine destroyed.
Because he was a Danan, he slew none of them, but all their
appurtenances of magic he piled and burned. The flames
smelled of everything from sacred herbs to ordure.

"You should have slaughtered them," Gui said. "They will

be at the place of battle casting spells because you allowed them to live.''

''Better than having the earth herself against us,'' Luchtan said. ''They have little to cast their spells with, now. Ask Cena what she thinks I should have done. If we take to slaughtering women we will have to kill the last Freth in the island before we attain peace.''

His apprentices fashioned spearshafts and launchers by the hundred, the latter a simple notched stick giving a javelin half the range again of one thrown unaided. They had been making them every day for years against the time of their use. Wicker and bullhide was assembled into shields in a hundred farmsteads. The strong shoes and warm, rainproof cloaks which meant as much to a fighting host as its weapons came from many a workshop and loom, to cover the bodies which ran and practiced daily. And the sea fed them.

Finally they marched. Cena rode at the head of the host, her red-gold hair covered by a helmet of *findrina,* the magic metal the hue of emeralds. A black tunic patterned with orange spirals covered her to the knees, while buckskin leggings clung loose, supple and soft below her waist. She carried three spears, while her cousin Naoling walked beside her horse with her shield on his arm. Macha her daughter rode on her other side, to see the battle but not to partake of it, and less than pleased on that account.

Behind Cena came her own royal bodyguard, a score of fighters drawn from the best Danan septs but the royal family itself. The horses and trappings of every one were her own individual gifts. They gave their loyalty to Cena, the woman, not to the one who happened to be their Rhi, and if Cena should be defeated they would all go down with her, or stand shamed before the living. If Cena should ever be deposed they would follow her into exile, dread though that word was to a Danan of Tirtangir.

Gui led the Rainbow Men, the force of riders that was his own creation. All seven troops were now below their full strength; their work of late had emptied saddles. Still they rode with pride, from the troop in purple leather, purple linen, and flashing amethysts which led, to the band in crimson, cerise, and garnets at the rear. Each man carried a sword of enamelled bronze, strong, slender things with the beauty of effectiveness.

Oghmal the battle champion was there, not greatly caring for
rank or precedence, with his troop of warriors. His scarlet tunic
and bronze belt flamed in the sun, while zigzags of red paint
marked his limbs, vivid against the white skin. The magician
who had made the paint swore it would protect him against all
infections and venoms. If wounded, he might bleed to death,
but die of lockjaw or gangrene he would not. His followers wore
paint themselves, in many contrasting designs, though none
wore armor.

Like Nemed, half the wanderers from Alba did, though
usually no more than a helmet and intricately worked breastplate. Full tunics of mail like the prince's were uncommon. The
foreign Danans marched, having no horses, and bore weapons
of every sort known, even to flint hatchets shining like polished,
blue-black metal. They mingled with chieftains from all over the
Danan realms of Tirtangir, followed by kinsmen of the farms,
the forests, the booming seacoast; by clients owing them service
in war and support in peace; by vagabonds and scroungers
hoping to get something for nothing when the battle had been
fought.

The War Crows flapped overhead. Sorcerers rode curious
beasts or "walked without legs," floating above the ground on
earth power like the many floatwains drawn by plodding oxen. A
woman with a face like an elegant red-haired skull rode beside a
man of two centuries' eld whose form was that of a freckled
youth. Enghan Skylock, squat and short-limbed, rode a carved
log which sucked air whistling through the flutings on its surface
as it floated. The grotesque face at its fore-end stared about and
commented upon the procession.

They arrived at the fighting ground where the Freths under
Sixarms had agreed to meet them. Here three great channels of
earth power met. Grass and trees grew richly tall. In the
background rose a conical hill with a carved stone on its crest,
barren as the country around it was fertile. A stream swung
around the area, sparkling, with alders and willows garbing its
bank.

The Freths came. Unlike their appearance of ten years before,
they went clad in wool and linen now, almost as much as the
Danans though less gaily. They still carried stone-headed clubs
and spears, but now bronze axes by the score winked in their
ranks, and they carried supplies to the battlefield in floatwains

of their own. Bullhide drums talked through the forest in booming voices. The lighter Danan drums answered, mingled with the music of harps and multiple flutes. It was all oddly beautiful in its way, and a strange setting for what had to come.

"The Freths have their own kind of ground, brother," Carbri commented, "but so have we."

"Yes. It's a little too fine," Oghmal said. "I'd like it better if I could see something wrong."

The Danans held a tongue of high ground, the light soil above limestone supporting rich grass and shrubs. Below them, on the other side of the stream, the Freths had dense forest at their backs and all around them, save for the road they had cut following the western channel of earth power. In the event of disaster, they could go to ground or retreat quickly, as they wished. Oghmal's gaze kept returning to that inexplicably barren hill.

He shrugged. Doubtless he was fancying things. His awareness of magic was about equal to a blind man's appreciation of color.

The music skirled, a weapon in Danan hands. Carbri played on his harp, and the lesser bards went to the triple crossroads where the Freth van awaited. They chanted their most virulent satires against their former rulers, disparaging their health, their courage in battle, their powers of sorcery, their appearance, generosity, and physical strength, wishing sickness and irresolution upon them all. Bitter and violent the satires began; scathing and hateful they ended.

Then Carbri strode down to the crossroads in a flutter of his blue and white mantle. His satire was subtle, almost gentle, by comparison, but it cut deeper than all the wild invective of his fellows because it was true.

He described the Freth way of living as it had been, and then outlined in mercilessly clear word-strokes what it had become since they had conquered the Danans. The former independent comrades of tree and beast were now a rabble of drunken thieves, battening on the folk they had conquered and fearing the day that folk would shatter their lordship. Carbri described that thievishness with many a burlesqued instance, and showed the foolishness of driving wide grassy roads through country a foe with horses might now traverse easily—and had.

Nor was there any turning back from that path. The day of

justice was here now. Carbri described in joyous detail the extreme defeat they would suffer, rubbing into raw skin the salty details of their fortress's overthrow, the ignominious flight of their bailiffs from Danan lands, and the raids into their own country. He excelled himself in describing the ignominious fate of their wise women. The Freths roared in wrath.

Lastly, Carbri turned his song to challenges, inviting any Freth warrior who wished to die before the others to come and be slain. He was welcome to meet Carbri. His brother Oghmal would gladly battle any Freth of prowess enough to honor him. Their sister, as Rhi and war-leader, might not fight save in the battle itself, but Nemed, Gui, Bava, and others were all eagerly ready. Who wished to die first?

A huge black-haired Freth walked to the circle where the three great roads met. He carried a shield like a small table, and an axe polished down from a ten-pound lump of flint to a balanced weapon weighing perhaps seven. Swinging it handily, he announced himself.

"I am Stag Who Wins All His Fights, of the Whitethorn Tribe. All who think they can make my name a lie, come and try! Come alone, come in threes! The first deaths of this day are for us and the Earth-Mother. Are Danans afraid?"

Varl, the man from Alba who had been at the destruction of the Revolving Fortress, bounded from among the Danans with his eyes shining. Long-limbed and sure, he approached Stag with his shield shifting back and forth, his wide-bladed spear questing for flesh. Stag watched him from glinting hazel eyes, feet planted widely in a fighting stance from which he could shift at once in any direction. His balance would be difficult to break.

Varl circled him, light-footed and tough, a man who had battled Firbolgs at home and other foes in many places since. Feinting at Stag's thigh, throat, and chest, he gained some measure of the Freth's nerve when Stag barely moved except to bring up his shield a little, covering his neck. He was not to be panicked by experimental jabs, and he moved swiftly.

Varl glared into the broad Freth face. Sooty stubble covered the barely existent chin, with numbers of inch-long bristles sprouting through it. He saw an opening, leaped in before most men could have blinked, and turned aside Stag's axe as it banged on his shield. He drove his spear home. The Freth's shield was before it at once, and Varl's spear skidded aside. He locked the edge of his own shield behind Stag's and tried to lever the Freth's heavier one out of the way, to make a hole in his defence.

He reckoned without the strength of a Freth. Stag Who Wins All His Fights stood fast, his shield never moving a nail's width. The flint axe rose, crashed down through Varl's shoulder and into his chest, almost severing his arm. He fell, aware of utter numbness in his limb, then staring in disbelief at the jumble of meat and bone it had become. Spurting blood covered it.

Knowing he was a dead man, Varl drove his spear upward with his undamaged arm. Perhaps he could slay his slayer yet. Stag rammed his broad foot down on the shaft, knocking it out of Varl's grasp, and struck again with an ox-chested roar. Varl's world vanished in a red blind storm, and he realized to his sorrow that he would not see Alba again, after all.

He died before the pain of his wounds could overwhelm him. Keir saw him die, and tears spilled hot from his eyes even as he began to move. He held a position towards the rear of the host, though, and others were before him.

Stag battled the first with harsh, bruising doggedness, until he was worn down and the Freth axed his trembling legs from under him. With the second, he rested all he could until he recovered his wind, using the fear of his two victories to keep his man at a distance. When he was ready, he lured him in, tripped him, and hewed off his head where he lay sprawling.

"The Earth-Mother drinks!" he shouted. "Who is next to feed her?"

"Three victories over Danans are three too many for that lob to enjoy," muttered a chief of the middle ranks. Taking a sword like a long cleaver, and a heavy shield, he trod into the reddened circle.

"Who are you?" Stag demanded. "I do not kill a man without knowing his name."

"Hol, the cattle chief of Tuirena. Your name I know. You have been bawling it loudly enough."

The bull-necked man sat down on the grass, fastidiously clear of bloodstains. He thumbed the edge of his weapon and held it against his shield.

"When you are ready," he said, "we shall begin. Don't hurry on my account, lad; you have just hewn three Danans and I am sure you need your rest."

The Freth frowned, puzzled by the corpulent chief's imperturbability. Three of his tribesmen's red corpses lay on the ground about him, and he was to make the fourth, and he sat as though taking his ease.

"I'll take the rest," Stag said, squatting himself. "Not a long one. They were brave, but their strength was small. You look like a man with some power, and one who enjoys his food. Hhurgn?"

The grunting cough seemed meant as an interrogative. Hol nodded. "You are not wrong. Food? Man, I give feasts which are the joy of the countryside, and all my friends come flocking to the scents which flow out of the cookhouse. The secret is to mate with the right woman and get her the right help. You seem to be one who knows what his jaws are used for, your own self."

"Yes! I like food. It's too bad that we cannot sit down and eat together someday, but one of us will be dead and it is going to be you."

"Well, that is for discovering, blanket-lip. Since you have started bragging, I take it you are rested now."

Stag became watchful. "Yes."

"We'd better begin, then." Hol bounced to his feet, his heavy sword raised, slanting backward over his shoulder. Stag rose also, his nicked and crusted stone axe steady in his hand.

The pair went at it carefully, with respect for each other's experience. Each used his shield as his main weapon, striking with the heavy boss or metal-bound edge, working around and over it with the subsidiary weapon. Once in a while Stag would strike like a thunderbolt with his axe, and it would boom loudly on Hol's shield. Occasionally Hol would send his blade snaking for the Freth's belly or throat, but he never felt dismayed when he failed to reach it. There was time.

Stag chopped away a segment of Hol's long shield with one of his thunderbolt blows. The Danan's hip was exposed, and Stag's attention kept returning to that weakness as might his tongue to a chipped tooth. Although he attempted other targets, different ploys, they were only feints, distractions from the tempting, vulnerable hip outlined by the missing segment of shield. Stag had allowed one thing to fill his mind, and it showed.

Hol began attacking more fiercely, while taking great care to protect his vulnerable spot. He kept his shield out of the active side of the fight, using his sword more aggressively now, and showed many signs of being worried.

He slashed twice in succession at the side of Stag's knee. The Freth's axe split the bullhide cover of his shield in a different place. Hol jerked it upward, trying to slam the rim into Stag's throat. Stag thrust him away, and might have known by how easy it was that he had been allowed to. Seeing his chance and seeing nothing else, Stag launched a crashing stroke at Hol's hip, which would have crippled him had it landed. The corpulent Danan moved quickly, lifting his shield higher in a half-second, so that Stag's axe-head boomed on the leather. It sank through bullhide and wicker, sticking fast. Hol dragged him off balance by heaving on the shield. Then he struck, sending the edge of his thick blade shearing through Stag's temple into the brain-pan. The blow jarred him to the bone.

Slowly, Stag's eyes rolled up into his head. He went to his knees, fighting his death each increment of the way down, yet sinking. Finally he lay huddled over his axe, while Hol remained standing. The Danans cheered him to the echo.

"So," Hol said, "it was you, my lad. But it could have been me. Maybe if you had been fresh . . ."

He left his shield discarded by the Freth's body and ran back to the Danan host.

Single combats filled the remainder of that day. The two sides bore away their dead, and living men went into the circle of gore looking for glory. Some found it. Many found death. Oghmal fought two Freths at once, and laid them dead beside each other, then did the same for three in succession. None seemed to like the work of fighting him thereafter.

A Freth champion named Ashbrother won twice in succession before he left the crossroads. One of his victims was a member of Cena's guard, and her eagle-shriek of anguish could be heard as far as the barren hilltop. Gui promptly spurred his horse to the crossroads and demanded that Ashbrother turn back to fight him. The Freth answered that he was too tired, and would fight Gui in the morning. Cena's consort did battle with one strong

Freth before dusk, and finished him, but it was Ashbrother he dreamed of through the night. Each one of Cena's nineteen surviving companions had marked the Freth as well, by appearance and name, and meant to give him personal attention if they met him in battle.

In the morning there were no more single combats. The Freth host had moved forward and massed itself behind a wall of shields. It looked solid as stone. Cena surveyed them soberly. Then she addressed her own war-host from her sorrel mare.

"Children of the goddess, of Earth-Mother Danu!"

They listened in utter silence as she faced them, their Rhi, judge, ruler, war-leader; woman and mother among a breed which held these things sacred. It was as though the great mother of them all had suddenly possessed Cena, and spoke with her voice.

"There are your enemies! You of Tirtangir, recall our defeat at the Waste; the shame of that, and the shame of ten years that followed. Recall the extortions, the fear of broken doors in the night, the taking of your crops, your goods, your very children —we, who had been the freest people on the ridge of the earth!

"Here we balance the debt and set ourselves free. Here we repay the full tally with something to spare! Is there one Danan here who will even consider going home to a new and harsher Freth rule? To groaning slavehood for life, to bearing Freth half-breeds, to eating Freth scraps after providing the meal? Will you give them *all* your children now, to come home after seven years and suffer the cruel name changeling? I know you will say with me, never!

"But if I were left alone to face every Freth in the island, I would leave my corpse here rather than submit to them. The Rhi who fails her people is not one.

"Some of you have no such debts to pay. Some of you are drawn here by the goddess's blood which runs in us both. Whether you are here for honor or to earn a new life, or for honorable gain, know this: Tirtangir is a Danan island! Alba has long been greatly troubled; my own forebears came here because invaders drove them out. So long as Danans rule here, there will be a place for you to come if you or your children stand in need, a place to speak your own tongue and live among your own folk.

"If we fail, there will be nowhere. Beyond Tirtangir there is nothing known, no land where an entire people can live. For yourselves, to have something to promise your children, we must win here, and on this day. Wipe out the shame of the past. Buy with your courage and your sorcery and your sharpened bronze all the good years to come! *Who is with me?"*

Their answer shook the sky, and Cena laughed through the mighty assent.

The Danan sorcerers had prepared illusions through the night. Now they cast them as the Danans moved forward. The Freths looked upon the approaching enemy and saw themselves mirrored there; the backward-bulging Freth heads and heavy Freth bodies, but as they would be in a nine-night, not as they were now, whole and living.

They saw rank mildew on their garments, and rotted black blood. They saw wounds puffed among grey flesh, and themselves holding severed limbs, or standing with half their heads. There were grisly wounds to the body, signs that wolves had been feeding, weapons broken in the injuries they had made, and dark cruor clotted around them. A smell of the devouring earth rolled from that army of corpses. The Freths saw themselves as the battle would leave them, and some did not stay to look again. They turned and ran.

They did not go far. Their own comrades brained them for cowardice and moved closer together, taking up the room. They raised a derisive roar against the Danans.

Then they moved. Their slow trot became a slow run, a steady run which ate distance in gulps, and finally a full charge. The wall of tough flesh split into individual faces as they drew nearer, holding rope-collared logs which they swung into the Danan lines, breaking their shield-lock so that Freths could tear the gaps wider.

The Danans did not rend. Ten years of enforced patience had made them stubborn. They assimilated the shock, stood fast against the onslaught, and piled a barrier of speared Freths between them and the next charge. The impact went up to the cloud-dappled sky.

Mahon was there, and his stomach had been a cold lump as he watched the Freth charge, dreading the sight of a foster-brother. All he did encounter was a scarred, angry stranger who swerved to meet him, came to grips, and almost gutted him. Mahon remembered a trick Oghmal had taught him, and broke the Freth's shin with the lower edge of his shield. When his

enemy hopped and staggered, Mahon was able to drive a spear
into his throat. After that, his frozen stomach melted. He forgot
that he had been a Freth foster-child and lived in the present,
with foes who tried their utmost to kill him.

The Freths came three more times, with their stones and logs
to break the Danan lines. Sixarms raced at their head, his great
body pulsing with earth power drawn from the crossroads,
unstoppable wherever he went. The Grinder broke shields like
crusts of bread, stove in chests, and shattered limbs. Sixarms
left ruin within the Danan lines, while Cena and Oghmal both
strove to reach him through the carnage. Neither succeeded. In
the event, it was an unknown dying man beneath his feet who
drove a piece of broken spear through Sixarms's thigh. The
Freth did not notice it when it happened, but at last he faltered,
and the Danans threw back that attack also. Sixarms limped
down the slope with a shield slung on his back for safety.
Missiles thudded into it from the Danan lines.

Now those lines opened, and with a magnificent shout the
Danan riders raced across the great open circle of the crossroads. The retreating Freths turned to face the charge, looking
into a line of wild eyes and bright, blowing cloaks. The Danans,
led by Gui, hurled short javelins into flesh, then wheeled to slash
with their long swords, gripping their horses hard with thighs
and knees to stay in the saddle. Fighting from horseback without
stirrups to brace their feet was work for experts, and even they
could not always keep their seat against a blow dealt or received.
More than one man was thrown or dragged down.

Sixarms stood on his one good leg, swung the Grinder with
all his might, and shattered the chest of Gui's rearing horse. A
flying hoof caught the Freth chieftain's shoulder as the animal
screamed hideously. It crashed to the turf. Gui sprang clear as it
fell. After one glance at the terrible, inward-driven injury, the
breastbone a broken crater a sheep's head could fit into, Gui
killed the beast at once before he thought of protecting his own
life. It was an unselfishness he would not have extended to many
human beings.

Sixarms stood before him. Freth, Freth, this is your last day!
Gui moved forward, his sword a strip of orange light in the sun,
but five of his foe's cousins from the Bear Tribe came between
them, while another quickly worked to stop the bleeding from
his tree-thick leg, which had started once more.

Five Freths. To reach Sixarms, Gui felt ready to deal with them all. He moved like an angry wildcat, sword flashing, drawing blood from the leader first; only a gash on the brow, but enough to blind with gore. Driving his point leftward, Gui sent it through a heavy forearm like a needle through snow, and twisted for additional damage as he withdrew. That maliciousness undid him. The blade stuck between thick Freth bones.

Gui wrenched to drag it clear. He glimpsed a lifted club, warded himself barely in time, and had his own shield driven down hard on his head by the impact. He fell, seeing crimson suns, but gripping his sword and dragging it clear as he rolled. From the ground, he rammed his point into a hairy side and felt it slip through soft organs.

The other Freths gathered about him to batter him where he lay. Gui glimpsed riders in daffodil cloaks urging their horses among them, shouldering them aside, trampling and swording to rescue their lord. The trained horses killed with their hooves and teeth.

Someone dropped beside Gui, lifted him, heaved him into the saddle he had just left, and took an axe-edge in the back while Gui groped for the reins. Gui felt the death-blow through the man's body as he was hurled against his lord's leg. He reached down, caught him, and hurled him bodily to the horse's back in front of Gui.

"Now grip fast!" he shouted, and kicked his horse to a canter over the ruined grass. The man clutched feebly at his mount's white mane, a stain of red spreading over his cloak, and as they reached the Danan positions he tumbled off. Gui sprang down, and saw the death-shadow spread across his rescuer's face. He made the sign a Danan makes over a slain brother, and wrapped the man soundly in his yellow shroud.

Cena approached; Gui saluted her.

"I missed Sixarms," he said. "He's wounded, but it was not my doing. His thigh's pierced."

"You did well to come back alive," she said. "We need you here, Gui. I am going to lead some horse-charges against the Freths, kill as many with darts as we can, but not drive home the charge. We will turn aside at the last minute. Perhaps we can lure them into another charge of their own, and catch them on the open ground."

"Yes!" Gui said harshly. "And if they are not deceived by it

the first time, we'll go on trying until they are!" He glanced at
the dabbled figure being lifted onto a bier. "That man's name
was Trahals. I want Carbri to give him a song that will be
remembered."

"I'm sure Carbri will. He'll have many songs to make when
this fight is over, though, my love."

Gui took her in his arms and kissed her. "Then let's win it
quickly, that his songs may be heard. How goes the sorcery?"

"The river turns back from the Freths whenever they try to
drink. Soon they will be distressed, and then they won't be able
to fight, though that other wickedness of binding the urine in
their bodies . . . is not working. Enghan is building an enchantment to send hail against them, instead, once we have lowered
their spirit a little more. Do you notice they have used no
sorcery of their own?"

"Yet. Well, we must give them no chance to."

"It makes me wonder what they are preparing. They have few
of their totem beasts with them, this time, except for the bears,
and none of the tree spirits or other faerie things. Can they have
changed so much in ten years?"

"Who knows? Mount and ride!"

Cena led the first charge, her own bodyguard and the depleted
Blue Troop following her wild gallop. Seeing her target, she
hurled three of the short saddle-javelins in quick succession at
Sixarms, but none reached him because of the shields his Freths
held before him. The hail of missiles which fell into the Freth
ranks slew a couple of score. The Freths retaliated, but Cena
wheeled her light-footed mare and was away so swiftly, her men
following, that none of the flint-tipped spears found a home.
Thereafter the Danans did the same thing again. And several
times again. Their horses' feet hardly left a mark on the ground
or disturbed the grass.

"They are angry," Gui reported, after taking his turn to lead
some charges. A smell of leather and horseflesh emanated from
him. "They will rush soon. I feel it."

"Good," Oghmal said. "A full charge by Freths needs some
breaking, but we will do it."

They brought forward all their throwers of long javelins and
their slingers, forming them in a wide crescent, with the slingers
at the crescent's tips. In the center the throwers were ranked four
deep, the butts of their spears settled snugly into the notches of

their launching sticks. Girls stood behind the ranks of throwers to cut open new bundles of javelins and pass them forward.

Danan horsemen raced across the little plateau once again, riding lightly as swallows, rushing down the slope towards the Freths. Again, led by Cena, they hurled their short spears at the closest possible range; again they swiftly turned around, racing back to the main host, up the whin-scattered slope. For men bred in the saddle, raiding and herding cattle, it was simple sport.

This time the Freths came after them. Heedless of the danger in the open, they splashed through the ford and slogged up the wide incline, determined to come to grips with the Danans. Armed with axes and heavy knives for hamstringing, they chased the hated Danan horses, their subjects' strongest weapon against them.

The riders disappeared around the tips of the crescent formation of foot fighters, reining in behind it. On came the charging Freths, knowing their foes' horses were tired, seeing a barrier of youthful, lightly-armed Danans, confident in their strength that they could smash through it. Their war-cry sent birds flying from nearby trees.

"Now!" Cena commanded, and the hundreds of sinewy arms shot forward. Hissing, the javelins arced through the sky, to come down ripping through mortal flesh and bone. Freths reeled, impaled, and clawed at the earth with bare hands in their torment. Deep-throated screams went up to the sky.

The deadly rain fell again, and a third time. The missiles drove through even the oaken shields of the Freths, or split them in half. They milled about, the unity of their charge spent.

Cena and Gui rode back, then, at the head of their horsemen, on as many fresh mounts as they had, into the chaos of decimated Freths, their long swords flaming. There on the slope they took revenge for ten years of misrule, as their trained war-horses killed in partnership with them. Hooves sank through curiously-shaped skulls or rib cages. Fallen Freths were stamped to death. One was lifted in the jaws of a furious stallion and shaken in the air, shaken until he dropped again with the muscle torn out of his arm, though he cut the stallion's throat before he fell. The ribbed bronze swords reaped their own particular grain.

The Freths gave back what they got. Many a horse was

crippled, many a rider torn from the saddle and butchered on the
reddened ground, or killed with the bare hands of some
infuriated Freth. Yet their ill-judged charge had been broken,
and they were soon in retreat. They withdrew past the crossroads and across the ford of the stream, herded like cattle by Gui
and Cena, until once again they stood with their backs to the
forest, and could be driven no farther. They held their ground.

"Yes, wait here for our pleasure!" Cena flung at them. "We
will be back."

The weary Freths began throwing up walls of earth against the
keeping of that promise. Thirst had become a torture from
which they would not be free until the battle ended. Yet they
could never yield. If they did . . .

"As surely as night follows day they will take the land from
us as they were doing before," said Owlet, one of the sorcerous
old women of Sixarms's tribe.

"We have their children," said another grimly.

"Ha! Has that stopped them?" Owlet's tone was grimmer
yet. "We took their children, we took their cattle, and still they
prospered. It is because of their magic, because they have
friends beyond the sea—because of their horses. The horses
most of all. This time we must take those. Forbid them to breed
the monsters."

"First we must defeat them again," croaked the oldest
woman there, "and our magic works more slowly than theirs.
That accursed Luchtan destroyed much of it. If they follow us
into the forest—"

"They won't. This ground suits them." Sixarms had never
interrupted a wise woman before. Now he looked towards the
Danan host with trouble in his lined face. "I smell sorcery of
theirs."

Enghan Skylock was the sorcerer. The squat man sent the
black hail of which he had boasted, in stones the size of sheep's
knuckles. They lashed and struck out of a clear sky, slashing
flesh, numbing skin which swiftly turned a dull, aching blue,
rattling off lifted shields, increasing the misery of wounded men
beyond bearing, adding cold and vicious drubbing to the pangs
of thirst. It went on for hours, and not one stone fell on the

Danans' little plateau. When at last Enghan had to stop, the Freths were bleeding and half frozen.

"This is their doing; let them bear it," Sixarms said. "We must unleash the Despoilers."

A murmur of sheer horror greeted that. The Despoilers were legend, yet some of these women were old enough to have known the reality, seven Danan generations before. Only Sixarms among men had lived long enough to say the same.

"Better if we won without that. We can hold fast until they give in!"

"Lacking water? No. Sixarms is the master of the Despoilers. They must obey him."

"I would not unleash them on a lifeless rock of the sea—and I am not so sure of their obedience, either."

They argued for another day, while Danan attacks grew fiercer and Freth resistance weaker. The forest people could not fill so much as their cupped hands from the nearby stream; it flowed away from them, and they had to watch the Danans coming down with jugs and skins at their pleasure. Many a watering party was attacked and driven back, and by night the Freths crept through the forest to slay Danan horses, but these were small actions. The Danans had gained the initiative, and they pressed their advantage without pause.

"We have them," Cena said passionately, lying in Gui's arms. "We are going to win, Gui. Win and be free!"

She covered his throat and chest with ardent kisses, and there in the tent of war he loved her with more tenderness than he ever had in time of peace. Afterward, though, his old black doubts filled his mind again.

What will happen once the Freths are defeated? It was because we were conquered and there were Freths to fight that you took me in the beginning, Cena—because I had an uncle and you a brother to avenge. When life is good again I will still need you. But you will not need me.

Although he had been Cena's lover for years, he did not know yet that it was not her way to discard a man the instant he had served her purpose.

The next morning, he came out of her tent to find that the Freths had gone.

All the thousands of their host had withdrawn into the

trackless forests, taking their wounded. The trampled, blood-mired crossroads stood empty. Beyond it, on the barren hill, around the carved stone on its crest, a dozen figures were gathered—and even at this distance, Gui scented magic.

Carbri the harper had a nose equally keen. He said quietly, "I mislike this. It's in my mind that if we do not stop it we will wish that we had! Fifty swift horses, Gui, and fifty good men, you and I among them. A sudden raid across the ford to that hilltop. Yes?"

"Yes!" Gui agreed. "We had better be ready to fight our way there. I see plenty of cover between here and there, nor do I believe that *all* the Freths have gone."

They rode with Oghmal and his band, for Gui's men had done more than their share on the previous day. They saddled and bridled in moments, the champion at their head, while Gui let Cena know what was happening.

"The War Crows are swifter!" she said. "Let them go."

"Aye, if you can find them in time!" Oghmal answered. "Meanwhile we will be there!"

They galloped through the camp and past the crossroads, along the one wide grassy highway which led westward. Thistledown blew on the wind, to gather on their rain-wet cloaks and the manes of their horses. Moving clouds filled the sky, and their shadows drifted across the world below in changing, foreboding shapes.

On the hillcrest, Sixarms chanted. The carved stone at his feet glowed with a vitreous sheen.

"Despoilers, hear me. Ochai speaks." Those who knew Sixarms's true name were few. "Once I drove you into darkness, bound you in prison. I offer you freedom now! For your release, do what pleases you to the war-host on yonder table, knowing they are yours so long as I permit it, no longer. The Grinder has not lost his power, nor have I grown too weak to wield him. Will you obey me, and crawl free of your prison for a space?"

Within the hill, as within a hollow jar, there sounded a rustling and hissing. In a liquid whisper, a unison of voices said, "We will obey you—in this."

"In all things! Or stay where you are!"

"In all things?" The voices laughed. "You are desperate even to think of releasing us. This is good to know. In *this* matter we will obey you. Let that be enough.''

"Danan riders come!'' a Freth magician said. "Oghmal is with them, and his brother.''

Sixarms never panicked. He said grimly, "Go beyond what I bid you and you will be the losers, not I. Your obedience for release—and bind yourselves to it by the heart of Tor which spawned you!''

The imprisoned beings rustled and conferred.

"By the foul heart of Tor, we take oath,'' they said at last.

"Be it so.'' Sixarms's own mighty heart jumped in his breast, but he took the Grinder and brought it down on the more brittle stone beneath, in one of the greatest blows he had ever struck. As the stone shattered, white flame enveloped the pieces, and the hillside split wide open. Two of the Freths, hurled from their feet, rolled down the steep sides.

Hideous shapes, twined and tangled about each other, crawled out of the rent. Under their belly scutes, the grass died. Writhing slowly, they untangled in the summer daylight, three monstrous crested serpents which slavered poison.

The Danan riders halted.

"Here is what comes against you if you will not surrender,'' Sixarms said in a somber voice. "Can you withstand it?''

Oghmal stared at the creatures in loathing. He said, "You will never do a worse deed than this, Sixarms. I mourn for your honor. What others will decide, I do not know—but I won't grovel for your poison worms!''

"Nor I!'' answered Carbri, and Gui echoed them.

The monsters moved sluggishly, for they had been long confined. One brushed against a hawthorn, which withered to the tips of its leaves, and then gazed malignly at the Danans. It had been too long in darkness to retain its sight; still, it sensed their warmth with the pits below its eyes, and writhed towards them. The venom from its mouth flowed in a steady rill.

Its brothers coiled after it.

Gui had a javelin in his hand. Balancing it, he took careful aim and threw, while his highly-bred horse shuddered beneath him. The spear missed its intended target, the eye, and sank into the flabby skin at the corner of the mouth instead, lodging in the angle of the jaw. Blood flowed out to mingle with the venom, and the Despoiler's sightless eyes glittered terribly.

"A gift from Lost Star Lake!" Gui yelled.

"Ride!" Oghmal was not a man for gestures. "To give them their quittance, we'll need nothing less than the Wailing Spear!"

Turning his horse's head, he raced for the birches, his twin beside him and Gui close behind. Fifty men followed as though the world was burning.

The Despoilers oozed through the grove, their scales rasping on silver-white birch bark. At their touch, the trees blackened from root to crown. At the gust of their envenomed breath, moles and birds fell dead. When the three serpents crawled from among the birches, nothing living remained behind them. The Freth sorcerers who had fallen to the foot of the hill lay there yet, withered as by the touch of pestilence.

The Despoilers creaked as they crawled, for pliability was slow in returning to bodies which had been so long pent in a narrow space. Otherwise, they would have caught the fleeing horses in a few moments. As it was they trailed them inexorably, thin tongues sliding in and out to taste the air.

"Break camp and leave now!" Oghmal roared as he thundered to Cena's tent. "You've seen what is coming, and by the goddess, it's worse than it looks! Half the host could leave its bones on the ground before we're rid of these vermin!"

Bursting into his own tent, he drew on a strange pair of gauntlets, and a helmet which covered his ears. Not until then did he approach the vat where the Wailing Spear lay imbrued. Pulling off the cover, he plunged his gloved hand into the fluid and drew forth the weapon.

"There's work for you, lady," he said, "and swift work."

The spear began to hum. Longer than Oghmal, forged of some curious black metal, with a three-bladed spiral head and a white grip, the Wailing Spear was one of the many things whose like even the Danans could no longer make. Although he had brought it to this battle, Oghmal had partly hoped not to have to use it, and had even begun to think that his wish might be granted. Foolishness.

He trod outside. The serpents, mottled madder and grey, had reached the Danans' camp and were gliding through its outskirts. Twenty men and women attacked them with blades. The foremost Despoiler blew a cloud of poison at them, and soon they moaned in blindness, clawing at their own flesh where they rolled on the ground. Horror and deadly rage tore Oghmal's heart.

"Hai, monster!" he bellowed. The creature turned its head towards the vibrations, for the Wailing Spear hummed more intensely now. Had Oghmal grasped it anywhere but by its own padded grip, its resonance would have shaken his hand to jelly, even through the special gauntlet. With a mirthless smile, he threw the weapon.

Its humming rose to a dreadful shriek as it flew. Piercing the Despoiler's neck, it lodged there and wailed ever more shrilly. The ophidian flesh turned to pulp in a dozen heartbeats; the head fell from the destroyed neck while the many-coiled body writhed. Oghmal's weapon hung in the air, vibrated until it was clean of mess, and returned to his hand.

As he ran after the remaining monsters, the Wailing Spear began to fume in his hand. The metal corroded to a dismal grey, and its vibration went swiftly out of control so that it stabbed Oghmal's ears, even through the helmet he wore.

The gauntlet no longer protected him. He cast the Wailing Spear at the nearest serpent, before his hand could be shaken asunder, and saw it sink into the Despoiler's tail. Then both spear and tail flew in pulverized bits.

Oghmal was caught in the open, unsheltered, while flecks of poison rained for yards around. He expected to die. After a full minute, he found himself still alive and knew a renewed faith in the battle-paint Diancet had mixed for him. He was immune, or appeared so.

One monster was dead, one maimed, and the Wailing Spear destroyed. The crippled Despoiler crawled on, leaving a trail of smoking blood, the fumes of which were deadly. Poison dribbled from its mouth; men and women died before it.

Madness had filled the camp. Screaming horses bolted the stable-lines or fought their tethers; oxen fled, goring whatever stood in their way; warriors either ran from the monsters or ran to fight them, and died of venom for their courage. Oghmal saw one man, Devor the Large-Hearted of his own band, charge with a loud war-cry and open a yard-long gash in the Despoiler's belly. Then fuming toxins spattered him, and Devor withered in convulsions. The Despoiler writhed on, spreading death.

"Oghmal!" Devor screamed, as his leader ran to him. "Cure my pain!"

The champion did, with a quick, merciful sword-stroke, for Devor's flesh was horrible to see, and the convulsions were breaking his bones. Then he coolly assessed his target and threw five javelins, like streaks of sunlight in the air, as fast as only Oghmal could throw. Each one transfixed the Despoiler's evil head, one entering through the eye, three piercing the brain. It began to roll and thrash, the javelin shafts sticking out of its skull.

Oghmal sought the third. He trod through devastation. A plague might have visited the camp. Blindness, sickness, death, and terror were everywhere. He passed a raving warrior cutting off his horribly swollen arm to escape the pain.

The last serpent writhed in a cloud of enormous crows. Bava's cult ripped at it in bird-form, while Cena and Nemed fought it on foot. The Alban prince's armor protected him, while Cena's sacred war paint, maybe, protected her. The Despoiler bore a number of ghastly wounds, and one of its eyes had gone; not that it depended much upon eyes.

The prince rushed close, sending a cut to deepen the wounds in the Despoiler's body. Cena crouched beneath her shield as the dripping head swayed above her, then stabbed the serpent's belly at the juncture of two tough scutes. Above, shrieking War Crows went on tearing at its head, while along its enormous length Danan warriors crowded to dismember it, dying after one or two strokes to make room for others.

Oghmal saw a laden floatwain drifting nearby, and acted. The carvings on them were magical signs which allowed them freely to drift above the ground, tapping the earth power; without them, a floatwain was so much inert weight.

"You, Brec, and Lygi, help me!" he ordered. "Four others, quickly! Push this over yon snake's back and hold it there!"

He could scarcely get the words out for coughing. Maybe death was in his lungs already. No matter, so long as he finished his work. Seizing a fallen axe, he mounted the floatwain's prow while his half-dozen aides threw their backs into moving the object. Since it drifted in the air, there was no friction to overcome, only the need to start the weight itself moving, and Oghmal's men were strong.

"Make way!" he commanded. "We'll hold it down before we kill it!"

The wain, with a yard of space between its keel and the

ground, scraped the writhing monster's back as it passed above. Oghmal swung his axe as though felling a tree for his life. Carved symbols and sacred writing flew from the wain's forepost in a shower of chips. A swift succession of blows obliterated them along the sides, and the floatwain dropped squarely across the huge serpent's back with all its crushing weight.

The Despoiler changed color and lashed about, spattering poison. War Crows fell out of the sky, cawing, and men crawled away in deadly pain. Oghmal's lungs felt like seared sponges. He drew painful breath into them and cried, "Spears now! Throwing axes, stones, whatever can kill at a distance—and bring more wains!"

He skewered the last blind, weaving head with javelins himself. With two more disabled wains holding the monster down, it was helpless, and could be killed in their own time. They severed the head at last. The mangled body lay slowly twitching.

Oghmal coughed foulness and felt dizzy.

Many others were worse. Diancet the healer gave them fragrant elixirs to breathe, but he could do little else for them for a long time. The dying, the blinded, and the poisoned required all his attention, besides that of his nephews and assistants.

The Despoilers' evil corpses had to be destroyed. Cena saw a pit dug, leaning on Oghmal a little, and had the fragments dragged there by oxen. The ropes, the spades, and other gear used were thrown into the pit as well, to burn with the Despoilers; and before they were reduced to ash, a column of noxious smoke had befouled the sky for most of a day, while the wind carried it eastward over Danan lands as though from purposeful malice.

"Oh, my brother," Cena said. "Without you, we would not have salvaged this much." She braced herself. "If Sixarms comes back we cannot fight him now—not and be victorious."

"If Sixarms comes back I will make it my business to kill him," Oghmal snarled. "Once I thought better of him! I'd have disputed the man who said he would ever fight with such weapons. Nay, we cannot fight!" His voice held anguish. "We have wounded and maimed to pack out of this place."

"Diancet and I will see to that." Cena's face hid her torment. "You and Nemed gather the healthy fighters, brother, and tally

their number. The horses, too. We must know what we have to
work with . . .''

Her voice trailed away. She sagged against the tall champion
and wept. *They had lost.* He held her for comfort, as he
sometimes had when they were children, always the strong one
on whom she could rely; on whom fighting men could rely with
their lives in the balance.

''Where is Gui?'' he asked.

''You didn't remember him until now! What were you
thinking, that he ran? Some horses rode him down. He will
mend.''

''Easy, sister. That Gui is not the man I love best in the
world, you know. But he's brave in a fight, few more so.'' He
gave her a tiny shake. ''Now let's to work.''

The ashes in the pit were death in themselves. Men had to
wear scarves over their faces to shovel them, and destroy their
clothing later. They threw the ash into the river, which hissed
and turned a lurid color, steaming all the way to the sea before
the Despoilers' venom was dissipated. The willows along its
banks were evil-hearted forever after.

Chapter
Ten

Mahon was beside his father when Gui regained consciousness. He raved for a while, then slept, and when he awoke his mind was clear.

"Defeat?" he whispered. "Again? Oh, goddess, no! It cannot be. We had them. Those venom-spewing monsters—who died, Mahon? Who? *Is Cena alive?*"

"Yes, father. She's unhurt, except for some poison in her lungs, and most of us have that. Diancet can cure it."

"You are sure?"

"Diancet is—and he cured me with the same medicine."

Gui sighed with relief, then asked other questions to which Mahon gave less welcome answers. The Freths marched behind them. Cena and others fought a desperate rearguard action while the maimed travelled slowly ahead. Sorcery and illusion delayed the Freths as much as weapons, yet the very trees and bushes fought against the Danans. They were trekking to Ridai for shelter—and a final stand within the royal fortress, perhaps.

"No," Gui husked. "No. This I will not bear. No matter

what it costs, it shall not end so . . . bring Cena to me, Mahon. I do not care what you must say; bring her here. We must go to Lost Star Lake, not to Ridai. My mother's a sorceress who can still snatch triumph from this. The Freths shall not outdo Danans when it comes to dreadfulness!''

Troubled, Mahon carried the message, and a weary Cena came to her man's litter. They talked for long. Mahon, like every hale man left in the war-host, forgot what sleep was. He scouted and fought night actions, dug pits, set stakes, warned of tree spirits waiting in ambush, flung himself down in his cloak for a lengthy half-hour's rest, and went out again. If it caused him suffering to be fighting against his foster-people so, nobody heard of it; and he tended the foul harms done by the Despoilers' poison with no more complaint than he ranged the forest. Many came to love and respect him on that appalling return from the Battle of the Serpents—perhaps even Gui, although he would not say it.

They came to Lost Star Lake with the Freths still at their heels. Sanhu met them, her normal bitterness the sweetness of honey to the bile she showed now. She knew what had happened, and she raged against Cena, Gui, and all the Danan sorcerers impartially.

''Fools! You have thrown away our freedom again! Two battles lost against those forest animals! Why did you not kill Sixarms? That at least you could have done. No, you were too occupied with your own honor, and now you have destroyed your people for it! You fools, you accursed fools!''

Beside herself, she tore her hair and shrieked. Gui said bleakly, ''Sixarms is coming. There may yet be time. We are not here to bleat of our losses, but to win, if we can. The Freths raised three mighty poisoned serpents, and it is in my mind that we should outdo them. Mother mine, is there such a power you can raise to send against the Freths?''

''Why should I? So that you can throw away the fruits? Listen to me,'' Sanhu said, breathing hard. ''There *is* a power of the earth that I can summon, a destructive force so fell that your precious Despoilers are harmless as earthworms before it. But you must swear to me by the womb of the Mother and your own lives to carry this thing through to the end, without mercy or relenting. You will demand the Freths' utter surrender, the life of Sixarms, the return of all tribute-children within the year.

They are to have nothing to fight with, and they are to supply us food. We make all the conditions; my voice is to utter the terms. Else there is no use. You will weakly throw away whatever I win.''

''What power will you raise, Lady Sanhu?'' Cena asked. ''How will you raise it, and how control it? Sixarms at least had mastered the Despoilers before, and knew he could control them. I must know something of the sort too.''

''Agree or surrender!'' Sanhu said harshly. ''My terms or the Freths'—and think of what terms they will give you now! You thought the child-tribute and fire-tax was harmful. They will make it seem like a lover's kiss.''

Cena thought about that, as she had often done on her return from the battle, and it was no more pleasant than it had ever been. She had twice failed her people, as Sanhu said. What worse power of devastation could there be than those three hate-born serpents? Yet looking into the small woman's taut-skinned face and vitriolic eyes, she believed that if there was one, Sanhu would know about it.

She said, ''Swear me an oath first. Swear that this being you speak of can stop the Freths.''

Sanhu laughed. ''It can stop the very sun!''

''Give the oath,'' Cena demanded, ''by the shade of your brother Mahon.''

''Will you stand havering until Sixarms arrives to demand your own children for his dinner? I swear by the shade of my brother, I can raise this being, that neither Sixarms nor any other sorcerer in the sacred island can withstand it, and that the one who raises it can send it back! I tell you further that they will view it with such alarm that they will plead to grant you your terms, for it is fearful!''

''So. And what do you want, Sanhu, more than you have said?''

''Nothing. But what I have said, I must have. The Freths are to pay at last.''

''This is why you are the Rhi, sister,'' Carbri murmured. ''For myself, I'd face the Despoilers again before I would give our people back to the Freths now.''

''Let them taste it,'' Oghmal said, his harshly handsome face cold. ''We have.''

Cena had made the same decision already. For her brothers,

the words they had uttered were just words. Hers would have lasting effect; as Carbri said, she was the Rhi.

"Granted," she said. "If you break the Freth host, and their power over us, you shall have what you desire. I will pay any price that is mine to give."

She swore the oaths demanded. Sanhu listened with a glitter of mad gratification in her eyes.

"You hear, my son?" she crooned. "Now the time of our vengeance is here. Now the Freths will suffer . . . Go, bring me the boy Mahon."

"Mahon?" Gui stiffened. "My son?"

"What other Mahons are there, since my brother died? You never called him your son before. Bring him here, Gui. I have preparations to make, and he must be part of them."

Gui grew suddenly pale. "Why, mother mine? Why?"

"Go!" she snapped. "Must I explain when I have so much to do? The Freths will be here before I have even begun. The boy won't be hurt, if you care so much." The last five words were a sneer.

Gui stalked out. When he returned with Mahon, Sanhu had cut an ornate quincunx in the turf beside the lake, and placed a bowl at each corner. They contained sand, pebbles, loam, and humus, while at the center burned a charcoal fire.

"I like this not at all, sister," Carbri said.

"Do not change your song now," she answered, with a flash from the fire-blue eyes so like his own. "If you can recommend it, you can see it."

"Remember what Sixarms did," Oghmal growled.

"You chatter like children," Sanhu spat. "The goddess improve our Danan breed if you are its best leaders! Goddess, goddess, goddess," she intoned, "send your child the blind boar into the sunlight. Send him from the black earth, from the red earth, from the sandy soil, from the lime turf, from the deep bogs, from the forest loam. Send him from all the earth of Tirtangir. Give him a single shape and a single place for so long as it takes him to destroy my enemies!"

From a rasp, Sanhu's voice rose to full-throated ecstasy. The charcoal at her feet burned hotter. The sand formed shifting patterns, the pebbles rattled in their bowl, and the humus smoldered. Sanhu continued to invoke the goddess and her child the blind boar.

Gui stood beside his son, his face a graven mask with secrets behind it. Mahon showed turmoil in each rigid line of his body. He remembered, too well, the last time he had been together with his father and grandam here at Lost Star Lake, and what had almost happened. For the presence of Cena and her brothers, he was strongly glad.

"Goddess, goddess, goddess," Sanhu groaned. "For the child of your womb, I give a child of mine. Send the blind boar! So. Come here, brat."

"No." Gui spoke in a voice flat, hard and cold as the ice of winter. "Run, Mahon. She still means to slay you. *Run!*"

Mahon stood where he was. Sanhu rushed forward with a knife in her hand, and Gui threw himself upon her, bearing her back into the ornate quincunx of trimmed earth. Genuine madness lay in both their faces as they struggled, and the tiny woman's force seemed equal to her warrior son's.

"You poisoned Airvith," Gui panted. "You won't have him as well."

"One will do . . . as well as another."

The knife sank into Gui's side. Cena uttered a wordless cry. Oghmal, a warrior's warrior, knew at once that Gui might have saved himself; any man with a fighter's training could have saved himself from a diminutive woman. The knife went in three times more, inhumanly, terribly, and Gui's blood splashed hissing into the charcoal. Oily smoke rose.

Mahon ran forward. Oghmal caught him back, and they too struggled while the charcoal fire hissed out. The youth cursed incoherently, and Cena reached for her sword while Carbri struggled with her to keep it in its sheath.

Sanhu looked at her son with tears streaming from eyes long dry, while hot blood dripped from the knife in her hand. He smiled a strange, twisted smile. It seemed to say that he had defeated her.

"Mahon, Airvith, and me," he whispered. "I knew. And—you will have to send the blind boar home, won't you? I know how that is done."

Blood spilled from his mouth. His feet drummed on the earth and a stink tainted the air. Men, even sacrifices, seldom die in a tidy manner. He had never looked towards Mahon or Cena.

Sanhu left the quincunx, stepping oddly, as though trying to walk on ground which wasn't there. Gui's blood still flowed feebly, soaking into the freshly turned earth, and the four witnesses ceased to fight one another. They drew back from Sanhu as though she had become a demon.

The quincunx incised in the earth of the garden upheaved, like a pot of boiling water. Heat smote them all, a radiating, baking heat of ancient decay bringing with it the stench of a thousand thousand thousand graveyards. A vast humped back thrust through the ground. Two monstrous forelegs came out of the earth with sucking noises. A featureless head rose between them, vaguely piglike, butting sightlessly about. It was the size of a bread-vat.

In emerging, the creature lifted Gui's body and sent it tumbling aside like a doll. It rotted instantly, consumed as though by centuries of corruption. Cena did not scream again, only gasped as though butted in the stomach, and sagged against Carbri.

Nothing was left of Gui now but dust and splinters of bone. The grass also withered, disintegrating, in the heat of the blind boar's presence. It moved clumsily, larger than a house, roughly formed and incomplete, made of putrescent black earth; and for yards around it, everything faded to decayed rubbish.

The witnesses ran. Sanhu was first to depart, and as she fled she panted to Oghmal, "It's done now. The thing is done. Better that changeling brat than Gui—far better—he could have fathered others. He has! Why did he do what he did?"

Oghmal shuddered. "I never thought he had it in him. But you! There's murder of what came from your own womb on you now, Sanhu. Does that even trouble you? Cena will slay you for it."

The sorceress laughed wildly. "That would not be wise. Tell her this, mighty champion! The blind boar cannot return whence it came until it has devoured the one who summoned it. There is no other way to be rid of it, and none at all to destroy it. None. Therefore Cena must keep me safe until the time is right, against all hatred. The blind boar will follow me through anything except the sea, but it moves slowly. We have a Freth war-host to destroy just now."

"And afterward—you will let it take you?" The champion was incredulous.

"Gladly! When it has served my purpose. Oh, Gui, my son!"

Oghmal felt contempt for that outcry. He had never known

her to show Gui any tenderness while he was alive. It rang false to him. Perhaps her other sayings were false too—but the blind boar was loose, and as terrible as she had claimed it to be. The Despoilers had at least needed to touch a man to slay him, and could be slain themselves.

He made for the stables, grasping Sanhu's arm. The touch of it made his skin contract. Never had he known or even heard of a mother slaying her child, until the Freths had imposed their tribute and the word *changeling* had come into use. This, though, had been done knowingly. Oghmal's mind recoiled bruised from the truth of it.

Why did he do what he did? Sanhu had asked.

Only the goddess knew. It hadn't been over Mahon, not really. There was something malign between Sanhu and Gui which had endured as long as they were both alive—and Sanhu spoke as though she would not long survive him. Nor would she, of course. If the blind boar did not see to that, Cena would.

But the blind boar had work to do, first.

Oghmal mounted a horse and rode with Sanhu through a darkening world.

The boar had crashed through the garden wall, leaving a trail of rankness behind it. Now it blundered along the lake shore. Sightless, moving on malformed legs, it stumbled without mind or senses, looking for the one who had summoned it.

Sanhu rode across its path. The featureless, blocky head swung towards her, and the thing shambled in a new direction, following her. Oghmal rode through the ripe grain fields beside the sorceress, taking the shortest way to the advancing Freth host. The monster lurched after them.

Beneath it, the grain brushed its belly and turned to black dust. The heat which smoldered and reeked from it made barley blacken ten paces away. Wherever it trod, dust was left as barren as powdered ash.

"Why do you not fight it, champion, Lord of Dar?" Sanhu mocked. "Take your vaunted sword. Approach it. The blade will begin to corrode while you are twenty paces away. Then your hair and teeth will fall out, or the stumps which *were* teeth! The flesh will slough from your bones, and the marrow within them dry up. Then it will trample over you, and your dust will blow away on the wind—if you're fortunate. Go and fight it! You slew the serpents, did you not?"

"Yes. But I don't battle the sun or the sea. When I want to make an end of the blind boar, Sanhu, I will throw you at it."

"And I'll thank you. Had you thought of that? Look, champion! There are the Freths!"

They had come out of the west, some riding horses, most afoot. Oghmal almost pitied them, but they were coming to conquer his people. He glanced back at the being which followed, then rode closely after Sanhu as she spurred her horse. The Freths gaped, watching the Danans ride by like the wind, with a towering, ridge-backed shape from evil dreams lumbering after them. Then it moved in among them, and they began to die.

Some withered completely in their tracks. They were fortunate. Others crawled aside with the blood curdled in their veins and lived for hours. Some stumbled out of the blind boar's radiating heat with the flesh rotting on one side of their bodies only. Some merely grew old in moments.

"Burn the fields!" one Freth chieftain howled. "Burn that beast with them!"

The grain went up in banners of crackling flame. Sanhu laughed again.

"Let it burn, you beasts! What is there to save it for? But if you think the blind boar will pause for that, you are fools!"

The creature of earth blundered through the flames without feeling them. Oghmal watched from slitted grey eyes as the inchoate form stumbled onward into the main body of Freths. Hearts grew moribund, buckskins and cloth became mildewed tatters, and floatwains fell apart in decay where it passed. Nor did it pass with no purpose. It cast about, rambling back and forth through the demoralized lines of invaders. Somehow, it knew that higher living things were present.

"You thought to prey upon the children of Danu!" the sorceress mocked. "See your reward now, children of ordure!"

"Yes, taste it!" Oghmal shouted, far louder. "You sent us serpents, and here is how we welcome you! You will know for the future, people of the forest, that nobody preys on Danans in safety. None conquers us forever!"

He felt fiercely alive again. That was the embodiment of his tribe's goddess, the giving and devouring earth, making ruin of his tribe's enemies! What else should it do? The Freths had come uninvited, and they must eat what they found in the cauldron! Maybe he could find and slay Sixarms, while the Freths were so confused.

No. Better to stay with Sanhu. There was no telling what she might do.

A band of wrinkle-browed young men advanced upon the beast with spears lifted. Oghmal saw the weapons fly and bite, but the lashings which held the head to the shaft perished in an instant, and the shafts crumbled as they slid down the beast's back. Only their flint heads remained, imbedded in earthly shoulders.

With sudden shock, Oghmal saw the blind boar rush. It had never moved other than slowly and deliberately yet. Now it charged, trampling, and Freths went down in utter dissolution between its hooves, or crawled aside in a torment of live corruption. The blind boar swung in a wide circle, reducing them also to dust, and they mingled with the barley as detritus of a thousand years. The boar trampled on, seeking, and the Freths fled. They were no longer a battle host, or anything threatening. They scattered in all directions, some clutching their weapons desperately, some throwing them away or letting them fall. Oghmal smiled.

"They'll be lying hidden in shaking ones and twos about the land for a time," he said, "and what is left of our host will not be too weary to rout them out and kill them. You have saved us, lady—but what will the boar do when it has finished here?"

The half-shaped, insensate thing now lurched restlessly onward, turning at random, tracing imperfect circles of decay through the fields. Then it blundered towards the northeast in aimless ramblings.

"Just what it is doing now," Sanhu answered. She began to tremble visibly, there on her horse, and Oghmal decided that perhaps she was flesh and blood after all. "It cannot sense me, so far away—but it will seek all over the island, until it finds, and there will be devastation wherever it goes. Do your killing well, champion! For that is the price of it."

Oghmal shook his head. "Hol and others can do that hunting. I must find Sixarms, for he won't be lurking in white fear. Without him—" Oghmal shrugged. "The Freths have other leaders, but none all their tribes will follow, and he freed the serpents."

"Do not tell me," Sanhu said viciously. "Be about it!"

Oghmal did. Giving Cena into the care of the master-poet, his uncle, he gathered one hundred riders with his twin among them, and set out, stained and weary, on the freshest horses he could obtain. Imperative though the need was to catch Sixarms, they had to rest, having fought and retreated for days. But Oghmal never rested more than three hours at a time, and seldom twice in the same day.

"There, brother," Carbri said, as they looked upon the tracks of a large band moving westward in coherent order. "That has the dye of Sixarms's leadership about it, and those tracks are not illusion." The bard could see the reality behind glamor; it was part of his training. "Must we lead the blind boar to them? By the goddess, they have earned it!"

"It won't follow any but Sanhu," the champion replied. "We can lead it into Freth holds later." His hands caressed the long-handled axe he now held, a heavy, beautifully fashioned thing made for shearing heads. "These are for us."

The band which had made the tracks in question proved not to be for them, after all. They hunted all day, but found nothing. The tracks scattered as though the group had not held together long, and Carbri could not believe that.

"Sixarms is with them!" he insisted. "Look, he drags his club behind him here, and there's no mistaking that. The Grinder leaves a mark like a territorial boundary, so. I even know the shamble of his great feet by now."

"Have I no eyes?" Oghmal had, and they were bloodshot with sleeplessness like every other man's, his temper short. "They may be Sixarms's tracks, but where is he? The earth has concealed him from trackers before. I'll find him, though, and lead the blind boar to him by a ring through its snout!"

Carbri lifted an eyebrow above a bleary but still questioning blue eye. Bombast was not like his brother. Well, Oghmal was allowed to show the effects of strain.

Before long, they lost the tracks, and never found them again though they searched for a league. It was as though the earth herself had refused to betray her powerful son. When Oghmal knew finally that he had lost his quarry, he gave a shout of raging frustration which rang from the hills around him, and hewed into the earth with his axe, cursing the goddess whose body it was. Twenty strokes and one he smote the ground, in outrage and deep betrayal, leaving as many long gashes while his curses hung vibrating in the air. Then he leaned on his axe, panting, while the red mist slowly cleared from his brain.

The goddess would not favor them now, if there had ever been any likelihood of it. Carbri said only, "Let's leave this place, brother, and have one full night's sleep before we turn home."

"One night's sleep? You milk-curd dreamer, you bleating lamb, we've let Sixarms escape!"

"No. He escaped without our permission, against all we could do, and you are close to falling down. Rave all you like, it will do no good. Fight the earth some more! And when you have finished, you will still need a night's sleep before we turn home."

"Where is your anger?" Oghmal demanded. He ground his teeth. "Remember all that Sixarms did!"

"We've done enough to him in return," Carbri said with satisfaction. "His fortress destroyed, his coasts ravaged, his war-host destroyed and scattered—and the blind boar still ours to bring against him, brother. Do not forget that."

"I don't," Oghmal said shortly. "No, by every power of earth, sky, and sea! We'll camp here awhile in case the Freths return. Loredan and Sanhu can see to the blind boar. I tell you, brother, I would not be that sorceress for the favor of a hundred gods."

"She has committed the worst enormity she can," Carbri said. "There's little left for her to do now. Her time must be short. Even now she can wreak only harm, not good. I pity her. Belike she'll be reborn as a wildcat which eats its kittens."

"I do not pity her," Oghmal declared, "any more than she pitied son or grandson, or would pity us while she watched us die."

Sanhu lay at Loredan's house even as the brothers spoke of her. Her small face gaunt over the sharp, birdlike bones, she gazed at the master-poet with the emptiness and chill of ancient space behind her eyes.

"You are afraid that having me in your house will curse it," she said, and showed the edges of her teeth. "Perhaps you are right. Perhaps you will have to burn it and build another."

Loredan, brown-haired, with a comfortably rounded face and belly, had larger matters on his mind. He said, "You may have cursed this entire isle! The folly of calling up a thing like the blind boar is beyond all! You knew how little we know of such beings. Tell me you can be sure it will return to its proper shape, even if it does—'' He stopped.

''Devour me? Make no poet's lovely phrases of it, lord, nor pretend that you would be sorrowful.''

''Then do not pretend that you truly care what the blind boar does! It could devastate the island from shore to shore, leaving rock, dead trees, and bones, and continue to wander seeking release. You might even delight in it. What you did was not done for the tribe, much less for your brother's soul.''

''The thing is done,'' Sanhu said. ''If it cannot be undone, so much the worse. But I will lead it against the Freths ere I try. Merely to have scattered their war-host is not enough.''

''Do you even know *what* it is?''

''Surely. It is the force which decays all dead things, drawing them back to the earth, from leaves to bones. Beneath the ground it is good; without it, there would be no new growth. Raised above the ground and given one compact shape, it rots everything living that it passes near.''

''Words!'' Loredan, the master of words, said vehemently. ''The empty words are all you know. You do not understand or feel the boar's nature. Nor do I. The Freths would. Maybe we will, too, after the tribute-children have become part of us—but for now we deal in glib ignorance when we deal with such beings. You summoned it, and you only hope that you can banish it again.''

''Best you hope the same, lord. And it would be a kindness if you did not speak of tribute-children.''

The half-formed, lurching shape of earth blundered through an oakwood. Above its back, the leaves changed color and fell, mildew touching them as they dropped. They were dust by the time they reached the earth-boar's feet. Its blind head butted a tree, which instantly rotted at the heart, split lengthwise, and crashed down, its naked branches crumbling. The boar left a dead, sapless grove behind it. Stubble and dust in a swathe marked its meandering track.

Coming to a farmstead by sheerest chance, it crashed into the palisade. Logs crumbled before it, and the unfinished head broke through into a herb-garden. A woman screamed, ''Freths!'' and hurled a trowel, which sank into the featureless snout and rotted away. A pair of immense shoulders rammed through the disintegrating stockade next, and putrescent warmth engulfed the woman. She moldered in heartbeats.

Two workmen who came running with mattocks dropped choking, as their lungs turned to rancid mud and their flesh sloughed away. A dog which leapt and clung to the deformed charcoal snout left its white bones on the ground.

The being did not know one person from another, but it sensed when men were near and attacked them, seeking the one whose death could release it. The horses which broke out of the stables and fled screaming survived, though the stables came down in a crash of dry rot. Bees lay like dusty gems among their combs of rotted black honey, and the cattle in the byres—because the horror passed close to them—were left piles of corrupt meat. But where the house had been, only post-holes and bones remained, as though disease had walked that way a century before.

The blind boar stood among the ruins and ached to return to its true state of being, in its right place. Release was not here, though. It lumbered on.

Where it went, fields and forests died. Dust and bones grew beneath its feet, while misshapen fungi sprouted in brilliant decay at a slightly greater distance. Once it crossed a stream, not liking the water's touch, and left scum on the surface.

Barley in the fields turned to black straw. Field mice became brittle skeletons in bags of dry fur. Pears rotted on the dead trees, and fences collapsed, but no beasts were left alive to walk out.

At last the blind boar's insensate course led it to the sea. It plodded along the margin, staggering into the waves at times, recoiling at once from the surge of chill brine about its deformed feet. Sightless, deaf, it followed the shore for miles before blundering inland again, and nothing checked its destructive course. Apart from the sea, one thing only could stop it, and Sanhu was in no haste.

Before she ended the thing she had initiated, she wanted an audience with the Freths.

Chapter
Eleven

"Your earthen demon made wreckage of four cantons," Loredan said, "before it left Danan territories again. That is the cost of the time we needed to arrange a council with Sixarms and the tribal mothers! Now it ravages the Golden Vale and is a Freth disaster again, but who knows how long it will be before that mindless beast swings back in our direction?"

"Not I," Sanhu answered, "so cease to blather. That is one being which is impressed neither by weapons nor satire, and I am another. Where shall we meet Sixarms? It were better that he died in the council circle."

"That is one place he will not be killed," Loredan snapped. He had taken omens from thrown sticks, the smoke of fires, and the flight of birds. All his auguries were inconclusive. It disturbed him. Sanhu disturbed him more, though, because she was mad and thought she controlled the situation. "Once murder is done there, war will be endless, and the tribute-children would never come home."

"That would be no bad thing, Loredan. I will not debate this with you. Cena and Oghmal are convinced; that is enough."

"Are they, now? A lie. I have spoken with them. Cena had but one thing to say about you. *'I will not look upon Sanhu again.'* "

"She need not. Much I care."

"We have strayed from the path, have we not? More than your word is required to convince me that they would kill where their honor has pledged safety."

"Do you know how desperate they are? How angry? They were at the morning practice each day, and then at the fighting, soft maker of word-tapestries, as you were not. When did you see your comrades poison-blinded? Diancet is attending them yet, and because he is only one man, they are still dying. Oghmal has visited them daily. I can promise you that his heart is not mild towards Sixarms, that walking blotch!"

"I see where Gui learned his attitudes," Loredan said dryly. "You know that in all the island, now, nothing decays as it should, except where the blind boar walks? Meat does not age; ale and wine do not ferment; even the mown hay smells fresh, day after day. It cannot be endured."

"That is why I did it, fool! Will the Freths make peace on our terms if the alternative is something they can bear? And you, you sit among your writings prating of what *you* cannot endure, when I slew my only son to bring this about. *I am already dead, do you not understand?*" she screamed.

"Who but yourself did it?" Loredan asked brutally. "I am sorry for Gui and Cena, and for the boy who witnessed it, not for you. I say you have lived far too long."

"You shall answer for that, Cena's errand-runner! What do you know of me? Come to the council fires and learn."

"I'll surely be there."

Loredan was generally the one who rode on embassies or acted as spokesman. Such were his talents—and neither Cena nor Oghmal was prepared to sit in a negotiator's circle with Sixarms now. Yet someone had to, and as mother's brother to the Rhi, Loredan was the only man with enough ability and standing.

"You had better come too, my hopeful," he said to Carbri, "and bring your harp. With a stream of loathing such as Sanhu at the council, we need all those we can find whose intentions are benign.''

"So? I'm pleased that you think the word describes me." Carbri smoothed his flowing coppery moustache. "Be warned, though. It's less than benign I feel towards Freths, even the best of them. The blind boar may leave them forestless and houseless before it goes home to the pit which spawned it.''

"You are saying that all Tirtangir may be laid waste because you bear a grudge?''

"Not Tirtangir. Only the Freth domains. Also, I'm in the humor to drive a hard bargain with them. Had you smelled the venom of the Despoilers, you would feel the same, mother's brother.''

"It's venom I am smelling now, from you, from Cena, from Oghmal, from Sanhu. Do you know how the Despoilers were spawned? In the cankered heart of a man full of hate, as three tiny worms. Rid yourself of some of that ill-will, if you want to come. I don't mind hard bargains being driven; I plan the same myself. But not for empty spite, my buck.''

Carbri stroked a melody of plangent sweetness from his golden-stringed harp, but harsh individual notes broke the flow like upthrusting rocks in a river. His playing matched his mood.

"So be it, then. Nothing for spite. But we must show them who Danans are.''

They appeared at the council tent leading a cavalcade of splendid riders on the long-legged, graceful horses of their tribe. Golden pendants chimed on the reins, while spiral ornaments clasped their tails, and bullion chinked on their thickly embroidered saddle-cloths. Their cloaks outdid nature in zigzags of red and green, yellow spirals against black, grey, crimson, and blue triskeles. Jewelled brooches pinned the bright mantles on their shoulders, and gems flashed on the buckles of their braided cinctures. Loredan wore a long tunic bordered in purple and green, with a similar tasselled sash.

The sorceress wore red, with a heavy silk mantle over the gown and her hair piled high on her birdlike head, dressed with jewelled combs. Her eyes were like pools of simmering lye when she gazed at the Freths.

Sixarms wore his accustomed leather and horsehide. The tribal mothers, squat women with broad faces and deeply lined skin, adorned with feathers, sat in a semicircle, before a low fire. The various male chiefs clustered at both ends.

Loredan's entourage filled the circle with brilliant colors. Carbri held his harp, the strings lines of shining light in the fireglow. The bog-oak frame had a satiny sheen.

They shared food, after swearing oaths of honesty and exchanging hostages. Most importantly, they accepted magical bonds against double-dealing. The preliminaries settled, they began to discuss.

"You haven't done well," Sixarms said.

"I might agree, if our choices had been wider," Loredan replied. "Where is the host that pursued the Danans back to their own lands? Gone. Where is the blind boar now? Ripping Freth soil as the Despoilers ravaged our warriors. We have avoided a second conquest at least—and if you could dismiss the Mother's child yourself, you would scarcely be here."

"You were evil to raise it, and fools besides," grated one of the tribal mothers.

"We had scarcely the best of examples before us when we did it," Sanhu purred, "and we are better off than we were as a result. Now. What terms will you take to see the blind boar dismissed from the ridge of the earth?"

"The ones about to be offered are the least *we* will take," Loredan said.

"Who is making them?" the same tribal mother demanded. "The woman or the man? While the boar roams at large we will all starve together, though it may take a long time. There is no room for terms in that."

"But it is Freth country the boar roams through now." Sanhu smiled. "The tribute-children must all come home, and you must supply us with food for them during the first winter."

She was by no means adamant on that point herself. It was Cena's condition, and many a family's. Sanhu would not have cared if they never returned. The Freths uttered roars of protest.

"That is the last thing you should name," Sixarms said. "The tribute-children are hostages, in a way. We mean them no harm, but they are as much at risk from the blind boar as we."

"That is why we want them back," Loredan told him.

"Second," Sanhu went on, "the Freths renounce all claim to lordship over the Danans until the end of time, and swear to

bring no war against us. Third, you make good our losses in the
war, and pay the honor-price of all the fighters maimed by your
serpents. Fourth, none of the fortresses we destroyed may be
rebuilt without the Rhi Cena's agreement, and it backed by the
tribe in assembly. Fifth, a hundred hostages from all the Freth
tribes must come to live among us as surety that these conditions
will be met—hostages of priest or chieftain's rank.''

The tribal mothers snickered.

"This is the least you will take? It's as well that we did not
hear the most. We have terms of our own.''

Loredan listened to them. They involved Danan surrender
and submission, for a beginning. The Freths would pay no
honor-price or other recompense. Their fortresses must be
rebuilt, with the help of the Danans' skills and resources. The
hostages might be given, upon the understanding that to mistreat
even one counted as cause for new war. The tribute-children
would be sent home over three years, beginning with the
youngest, and no food would be supplied. The Danans must find
it.

They disputed, bargained, and chaffered until the evening of
the third day. Freth bellows and Danan shouts issued from the
tent many times, with Sanhu's voice the harshest and Loredan's
mellifluous tones soothing the abrasion. Carbri's music often
rippled beneath the spoken words.

They agreed at last. The terms were sworn to, by Freth and
Danan customs, with a sacrifice of calves on the one side and
written words in the script of Loredan's devising on the other.
His characters flamed with potency on the ramskin sheet.

Finally they made their vows in blood, bread, and salt, letting
the drops from their mingled cuts flow into the earth, dropping
salt on their arms and on the ground below, then eating part of
the bread before crushing the rest into the soil. Breaking such
vows would mean that the Earth-Goddess ceased to nourish
their tribes, which would then die of hunger to the smallest
infant. It was enough to freeze the heart of anyone mad enough
to swear it falsely.

"You know how the blind boar is to be sent home?" Sixarms
asked. "You Danans are ignorant of so much."

"We know indeed." Sanhu's head lifted in a gesture of
terrible pride. "You may come and see this bargain kept, if you
have the courage."

Challenge and counter-challenge again; Freth knowledge

against Danan rashness. Sixarms said, "Tell us how you will do one thing: remove the boar?"

"Is this a test? It must have a sacrifice of the one who raised it. Then it is free of its constraint in a single shape. We have the responsible one ready; you need not doubt it. The question is only of when the sacrifice should be given."

"Now," Sixarms said inexorably.

"So said my brave companions," Sanhu sneered. "I say we should wait until three parts of your tribal land is barren, and the children you ruined a memory, but they would not accede. So willing are they to see another pay for their weakness. They will do their own paying in the future, I think, because they would not listen to me. Pah! Tell me where the boar is to be found now. We will see that the sacrifice is taken to meet it."

Before Sixarms could answer, a frothing pony raced to the council tent, ridden by a youth of the Bear Tribe. Hurling himself from its back, the Freth stood before his chief and made a gesture of respect.

"Earth-Mother's son," he said, "the boar comes north! By morning it will enter Macilory Slough, and none will see it again afterward. The bog will swallow it."

"Pretending to know what you do not is a mistake," Sixarms said. "Learn that while you are still young. The boar is more likely to swallow the slough."

"But that will take time." Sanhu shivered, not wanting to wait. "Let us go there now. The magician will meet us. He's within my control."

Sixarms bent his brown, encompassing gaze upon her. "Is he your son?"

Loredan flinched. Sanhu smiled bitterly.

"My son indeed had a part in raising the boar."

"I am sorry."

"So I think was he. Your sorrow is not wanted, Freth! Let's ride to the slough and end this bad joke."

Within the hour they were cantering through the starlit night, the Danans on their wind-swift, wind-light horses in a chiming of ornaments, the Freths straddling surefooted ponies. The place of their council stood deserted. In the east, a bar of grey appeared across the sky. To Sanhu everything was sharply, brightly clear, and more precious than it had seemed for years, as it should have been on her final journey.

Chapter
Twelve

The bog called Macilory Slough quaked to the lightest tread.
Islands and ponds stretched across it in chains. Willows grew
green; sedges covered the margins of hidden pools. In other
places, water-plants grew so matted and thick on the surface of
the bog that they appeared to be firm earth, and could even give
solid footing to bog-men or Danan horses.

Mandrake and aconite grew in the shadows. Odd trillings
sounded among the leaves. Having reached this eerie place in a
night's hard riding, the Danans now rested on a few hummocks
of islands and tended their horses. These were restive, snorting,
and whinnying too much.

"They sense something dark about to happen," Carbri said
to his uncle.

"Horses are not gifted with second sight. It's the place itself.
Maybe the blind boar has gone somewhere else, Carbri."

"Maybe. Myself, I'm none so sure that horses cannot sense
what is coming."

The harper's music reached across the water. Marsh violets trembled in the shadow of oaks and ferns. Aside from that, nothing moved. Carbri began to think that his mother's brother was right, and the blind boar's random blunderings had taken it elsewhere. One thing was certain; its trail would be easy to find.

That moment's flippancy chilled within his skull as he saw something huge shamble between the trees. Fungi erupted; the violets decayed. Black, malformed, and smoldering, the earth-boar lumbered into view between disintegrating trees. Carbri felt his throat contract as its hot reek blew across the bog to him.

Sanhu's eyes widened in half-ecstatic horror at the vision. She inhaled a hard, shuddering breath. Carbri and Loredan watched intently, with some of Sanhu's own fascinated abhorrence. Sixarms scowled, changing his grip on the Grinder. Both he and the club surged with earth power, and he would fight the blind boar if he must.

It staggered onto the green, crusted surface of the bog, and immediately broke through the moss. The floating plants rotted apart at the boar's touch. It sank like iron. Slime and bubbles erupted through the hole where it had vanished.

"Water may dissolve it," a young Danan warrior said hopefully. "It does not like the sea."

"Pray it doesn't happen," Sixarms advised. "Tirtangir would be barren forever. We might destroy it, but the thing to do is restore it."

"We cannot even reach it, now," Loredan said. "We'd require a boat, and the power to breathe beneath the water. Ha, there! The monster still moves!"

The mossy surface crust undulated like a flag in a slow breeze. Here and there it cracked. Foul, bubbling water appeared in little pools, clouded with bits of rotting vegetation. The unrest subsided.

"If it emerges, help me to lure it deeper into Freth country," Sanhu said to the master-poet, whispering. "Why should they escape so lightly, with what they have made us suffer?"

"Because we have sworn the treaty, lady, and if that does not suffice, because we need the reparations they will pay. They cannot recompense us if they are decimated and starving."

"We'd have no need of their goods—*our* goods! We could take the island from them."

"If it was worth having by then! No, lady. Is it that you do not wish to undo what you did? To leave this terror at large until all Tirtangir is blighted and dead?"

Sanhu gazed over the disturbed bog. "Do not insult me. I want to be sure my work is thoroughly done before I die. Do you think I murdered my son to deal in half-measures now? Why, why, why would he not let me sacrifice that worthless brat in his place?"

"Perhaps," Loredan said dryly, "he too had some feeling for a son."

"A father's part is nothing! He does not carry or bear; he does not even know. Nor did Gui love him."

It occurred to Loredan that perhaps the cold, warlike master of Lost Star Lake had loved Mahon's mother, and remembered it after too long. There was no purpose in saying it, for only the dead could confirm that guess, and nothing could comfort Sanhu now.

"He may have done," Loredan suggested. "He may even have felt he had wronged the lad."

"When he was caught spying, and deserved to die?" Sanhu spat. "Now he will inherit Lost Star Lake, since Gui has no sisters or sister's children living. It makes me ill to think of him ruling those lands, a barking, grunting Freth changeling!" Her face worked hideously, her teeth showing. "And I must die and leave them to him!"

"I wonder why you hate him so."

"I have said why."

She lied. It had been Mahon's mother she hated, because Gui had loved her better than Sanhu until the moment of his death. Sanhu disliked Cena for a similar reason, though not so much; Gui had mated with her to serve his schemes and ambitions, inspired by Sanhu herself, and had loved her only a little. But now Airvith, whom the sorceress had poisoned, would triumph after all.

No. Mahon must not rule at Lost Star Lake! Shall I let that whelp live when I slaughtered Gui, whom I loved better than my own heart? The blind boar can wait.

With the force of that sudden decision came the renewed power to think and act. Escape would not be easy, surrounded as she was by Freths and traitor Danans. Carbri was horseman enough to ride her down in any country; so were most of the others, perhaps even Loredan. There remained the heavy canoes drawn up on the bog's margin—too heavy, indeed, for one slight woman to paddle. Sorcery must serve her.

Two great magicians and a lesser but skillful one were present. They would thwart her if they could. She could not allow that. With the leap of a purpose within her, destructive though it was, she felt a borrowed urge to live and strive, brief though it might prove, and a normal horror of death. It was almost like being young. Sanhu's cold heart flamed.

"I must prepare something," she said. "Quickly, before the monster breaks clear of the slough! It will be better if I welcome it standing in a quincunx, as I was when I raised it. This patch of moss will do."

"You never thought of it until now?" Sixarms frowned. "You, a sorceress of rank?"

"I've had much else to grip my mind, you thing," Sanhu said. "There is time if I hasten, and it is my death we talk about. So."

She cut the intricate figure in the moss with the skill of long practice, slicing the interwoven lines in their four-sided pattern; the corners and the center, four and one, equalling the five which meant wholeness and stood for everything which was. Four seasons of one year, four provinces of one island, four directions of one world. She had no bowls here to contain the different soils. Instead she placed piles of peat, stones, sand, and bones in the four corners, and then kindled a fire of twigs. This was all unnecessary, in any case, except to fool those watching. A quincunx figure had many uses, including one which nobody knew Sanhu had mastered.

The surface of the bog rippled again.

Sanhu stood in the quincunx, concentrating. One such figure was also every one of the others. They could aid a sorcerer to travel instantly whither he would go—so long as a matching quincunx was at his destination to receive him. Loredan knew that, of course, and was watching her closely. If she disappeared, he would follow her at once, and he was a master of such sorceries, more so than she. Did he play with her? She could believe it of him, the bland, supercilious mouse!

Clearing her mind of such things, she envisioned a quincunx of gold wire set in malachite, on a dais at the center of a ruined hall. Beech pillars surrounded it in triple circles, although the walls and roof had long vanished. Sun-yellow tiles covered the floor, some cracked, a few missing. Sanhu focussed her mind on the dais, each volute of wire, each crack in the stone, and anchored her awareness there. Few could do that, even among sorcerers, and fewer yet could take the next step. Travel by quincunx was accordingly rare.

Sanhu imagined a pulsing red womb around herself, ready to expel her from one place to another, its contractions waxing in power. She fitted the quincunx beneath her feet to the one in the ruined hall, imagining the two patterns one atop the other, in precise alignment.

Now!

She was gone with a coruscation of white light, and Loredan sprang into the quincunx she had left empty. "Trickery!" he cried to Sixarms, knowing his amazement was feigned; he had half expected this, and still allowed it to happen. "She thinks she has escaped her charge, but I'll find her!"

He sent his mind through the quincunx, following Sanhu's trail of imagination as Sixarms might have tracked a deer. He, too, saw the ruined hall in his mind, and recognized the place. Sanhu was there, beside the golden quincunx on the dais. Even as he mindwatched her, she prised a length of the gold wire from its setting and threw it away. With the quincunx incomplete, he could not travel to the hall on Sanhu's small flashing heels. She had gained time.

Loredan was granted none. Sixarms's hands clamped upon his shoulders, and the mighty Freth plucked him from the quincunx like an ear of wheat from the stalk. The master-poet felt the boiling outrage of one whose person had always been sacrosanct. He brought up his arms quickly between the other's wrists, but he might as well have tried to lift a cromlech. Sixarms increased the power of his grip until Loredan sank gasping to his knees.

Carbri's bronze sword pricked Sixarms's neck, ever so lightly. "Just be freeing my mother's brother, chieftain," the harper advised, "as a small courtesy."

Sixarms grunted a laugh. "Draw my blood," he said, "and not you nor he nor one of your men will ever lie beside a Danan woman again. Also, remember what waits beneath the bog."

"I've not forgotten." Carbri did lower his blade. "Let our poet rise and we will discuss it—or simply leg it out of here, now that Sanhu has betrayed us. Sun, Moon, and stars! How she betrayed us! Not wanting to live after murdering Gui! No, surely she does not, the false hag!''

"Stay away from *that*," Sixarms ordered, stamping on one edge of the quincunx and lifting his club in menace. "Did she betray us? *You* let her go."

"It was betrayal, by her," Loredan said. "Still, I did not trust her. While in the figure there—do not deface it—I sent my mind following her. I know where she is now."

It was perhaps not the wisest thing to confess. Several Freths growled like savage beasts scenting prey. Sixarms, who knew the poet was also a master sorcerer, understood better, though he too was angry and deeply suspicious.

He said, "Somewhere in Danan lands, ha?"

"She's near Ohivala, the remnant of a great hall built long ago by Danans. She will not be there any longer than it takes her to leave, cut a new quincunx in the ground nearby, and traverse to another of her choice. That could be situated in any place at all; there is no way to tell. Yet it's in my mind that I know whom she seeks."

"The lad Stagshanks?" rumbled Sixarms.

"You know him? I'd supposed he was one tribute-child among many to you."

"Foolish. He's the son of my blackest enemy. Did you think I would not take the trouble to know? Let's depart from here before we talk more."

They mounted their steeds to leave. Before they had gone three furlongs, the crust of moss edging the slough burst upward. A humped, ridged back rose into view. Emerald plants turned grey with putrefaction and slid down the monster's muddy, steaming flanks. It lurched ashore on the quaking island, shedding water. Its blind blank head swung back and forth.

Mindless yet knowing, it trod squelching to the quincunx which Sixarms had defaced. Its own misshapen hoof completed the wreckage, and Sanhu was again far beyond its reach. Stretching its head skyward, it looked as though it would have bellowed in anguish had it not been devoid of a mouth, entirely mute.

Trampling the length of the island, the blind boar reduced it to a garden of corruption. Afterward it plunged into the water, following a submerged path known only to Freths, sensing somehow that here was a convenient way across the bog. It moved like something ancient, crippled and weary to exhaustion, yet it went on, searching.

This time it blundered in the wrong direction, westward. The lakes and bogs at the heart of Tirtangir would delay it for years, perhaps, but at last it would walk out on a trackway of carrion, and nothing would remain living behind it save starving birds.

"This I'll never allow," Sixarms said, in a voice as final as the capstone sealing a tomb. "Loredan of the Danans, make a quincunx of your own and send the blind boar back to Danan lands. Then follow it yourself." His voice grew deeper. "Find that woman, if you can, and it had better be possible. See that she sends the blind boar home whether she wishes to or not. She drove a bargain for your people, but now I hold that she has broken it. I lay it upon you to see that it is kept."

"And if it is not?"

Sixarms's brown eyes were harder than agates. "Then there will be no food from us to you, this winter, and if the blind boar leaves us helpless, we will see that you are left the same way. You lied by not telling us that the woman Sanhu had raised it. Undo that lie before you talk with me again."

"That shall be done," Loredan said. "I cannot take the monster back to Danan lands, though. A quincunx can only be traversed by your own mind, choice, and will; it helps in concentrating those powers, it is not the means of traversing in itself. The blind boar is not a trained magician, as it would have to be, and wholly willing, no, *dedicated* to making the traverse. I don't believe it even thinks. I would not do what you demand if I could. Be certain of that. But in any case I cannot."

"If that is true, then your nephew and all of your men remain here with us while you seek the woman."

"As if you did not plan to hold them for hostages all the time. Of course they stay. But I will find Sanhu, thwart her scheme if I've guessed aright what it is—and then I will bring her back here in a cage as her treachery merits!"

"Meanwhile our bogs are turned to middens of death," Sixarms roared. "Words are easy! Go bring me the proof!"

Settled in that way, the agreement soon became action, and Loredan stood in the moss-cut pattern he had devised himself. A flock of birds flew above him, calling in terror as the blind boar advanced. He visualized, concentrated, pictured a small closed chamber in his own house with a quincunx pattern on the floor, and vanished from the bogs.

Standing in the dim chamber, he sensed at once that the house had few people in it. He'd earlier given them leave to depart, in case the blind boar should appear there. It suited him well enough now.

Loredan was no breakneck rider like his twin nephews or Cena. For a Danan, he sat a horse rather poorly. His favorite way of travelling, other than through a quincunx, was a wooden litter made for him by Luchtan the carpenter, which walked smoothly on six jointed wooden legs. Since it was distinctive, he cast a glamor over it and himself before he set out. The figure which travelled along the track to Ridai was a potter in a pony-drawn cart, to outward seeming. It even smelled as it should, and the masters of illusion who could deceive the sense of smell were rare indeed.

Loredan had chosen the royal dun because Mahon might well be there. If he was not, then the most likely places were Dar and Lost Star Lake, equal distances from Ridai, and Cena could tell him which one to approach. Where Mahon was, there sooner or later Sanhu would be.

Were she seeking only to escape with her life, she would find a ship and leave Tirtangir. Sanhu, though, did not care to live; that much of her bitterness the master-poet did believe. He remembered the scalding things she had said of her grandson. Mahon Stagshanks was her unfinished task.

Loredan hurried. More than one traveller marvelled at the speed of the potter's pony-cart as it rattled along the track.

He saw the royal dun at Ridai from far away. Cena's feather-shingled roof with its wide sun-balcony commanded a view of the country from the crest of a hill, and the feasting hall below could seat four hundred in its partitioned booths alone. Outbuildings surrounded it; cookhouses, brew-houses, a dairy, barns and byres and sties, three long barrack-buildings for the large musters of fighting men which gathered there at times, granaries and wells. Strong palisades, gates, and series of earthworks surrounded the whole. Ridai had never yet faced a concerted attack by a large host, and if it did, it would not be easily taken.

Loredan gained entry with no trouble. The guards at the outer gate let him through cheerfully, drunk on the wine of freedom. He followed the winding road upward between two stockade walls, until the spiral narrowed at the top of the hill and he passed into Ridai proper. Almost the first man he saw there was Oghmal.

The champion had all the fine discrimination of a new-born calf where sorcery was concerned, and could no more see through an illusion than through an oak tree. When Loredan passed him with a hearty, "Good day, lord," Oghmal replied with barely a second glance. He did look twice when Loredan halted his supposed cart before him, but did not recognize his uncle even then. At most he experienced a sense of familiarity, for Loredan had not changed his appearance completely. His fresh skin had become coarser, like his hair, his mouth thicker and himself somewhat leaner. He'd also changed his speaking voice, vain though he was of it, but now he destroyed that part of his illusion and addressed Oghmal in his own accents.

"Be careful, sister's son. An enemy might approach you in this fashion someday."

If Oghmal was good at anything besides fighting, it was concealing surprise or dismay. He responded with a startled blink and a moment's rigid astonishment; then, muscle by muscle, he relaxed. "What became of the council?" he asked, and pointed to a nearby stable as he spoke, so that any who noticed would think he was giving the potter advice.

"Sanhu betrayed us. She fled through a quincunx; I bungled, to let her. Your dearest comrade Sixarms is very angry, and I believe Sanhu means harm to her grandson. Is he here?"

"Wait! This is too swift. Sanhu is at Ridai? What of the monster, then? The blind boar?"

"At large in the bogs. Sanhu, I think, will be found where young Mahon is. I've two things to do; protect him, and take her back in a cage to satiate the blind boar. I grew careless because I pitied her, despite all, and this is the outcome. The boar is ravaging Sixarms's darling bogs this instant, and every Freth in those parts is wondering when spoilage, putrescence, and rot will come blundering through the walls of his home on half-formed feet. Mahon is the answer, sister's son. Is he here?—for I must know."

"He's here. You will find him playing hurley, he and a band of other tribute-children against Danans bred, out on the liss.

Now take your cart to the stable, mother's brother, before someone wonders why we are talking so long."

Loredan did that sensible thing. Then he strolled to the liss, the open space before the hall, as though he had ample time to watch games. Despite his easy gait, he moved without wasting an instant. While difficult to assassinate a young man on a playing field, it would be possible, and especially for a sorceress guised as one of the players. A hurley game was a scramble of mayhem, and a game which caused less than several broken bones was reckoned tame. Loredan did not think it beyond Sanhu to be on the field herself, with a poisoned spear made by glamor to seem a hurley stick.

The lithe youngsters raced and fought in their gaudy kilts. Loredan heard a crack as two sticks met in a parried attempt by a Danan bred to knock out a tribute-child. The ball flew high in the air. Someone sprang after it, snatching it out of the sky with the tip of his stick and knocking it far down the field. Loredan joined in the yell of approbation.

The youngster who had made that telling hit now sped after the ball, determined to cover more distance with it. Although Loredan knew him but slightly, he recognized the lad by his shock of undisciplined hair and the disproportion of heavy shoulders to lean, tough-sinewed legs. He did not so much run as lope and spring in bursting explosions of power. None could catch him. Some could intercept him, though, and two did. They crashed into him, brought him down in a furious tangle, and struggled there while others chased the ball. Another tribute-child threw himself into the pile. When Mahon struggled out of the brawl he wore only a breechclout, his tunic now being a rag in the dirt, while a bloody nose reddened his lower face.

The ball by then had nearly returned to him, driven by young Danans who had escaped the Freth tribute. Mahon lifted it as neatly as they would have lifted cattle from a field, racing away with it. Loredan chuckled with appreciation.

He could not imagine Sanhu in such a free-for-all. No matter how well disguised, she would still be a light-boned small woman past her youth. Glamor would not change that, and she would be likely to have her neck broken in the first scuffle which involved her. Besides, she would scorn to rush about on that sweaty field.

She might well be watching, though. Loredan scanned the

crowd, asking himself what semblance he would wear in her place. Not a warrior's or noble's, for that would be too conspicuous, nor yet that of someone with duties, for then his movements would be too restricted. He'd pass for a guest, he decided; a craftsman or -woman with a right to sit in the hall, neither too high nor too low, and to go anywhere.

He wondered whether Sanhu would assume the appearance of a man. As a woman, she would make fewer mistakes. All weavers and dyers were women; so were many poets, sorcerers, and farmers, as well as some fighters. She might even decide to pass as one of the surviving War Crows. Certainly none would meddle with her then.

Loredan looked back to the playing field. The Danans had won, despite Mahon's swiftness, and now he was leaving the grass with a plain cloak wrapped around him. He'd require a bath. The question was whether, being a Freth by rearing, he would take one; but surely some mentor of his would advise him.

The bath-house was a perfect place to commit stealthy murder.

"A bonny player, that tribute-lad, isn't he?"

Loredan recognized the one who addressed him as a herald of Cena's. The master-poet had trained him. It could not be chance that he was speaking to Loredan of all men now. Oghmal had been busy, and sent the herald to find a certain potter.

"He is, Cahad," Loredan agreed. "Do you know me?"

The herald looked at him closely, with the sight Loredan had trained. A messenger in a land so filled with sorcery and illusion had to know how to resist such deceptions, and know whom he confronted.

"I do, lord. Others are seeking the lady you know of, but with care. She may not have arrived yet . . . if she is truly coming."

Loredan shook his head. "She has had ample time. I was slow to leave my own house and travel here. Before that, I was delayed in the bogs. If Sanhu is not here, then I'm wrong about what she intends, and I doubt that. Follow Mahon to the bath-house, Cahad. He's open to attack there. I'll go with you as your servant."

The herald laughed. ''That is a thing I never thought would befall when I struggled with feats of memory at your college.''

''Many strange things have happened since then. I promise you, this is a little one. Now, there goes Mahon. After him, man, and scan everybody who goes near him.''

The pair followed Mahon to Ridai's bath-house, through crowds of cooks, leather-workers, wheelwrights, stable boys, and slaves, the latter but lightly afflicted compared with those who were called slaves in the eastern lands of the world. Loredan wished for once that Ridai was less boisterously crowded, and a smaller place. There must be almost two thousand souls here on this day!

The stone bath-house, roofed with slate so that it would not burn down, seeped plumes of vapor. Beds of coal were kept simmering constantly whenever Ridai held many guests, as it did now. Nor were the attendants always the same.

Loredan had some time now for trepidation. He'd been a woeful fool to allow Sanhu to escape from the bogs. He had felt sorry for her despite himself, he knew now, and sickened by the prospect of her death to come. Suppose she was fleeing the land instead of following Mahon to murder him? Renewed war would be Loredan's fault. She might send an accomplice, though he doubted it. Sanhu would come herself.

He glanced back and forth, even as he fetched a bucket to rinse Cahad. The tribute-youths were splashing one another, wrestling, boasting of what they would do to their opponents in the next game, and none was anything but what he seemed.

Having sluiced away the outer dirt, they passed into the sweating room, where hot stones were doused with water. Loredan had a hideous vision of Sanhu braining her grandson with such a heated stone, gripping it hard in both hands with the strength and self-hatred of madness. Thoughts like that were not good. He had never had them of anyone but the sorceress.

Still, they were his own thoughts. Sanhu might well be subtler. Her legend said that she had used poison once.

Cahad sat opposite Mahon on an oaken form and breathed the herb-laden steam. This was no bad way to search for a murderess, save that it hindered the vision. She might come in at any time. She would be one more indistinct shape in the steam, hardly needing a glamor to conceal her.

Loredan watched Mahon with his mind, not his eyes, and all those close to him, even as he went through the motions of serving Cahad. None attempted anything evil. All were precisely what they seemed, unless they were deceiving a master of enchantment. Yet Loredan's sense that Sanhu lurked nearby only grew stronger.

Glistening, Mahon strode out of the bath-house to scrub and rinse. Loredan's sense that death hung above the youth with talons flexing was so strong by now that he almost felt them pricking his own hide. He said hurriedly to Cahad, "Lord, I forgot your sandals. I'll fetch them now." With that he virtually ran from the long stone room.

Mahon stood outside, with a small crookbacked attendant near him. Loredan recognized the fellow, having seen him before—at Ridai, he was certain. Nothing appeared amiss, and now he would have to produce some sandals or look like a dolt.

Mahon turned his back. The attendant lifted a stiff-bristled brush in both hands. In that instant Loredan remembered *where* he had seen him before; in Sanhu's retinue, the single time that she and Loredan had visited Ridai simultaneously.

Loredan vented a yell which would have startled a rock, and hurled himself upon the little servant. Knocked sprawling, he rolled over with a weasel's swiftness and thrust the brush at Loredan's face like a weapon, which the master-poet by now felt certain it was. Catching both the other's wrists, he squeezed and twisted desperately, while the other tried with transcendent frenzy to grind his brush into the poet's face. As Loredan fought to hold it back, he stared through the ruddy, snarling visage to another set of features behind it. He saw sharp cheekbones, a pointed chin, round forehead, black hair stranded with grey—and furiously bitter eyes.

"Lord!" Loredan cried, knowing that Mahon was about to interfere—and undoubtedly, in his ignorance, upon the wrong side. "This cur was paid to murder you!"

Twisting the deadly brush out of Sanhu's hands, he kicked it against the wall. Hearing the commotion, Cahad the herald rushed out of the bath-house in time to see Loredan seized by the youngster he had tried to protect. For a moment it seemed that a general brawl would start, and that Sanhu would escape in the confusion, but the herald caught her as she rushed away, bringing her down by her ankle. They fell together.

"No murderer am I!" Sanhu shouted, in her counterfeit of a man's voice. "He is mad!"

"Mad, you say?" Cahad spoke with enjoyment. "He's my servant, and I, Cahad, herald to the Rhi, attest that he knows what he is about."

"I'd hope so," Loredan said, playing his role, "for you gave me the commands. The brush he was about to use on this lad's back would have baned him quickly, or I'm far wrong. There it lies, and who touches it should touch it carefully, so."

One of the hurley-players recovered it, sniffed at the bristles, and grimaced. "Maybe it's liniment or salve of some kind," he said, "but something anoints this brush that I do not enjoy smelling."

"A lotion for bruises!" Sanhu said. She bared her teeth. "Here, scrub me with it and see whether I die. That's the quickest way to end this foolishness."

That was an impressive sign of innocence to most of those present. Only Loredan knew something like the full truth; that having failed, Sanhu was prepared to die, and preferred to die leaving the blind boar at large, so that the Freths would suffer and the war against them—or their war against the Danans—would continue.

Loredan, playing the servant yet, scoffed. "Never know who paid you then, will we? Maybe you'd rather be poisoned than give that away. What's your word, master?"

His "master" took the hint adroitly. "This is not something to decide in a bath-house. Mahon of Lost Star Lake, you know best who might desire to murder you. The Rhi is here. She can judge the matter, and who better, since you are her man's heir? I'll say that it is no happenstance that my servant and I were here. I've suspected that this fellow meant harm."

"I know him from a time when he was here with your grandam, lord," Loredan added. "Maybe if you look at him again, you'll know him too."

Mahon inspected the bogus attendant closely. Puzzled, he shook his head. "I never saw him at Lost Star Lake, or with my father's mother."

"I was never there!" the disguised Sanhu protested.

Loredan saw that he had made a mistake. Sanhu would not have appeared to her hated grandson in a guise she expected him to know. The man with the twisted back evidently was some creature of hers, but one seldom seen in public, whose appearance she had assumed for that reason. Once he learned of her undoing, he might well take care that he was never seen again—but that was his affair. Clearing away the immediate confusion was Loredan's.

Telling his true identity, and Sanhu's, to a boisterous gang in a bath-house was no way to simplify the matter. More likely it would confuse it further. The best way was to take the matter before the Rhi, as Cahad said.

"Bring someone who knows you to vouch for you," Cahad suggested. "I do not think you can. Like my servant, I say you were paid by the Lady Sanhu to murder this young man, and are no proper bath-house attendant at all, yet I am willing to be proved wrong. Can you do that?"

Silence, seething with malevolence, answered him.

"Then speak before the Rhi. You will have the chance to say your full say, and she will hear you fairly. All know that. More, we will scrub a piglet with this brush of yours, and see how long it lives thereafter. If I've accused you falsely, the Rhi will see me shamed for it and yourself compensated, if you are a slave who cleans privies. You can speak out like a man." Cahad smiled at his unplanned joke. "Tell us your name."

"*Sanhu of Lost Star Lake,*" she hissed defiantly, and when the truth was uttered, the illusion cloaking her disappeared. "My life's curse on you all—and it's a foolish man who takes Sanhu's curses lightly."

Mahon took a backward step.

"Cursed are you above all, whelp," she snarled at him. "May you never know peace or rest or an hour of honest pride in the house you steal! May Danans despise you, your own kindred persecute you, and your stinking Freths refuse to accept you when you run back to their hovels! May you love a woman forever who will dance on your heart and bring you only grief! May you live a hundred years in that condition! May—"

Loredan stepped forward, made a sign, and struck Sanhu mute in mid-malediction. The master of language did not care to have it used so unless the recipient deserved it. While Sanhu struggled with a larynx bereft of the power to form words, the master-poet spoke to Mahon.

"You had to listen to her. Now listen to me. My words are stronger than hers. If you know unhappiness in the house at Lost

Star Lake, you will be content in a different house. For every Danan who despises you, ten will prove friends who stand by you, so long as you merit it. Should your own kindred persecute you, greater folk will aid you. Maybe you will always be part Danan, part Freth, and never find it easy. As for the curse of hopeless love, I've never heard of any suffering that for a hundred years without surcease. The Lady Sanhu hasn't any power over love that I've seen, withal. And if you do live a hundred years, you will live them in health, with all your teeth, clear sight, and clear wits to the very end. I have known men to suffer worse fates than that.''

Mahon smiled, though Sanhu's viciousness had shaken him. ''I think, friend, that you are something more than a servant.''

''Just a servant,'' Loredan said, ''but do not ask whose.''

''Now let us take this matter to the Rhi.''

Cena heard the full tale, and gave judgement from her throne. No decision but one was possible. Sanhu must return to the land where the blind boar ranged, not in the free fulfillment of an oath she had sworn, but helpless in a cage. Then she should be left in the earth-boar's path.

Sanhu raged and fought as the wooden bars of her cage were lashed in place around her. She screamed as she was carried into the bogs by boat, and across slippery ground by sledge. She glared silently at Sixarms when she was brought back to his camp in a stretch of bogland where stagnant water showed a thick, greasy sheen on its surface. The corpses of trees and the rotten tatters of undergrowth surrounded them. Clearly the monster Sanhu had raised still wandered.

Elsewhere, throughout the land, nothing which died decayed.

The boar had passed to the north. It travelled slowly, and at last they found it, trampling a thicket of brambles to ruin. Sanhu gripped the bars of her cage, staring in disgusted horror at her doom. Festooned with rotting thorns, the creature shambled towards her. Sanhu hurled herself so violently back that her cage toppled over.

Crouched within it, she felt the smoldering heat of the earth-boar's advance. The garments she wore rotted on her body; patches of canker spread on her skin. She uttered one gasp, and her lungs decomposed in her chest as she drew in the tainted air. Her last vision was the black, half-fashioned demon looming above her. Then the cage broke apart, mingling with the earth, as the blind boar scattered the fragments. Scraps of pitted bone rolled aside with the rotted cage bars, turning to dust.

The watchers dared not breathe. They did not even wish to. Loredan wondered if the sacrifice would be enough, or if the monster would remain above ground. Sixarms bent forward, glaring, and Carbri asked the Earth-Mother's mercy in the most fervent prayer he had ever uttered.

The blind shape sank into the earth as into a morass. Its shape melted even as it sank from sight, and then it was gone without trace, as was Sanhu. From the place where both had vanished, something spread through the living soil of Tirtangir, something which had been stolen and concentrated in an unnatural shape, and was now restored. Through heavy peat, through the ooze at the bottom of lakes, through lowland clays and light upland soils, the power of wholesome decay was restored for league upon league.

Fallen leaves mildewed. Dead beetles softened within their shards and provided banquets for ants. Broken bird's eggs spoiled as they should. Compost piles in many a garden moldered again.

But those consumed by the terrible blind boar remained dead. The wasted fields were still barren. Not for a hundred years would the rotted forests have great trees in them again. The black, incomplete figure of earth which carried destruction with it would stalk through Freth and Danan nightmares for much longer.

"Goddess, endure us all," Loredan muttered.

Sixarms signed himself with a thumb like an oak gall.

Carbri harped notes like the onset of autumn.

It was over.

At Ridai, young Mahon spoke with Cena. He felt disenchanted, in the hardest sense of the word, with his birth-people. His father had given him recognition, grudgingly and late; his father's mother had proved wholly unrelenting. Now they were both dead. Many more tribute-children would be returning to Danan lands, and to Mahon they were like unnamed brothers and sisters.

"I want to receive some of them at Lost Star Lake," he said, "and help them as you and your brothers have helped me, Rhi."

"It's a great-hearted thought, Mahon," Cena said, "but that takes more than wanting. It takes work. You will need a good steward, for a beginning. But assuredly there will be no stronger lord than you among the tribute-children. You can do much, and we will all be glad of it, not tribute-children only."

"Better they come to Lost Star Lake than go to their own kindred, I'm thinking," Mahon said bleakly.

"Ah! Listen, Stagshanks! Try your utmost to forgive your father those things he did against you. One day you may want that kind of forgiveness yourself. Sanhu poisoned lives by never dealing in forgiveness. You know how she ended. She had a wasting blind boar within her, to match the one she conjured into this world of matter. Oh, I wanted her to do it! Because we were defeated again, I called on a weapon worse than Sixarms used, eager that one I had never trusted should do my grimy tasks for me. Take warning by this, Mahon. When work is your own, don't give it to another because you find it disagreeable. Gui never did that."

"Lady, you had little choice," Mahon protested. He knew, uncomfortably, that Cena had cause to blame herself, but he did not like hearing her do it. He would have preferred to blame Sanhu and Gui wholly.

"Maybe that is true. This other truth stands; if I wanted the blind boar raised, I should have raised it myself, and parleyed with Sixarms myself. Remember that, Mahon. You will not be able to do everything yourself, and will have to trust others to do their part. But when something is yours to do, never neglect it. You live with knowing, afterward."

"The tribute-children will help, lady. In what is to be done. What will you do next?"

"What I should have done before, child. Hold council with Sixarms to confirm Loredan's treaty. Talk with him again, and again after that, if need be. Hammer out the terms anew if he holds that our agreement is voided. But the Freths will never rule Danans again. That is one demand I will never accede to, and I am glad he lacks the power to make it."

Sixarms had the power to do much, but with his long store of patience he refrained. They arrived at conditions of peace all over again, and did not try to debate which was the more wicked deed; using the Despoilers as weapons in a battle, or one earthen monster. But Sanhu's treachery was an issue, and the fact that

Cena had sent her instead of confronting Sixarms in person. Because of that, the terms were less handsome than they might have been.

"The child-tribute ends," Sixarms said, "and we restore them to you year by year as their time ends, in case there is more treachery."

"No, by the Mother! Those are our children, Sixarms. We must have them back in three years at the most. I would ask for them all now, save that we cannot feed them. What of the meat you were to supply us through the winter?"

"Your blind boar has left us too little to spare. Maybe your friend the sea lord can aid you. He's done that before."

"Manahu aided us the once." Cena thought that he would call for repayment in his own good time, as well, and hoped it would not be while their pledges to the Freths remained unredeemed. "Your old women's curses on our cattle and harvests have ripened, and my curses go back to them! Sixarms, are we to continue thus until the entire sacred isle is barren? We have the eastern plain; you hold most of the bogs, the lakes, forests, and mountains, and despite what the blind boar did there is enough to feed your people. Do you think I have not flown over them as an eagle, or run in your woods as a doe? I've other spies besides!"

Brown eyes, steady and stubborn, looked into orbs of a fiery, impatient blue. At length the chieftain said, "Seven years for the children, and you must aid me to rebuild the Revolving Fortress, though that work will not begin sooner than three years from tonight. We will not be ready until then . . . and if that is agreed, then I will feed your people through this winter, unfailingly."

"Unfailingly is a large word," Cena said. "How can you be sure? It may be the worst winter for a generation! The snow and ice may shackle the world."

"That will make no difference." Sixarms raised his bull's voice. "Beartooth, fetch in the Undry!"

Cena nearly gasped. The Undry was Sixarm's other treasure, the first being his club, Grinder. She watched as two gigantic Freths carried what he had called for into Sixarms's council tent.

It did not look so wonderful. Indeed, Cena would have called it a lumpy, graceless earthenware cooking pot, unusual only in being strong enough to resist spear-thrusts. She never would have identified it as the fabulous Undry had she seen it on some lowly hearth, or for that matter thought twice about it. It had another name: the cauldron of plenty.

"None ever goes hungry away from this, no matter how many must eat," Sixarms rumbled, "and it will cook rubbish and offal into savory food. Withal, no poison can survive in it. Any food ladled out of this is sound. If you cooked the flesh of the Despoilers in it, the Undry would render it wholesome. I lend it to you, Rhi of the Danans, for this one winter. You must return it in the spring."

Tears came to Cena's eyes. She said huskily, "Sixarms, this is generous indeed. Maybe . . . maybe we can escape further war after all."

"For how long?" Sixarms asked realistically. "Once the food is digested, your folk will not trouble their memories with it. We're both too worn to fight for a while. Even so, we will not have as much as a decade of peace if Danans keep coming from Alba."

"Nemed is returning there."

"What of the fighters who came with him, seeking land? Are they returning too?"

Cena said rather grimly, "They barely make up the loss of those who died before the Despoilers, and your other weapons. Nay, I doubt they can even do that."

Sixarms rubbed his bristly, thick-boned jaw. "Let them stay, then. But forbid your shores to others until the Revolving Fortress stands once more. Can we make the pact so?"

"Consider it made now," Cena said, looking again at the Undry. "My people must confirm it at the tribal assembly—but that is at Winter Eve, and they won't refuse if I bring this to their tables."

"Yes," Sixarms endorsed. "As I said, while their bellies are filled they will be happy, and when they grow hungry or cold, beware of them. That is when they will cry to depose you."

"You have it wrong," Cena told him. "That may be true of your folk, but then they are simpler than Danans. Mine are ripest for mischief when they are fed, drunken, and idle."

Gui, my man, she thought with a sudden pang, *do not think me a traitor if I reflect that you were the worst such. I'm sure you were sometimes a traitor to me, and that Sanhu always was. We*

*had some fine loving and sweet times between the quarrels, but
there was never full trust—never any, indeed. What kept us
together was having a war to fight.*

Sixarms, my enemy, was the one I trusted.

Her enemy waved at the cauldron of plenty. Freth women
were filling it with bones, grass, and ancient leather. Others
blew up a fire in the simple hearth.

"Tonight I will show you that the Undry is all her reputation
makes her," he said. "I'll feed you, your party, and the
hundred hostages, before you all depart for Ridai. Then,
perhaps, I'll come and be your guest there in the spring."

"I guarantee your safety if you do—but then you can assure
your own safety, can you not, Sixarms?" Cena laughed suddenly, and punched his thickly muscled arm. "Tonight at least there
is no trouble. Let us savor that while we may."

A copper-colored harvest moon arose. The rubbish in Undry,
cooking, altered to spread a luscious aroma through the tent.
Outside, Carbri played a cheerful song. Hearing her brother's
melodious voice and sitting beside the earthy bulk of Sixarms,
Cena, Rhi of all the Danans in Tirtangir, felt a rebirth of hope.

They were free once more, whatever it had cost.

They were free.